BITTEN VAMPIRE

AN URBAN FANTASY
STAND-ALONE

BITTEN VAMPIRE

THE BITTEN CHRONICLES

BROGAN THOMAS

This is a work of fiction. Names, characters, places, and incidents either are the product of the author's imagination or are used fictitiously.

No part of this book may be reproduced or used in any manner without written permission of the copyright owner except for the use of quotations in a book review.

BITTEN VAMPIRE - THE BITTEN CHRONICLES
WWW.BROGANTHOMAS.COM

Copyright © 2025 by Brogan Thomas

All rights reserved.

Ebook ASIN: B0DFXZCPHV
Paperback ISBN: 978-1-915946-61-4
Hardcover ISBN: 978-1-915946-62-1

Edited by M.D. Bowling, Tina Reber, and proofread by Sam Everard
Cover design by Melony Paradise of Paradise Cover Design
Character art by efa_finearts

For my hubby

Chapter One

The front door slams, and my heart jolts. A sharp blend of dread and anticipation twists in my chest. I drop the tea towel on the counter and rush into the hallway.

"Perfect timing! Dinner's nearly ready. I made your favourite."

Jay shrugs off his snow-dusted coat. "Hi, babe." He kisses my cheek, and as he squeezes past, clips my collarbone with his bony elbow.

I gasp and rebound off the wall.

"You okay down there, shorty?"

"It's all right. My fault." I wince and rub the throbbing spot.

He's never had good spatial awareness. He's all elbows and knees, and I ought to know better than to greet him in the narrow hallway. Besides, he's always extra clumsy after working late.

He vanishes into the kitchen, the smell of Chinese food wafting from the brown bag he's carrying.

Oh no. I hurry after him.

"I—I cooked. I said I'd cook." The once-cosy kitchen suddenly feels stifling.

He waves me off. "Yeah, yeah, but I don't fancy your cooking tonight. I wanted a takeaway." Without even looking at me, he dumps the bag, tears it open, and yanks out a plastic carton. Sauce splatters the spotless white countertop as he lifts the lid. He doesn't wipe it—doesn't even notice—just snatches a fork and strides into the living room with his prize.

Jay slumps in the recliner and kicks up his feet, the television droning while he shovels food into his mouth as though he hasn't eaten in days.

My hands clench at my sides. *Hours.* I spent hours perfecting a Beef Wellington, yet he couldn't be bothered to text and say he had other plans. I grind my teeth when a blob of orange sauce splashes onto his shirt. He curses, pinches the fabric to his lips, and licks the stain away.

I average fourteen-hour days. On my single day off, I scrubbed the house until it gleamed, ironed his shirts, and cooked his favourite meal. The least he could do was eat it.

But arguing changes nothing.

Over the past year he has been busy—entertaining mysterious clients, coming home at all hours—and through it all I've supported him and the family business. I handle the marketing, yet somehow I have become the office dogsbody: accounts, payroll, even coffee runs. I do so much that there are never enough hours in the day, but we are supposed to be working towards something—our future.

I force my shoulders to drop, unclench my fists, and flex my fingers. No reason to lose my temper. He means nothing by it. Fighting with him just shuts him down further. I can count on my fingers how many times I have managed to win an argument.

Besides, there's something more important we need to discuss tonight.

I watch him, silently rehearsing the speech I have run through my head a thousand times. I have listened to countless motivational podcasts to work up my nerve. I deserve to ask for what I want.

We have been together ten years. In that time, we have celebrated everyone else's engagements and weddings. Never ours.

In the Human Sector, marriage isn't merely romantic; it's protection from being snatched off the street and turned into a creature's plaything. Being human is dangerous in a world of monsters. Long-term relationships without marriage count for little in our laws and theirs.

But Jay doesn't see it that way.

I never wanted to beg for a 'shut-up ring,' to nag for commitment. Jay's a free spirit—marriage isn't for him, and for years I pretended I was fine with that. But I'm not.

Mum's voice still echoes: *"Why would a man buy the cow if he's getting the milk for free?"* I detest that saying. Yet perhaps she wasn't entirely wrong. I thought time would change his mind.

Ten years. Deep down, I cringe. I thought I was doing right by him, putting his needs before mine. But I'm forty now. Each birthday gnaws at me; friends' pitying looks pile up, and my doubts grow louder. What's wrong with me? Why doesn't the man I love want to marry me? Each special occasion, I hold my breath, thinking, *Is today the day?* And every time, nothing.

The disappointment chips away at me until I barely recognise myself.

No more. I've invested too much to leave without a fight. I hope he will meet me halfway, catch me when I leap from that proverbial cliff, admit he's been a fool and is finally ready to commit.

Together we could have a happy and safe life.

I reach for the remote and switch off the television.

Jay glares. "Football's on in a bit, babe."

"I know." My pulse hammers. I perch on the edge of the coffee table, facing him. "We need to talk."

He rolls his eyes, crams another piece of chicken into his mouth, and gestures vaguely with his fork. "Go on, then. Spit it out. If you're pissed about the food, put mine in the fridge. We've got Tupperware, haven't we?"

Be brave, Winifred.

I lean closer. "Jay, I know this isn't your favourite topic, but it is important to me—"

He's barely listening, more focused on chasing a stray slice of carrot around the carton. "Go on," he mutters.

I reach over and brush his hand, but he shakes me off as though I were a nuisance. *Dismissed.* Dismissed, again. No, like he always says, I'm overreacting. Being too sensitive. I pull back and toy with the remote.

"Jay," I begin once more, inhaling sharply. My instincts

scream to let it drop, but I can't. Not this time. "I want to talk about us."

He raises a finger for silence. The pause stretches, thick and tense. His expression shifts: blank, annoyed, then something else entirely.

Then he laughs.

He laughs.

Not a nervous or surprised laugh—a mean, sharp one that pricks my skin. A knife slicing through my brave façade. Slicing through my confidence yet again.

Jay drops the fork into the carton and reclines, a nasty grin spreading. "Us," he repeats. Then his voice hardens. "Oh, I get it. This again. You don't know when to leave things alone. Come on, babe. Don't you have everything you want? Nice house, nice cars. Why slap a label on it?" He grabs the fork in his fist and stabs another chunk of chicken.

I swallow, my throat tight. "It's not a label. It is safety."

He sighs through his nose. "Not this again. No vampires are dragging you out of bed. No shifters are humping your leg. You're perfectly safe. Stop being so dramatic. And you wonder why I don't want to marry you."

"Jay—"

"No." Flat. Final.

"But... I—I want us to—"

"No."

That's it. No discussion.

Good enough to share his bed, not good enough to be his wife.

Dread knots my stomach. "If I'm not good enough to marry—"

He cuts me off with another short laugh. "Don't do this, Winifred. You know you love looking after me. The house is in my name. You leave, you lose everything. And your job? Think my parents will keep you on if you're not my girl? Walk out that door, and you're dead to them. Dead to all of us."

Dead.

I stare, numb.

"Thought so. Now stop being silly and get me a beer." He snatches the remote and turns the television back on.

Right.

Right. Okay.

My hand shakes as I tuck a strand of blonde hair behind my ear. My chest is tight, disappointment pressing in, but autopilot takes over. I fetch a beer, set it in his waiting hand, collect the empty carton, and wipe the sticky mess in the kitchen.

My mind whirls.

I hunch against the kitchen counter and let reality settle. A sob traps in my throat, and my arms fall to my sides, lifeless. That went exactly as I feared. I barely managed two sentences before he shut me down.

I'm disappointed in him, but... I'm more disappointed in myself.

I'm embarrassed.

Embarrassed I dared to hope. Dared to want more, dared to believe I was worth loving. Worth fighting for.

I feel so ashamed.

I press a trembling hand to my mouth, tears slipping

down my cheeks as the sad reality burns my throat. Deep down I always knew I wasn't enough for him—or at least not in his eyes. He shows me in a hundred small ways: every dismissive comment, every selfish choice. Even tonight he brought food only for himself.

Yet I clung to him, pretending not to notice, numbing myself because admitting the truth meant leaving, and I wasn't ready.

I wasn't ready until now.

I'm still not ready.

Winifred, do you want to be loved like this for the rest of your life?

A hollow, bitter laugh escapes through my hand. I have been so in love, so befuddled by hope, that I overlooked the glaring red flags, like bunting wrapped around him, chaining us both.

Mum would have hated Jay. Hated how he treated me. I met him just after she died, when I was broken with grief and utterly vulnerable. She had been caught in the crossfire of a magical skirmish—a spell had misfired into a crowd of onlookers and killed her instantly. Old, familiar pain carves another hole in my chest. It was my fault. If only I hadn't asked her to pick up that parcel.

Perhaps that's why I let Jay in.

Why I pursued a relationship I would never have tolerated if she had been alive. Even in the early days, Jay was dismissive of my feelings.

I wipe my face as something shifts inside. Even the kindest souls have limits, and Jay is about to learn that he does not get unlimited chances. He had two choices tonight: commit or watch me walk away.

I'm done.

Staying will only hurt me now.

I stare at the Beef Wellington resting on its wire rack, at its golden-crusted puff pastry encasing savoury mushroom duxelles and perfectly medium-rare beef tenderloin. I stamp on the pedal-operated bin; its lid flips open. Snatching the Wellington from the rack—burning my fingers, flakes of pastry lodging under my nails—I drop it inside. The dauphinoise potatoes and green beans follow.

He's not getting anything nice from me again.

I will need somewhere to live and a new job. His mother will make my life hell. It's going to be a nightmare. I have no family; there is no safety net. But the rose-coloured glasses are off, and I cannot stay.

I won't.

Chapter Two

Four Months Later

"Don't come back!" my landlord yells as he tosses my belongings out of the first-floor window of the scruffy little house. They rain down around me, scattering across the grass and snagging on the thorny hedge bordering the street.

Wow. He's angry. Like a proper numpty, I stand there frozen with my mouth open, staring.

There's a thump of a wagging tail hitting the grass and a playful growl. I glance at the dog who started all this, happily gnawing on a piece of black fabric clutched between his grey and white paws.

"Baylor, no, really? Do you have to?"

He's slobbering, tearing into my favourite pair of knickers, the expensive satin-and-lace kind. I groan and rub my eyes. I know better than to try to take them from him. A Saturday morning Husky-underwear-tug-of-war isn't on my to-do list.

At least the distraction keeps him occupied and stops him from ruining anything else.

I hope.

I stare at the growing mess and rub the back of my sweaty neck. Seeing my things on the ground is almost overwhelming, especially the things that landed in the flowerbeds and are now streaked with dirt.

I'll have to wash everything. I love clothes, but now that I'm on a strict budget, each piece must be chosen with care. My carefully curated capsule wardrobe—where everything mixes and matches—is a source of pride, along with my makeup.

My makeup... Bile fills my mouth. I close my eyes. Most of it won't survive the drop from the window. A few palettes are already broken, and I don't dare look closer. I refuse to cry, not with onlookers enjoying the show.

A few neighbours peek out from their windows, while the bolder ones linger in their doorways, coffee mugs clutched in their hands, clearly entertained at my expense.

I know how people see me—blonde, blue eyes, petite, unassuming. They decide who I am before I open my mouth: stupid. Soft. Weak. Middle-aged.

It doesn't bother me. Let them think what they want. The version of me they have in their heads isn't real. Only my own perception of myself matters.

"That's what you get when you cheat!" a woman calls

out before slamming her door. The sound echoes down the street.

My cheeks burn. "I didn't cheat," I mutter. Louder, I yell, "He's my landlord!" As if I would have a relationship with Derek. "He's not even a friend."

I flinch as something smacks me in the forehead. *Ouch.* The rubber chicken dog toy squawks comically as it hits the grass. Baylor eyes it and lets out a soft "awoo" before returning to his work of tearing at the wet, silky fabric under his paws.

This is all his fault. Bloody dog.

I sigh, hunch my shoulders and—with one eye on Baylor and the other on the window above—begin gathering my things, yanking them out of the shrubs. The stems catch on my sleeves and scratch my hands. I sweep my scattered possessions into a pile, hoping Derek will eventually toss down my bags.

Baylor's a good dog, really. It's not his fault, it's mine. He's been through a lot. He has separation anxiety, and I don't blame him—his humans passed away a couple of weeks ago, and I'm a poor substitute.

I don't know what the heck I'm doing.

What I do know is that a three-year-old Husky isn't ideal for a first-time pet owner.

First, he chewed the wires in the back of my car and damaged the lights. I thought I was being thoughtful when I lowered the seats so he would have more room to curl his fluffy bum and grumpy attitude into the boot. I had no idea he'd make a meal out of it.

I couldn't afford the repair, but I had no choice since I need a vehicle for work. So, today I got it fixed, bought a waterproof cover to protect the back seat, and invested in two dog guards: one to block the front, and one to protect the boot and its tasty lights.

I assumed locking him in my room while I ran to the dealership would be safe.

Turns out, it wasn't.

I wasn't gone long, maybe forty-five minutes. But when I returned, there was a hole in my bedsit's door, and Baylor's head was sticking through it, tail wagging, a huge doggy grin on his face.

He was thrilled to see me.

Derek was there to fix a leaky tap and saw the damage at the same time I did.

I rub my sore biceps, where finger-shaped bruises circle my arm. The tender flesh pulses under my touch. He dragged me downstairs and threw us both out. I scowl up at the window. No, Derek is not my friend.

My hairdryer lands next, its plastic shattering on the path. "Oh no." I dash towards Baylor, deciding he's safer in the car.

There's no dog lead in sight. I improvise with a knee sock, loop it around his collar and let him drag me to the vehicle. He leaps into the back and wriggles, smoke-grey tail thumping against me as he inspects the new 'anti-Husky décor.'

The spring weather still holds a chill, but I crack the windows for him before running back to salvage my belongings. At least I don't have to haul them downstairs.

A threadbare bag scrapes the red brick on its way down. Finally. I scoop up armfuls of clothes and shove them inside.

What's sad is that this doesn't even make the top ten worst things that have happened these past four months. Just thinking about everything churns my stomach. If I dwell on it too long, I'll be sick.

Four months ago, with my pride in tatters, I moved out and rented a dingy, mouldy room. Jay didn't call, but his mum sent me an email at 2 a.m. terminating me 'effective immediately.'

Deep down, I wanted Jay to miss me. To fight for me. As days turned into weeks, his family waged war on my reputation, but Jay remained suspiciously silent.

Seven weeks later, I was scrolling through my mobile when my thumb froze. Jay's face flashed on the screen, smiling, his arm around another woman.

For reasons I still can't explain, I read the caption: he was getting married to *her*.

I didn't realise I had stopped breathing until my chest started to burn. A dull roar filled my ears as I stared at my phone, hands trembling. The betrayal—the finality—hit me like a punch.

I wiped every social media account. One more 'I'm so sorry' or 'serves you right' from my so-called friends, and I would have screamed.

As if to twist the knife, Jay tracked me down just to send me a wedding invitation.

A bloody wedding invitation! I was mortified. The wedding day is in June, on my birthday. Humiliation scorched beneath my skin. I felt small, foolish, desperate to curl up and disappear.

I keep telling myself it wasn't my fault. Our relationship was like a book held too close to my face—only when I moved it to arm's length could I read the words. With distance I could finally see the whole story, and now I shove the memories aside just to function.

I can't believe I was with a man for so long who was so deliberately cruel.

I grab another item and stuff it into the bag. People are no better than the monsters who lurk in the darkness, just waiting for us silly humans to show a sliver of weakness.

The only person I stayed in contact with was the wife of one of Jay's friends, Amy. She chose to stand by me, which surprised me. Amy wasn't gentle with her opinions; she never patted my arm or said, 'You'll be okay.' She was livid —furious on my behalf—and never once said, 'I told you so.' Instead, she stood beside me, letting me be angry, letting me grieve, letting me hate. Letting me cry on her shoulder. Amy was a true friend.

And then she was gone.

A simple dinner date. A fun night out in the Vampire Sector with her husband, Max. They never came home.

A vampire killed them.

I swallow the lump in my throat. That's how I ended up with Baylor. Nobody here cares about animals—no shelters, no rescue groups—so it's just him and me.

Losing Amy was the wake-up call I needed. It wrenched me out of any lingering daydreams about Jay, forcing me to face a real tragedy. My broken relationship was nothing compared to my best friend's murder.

Now I'm left with a heart full of grief and a depressed, clingy dog.

And now this.

Yeah, it doesn't even make the top ten.

I sniff, throat tight, chest aching under the weight of it all.

We will be fine. We have to be.

Things must get better. This has to be the worst of it. This has to be rock bottom.

... Right?

When the window opens again, I gather my courage. I'm not the doormat I used to be. I'm learning to speak up for myself.

"You owe me rent!" I shout. "I've paid for the entire month, and we have a contract!" I don't expect to see my deposit again.

"Get lost, Winifred!" Derek yells, sticking his greasy head out the window to glare at me. "Thanks to your mutt, you owe me a new door."

It begins to rain. "Will you please just stop? I said I was sorry. He didn't mean to eat the door."

"I warned you that you could only have the dog stay for a week. It's been two. I told you no pets! By the time I'm finished with you, no one will rent you a room. You are finished in this town." It's not as though he's landlord of the year. "You should have done the world a favour and had that animal put down!"

I gasp. "So you are a dog killer now?"

"That dog I am. He peed all over my flowerpots. He's an untrainable menace."

"Derek, you can't do this. I have tenant rights. You can't throw us out with nowhere to go. It's a death sentence!"

As soon as I say 'death sentence,' the nosy neighbours vanish, and the street falls silent.

I stand alone in the cold, drizzle spattering my face and wind tugging at my hair. Is this really happening?

"You should have thought of that when you let that uncontrollable beast into my home. Actions have consequences, Winifred."

"I'll fix the door, and I will wash all the flowerpots. Please, Derek—" I will beg on my knees for a roof over our heads. Pride is useless if we end up dead.

"No," he snaps, and the window slams shut.

Stunned, I stare at the glass, a deep sigh building in my chest. Then I keep moving. What else can I do?

One by one I rescue the rest of my belongings. It's like playing Tetris, cramming everything into the tiny boot, the footwell and the passenger seat. The large bag of dog food —for sensitive skin and stomachs—that was shoved out of the front door gets wedged in next, followed by Baylor's bowls. The dog eats better than I do.

I slide into the driver's seat and slam the door, letting out a shaky breath. No tissues in sight; they are likely buried behind half my life. I wipe my nose on the back of my hand, determined not to break down.

"Come on, Fred. Everything will be all right. This is just a blip." It has to be. Everything happens for a reason, otherwise the universe would be chaos. Yeah, everything happens for a reason and the good people, the special people, die first.

My lower lip trembles. Amy would be so disappointed in me. We have nowhere to go, and we can't even stay in a guest house or hotel. They won't take a dog and me. I refuse to abandon Baylor.

I have no idea what to do next.

If only Derek would let me fix things. I understand why he's angry. The hole in the door was huge, with wood chunks all over the carpet, but he didn't need to hurt me or throw us out.

It's a nightmare.

Baylor whines, snuffles and pokes his tongue through the grille, trying to reach me.

"It's all right, buddy," I murmur, trying to convince us both. Something else occurs to me: I didn't get a chance to compare the splinters on the floor with the size of the hole before we were shoved outside. So I have no idea if he swallowed any.

For all I know he munched on a chunk of '80s lead-painted wood. Who knows what that will do to his stomach. My gut twists. We are looking at an expensive emergency vet visit.

"We will see the doggy doctor to make sure your tummy is all right, and then we'll find a new home." I rest my hand against the mesh. "Everything's going to be fine. I won't let you down."

I can't let him down. Amy adored him—her fur baby. What kind of person would I be if I gave up on him?

I still can't believe I'm in this situation.

From the corner of my eye, I spot Derek glaring through the window as he sticks a sign on the glass: ROOM FOR RENT.

I huff out a bitter laugh. If I stay here much longer, he will call the police. I groan and start the car, the engine rumbling to life. Slowly I pull out of the driveway. Surely everything's going to be fine.

It can't get any worse.

Chapter Three

With Baylor chewing his way through plastic, wires and wood, I'm beginning to feel embarrassed every time we set foot in the vet's office. Like I'm the incompetent fool, the hapless pet parent dragging in her Husky sidekick yet again.

I half-expect them to report me. But after a thorough exam, the vet concludes he's fine—no splinters, no paint ingestion—and sends us home with orders to keep an eye on him. Looks like I'll be on poo patrol for the next few days. Lovely.

I drive to a nearby supermarket and park at the far edge of the car park, away from the bustle. Rain patters against the windscreen, and behind the ominous clouds, the sun hangs low, stretching shadows across the tarmac. Daylight is fading fast, and I'm no closer to finding a place for us to stay tonight. I need to find a place for us to live.

My shoulders ache, my eyes burn, and anxiety gnaws at me. Since online searches in the vet's waiting room haven't worked out, I decide to try the old-school route: I unfold a local newspaper and circle listings with growing desperation.

"Hello, yes, I'm calling about the room—"

"The room's gone." Click.

That listing only went live on Friday. I sigh, press the phone to my forehead, then move on.

I try another. "Good afternoon. I'm calling about the room you have for rent?"

A pause, then a quiet throat-clear. "Look, love," a woman says gently, "is your name Winifred Crowsdale, by any chance?"

"Um... yes."

"You're not gonna get a room, love."

"It was my dog. I didn't do any damage," I whisper.

"I know. I didn't think you'd gone full shifter and chewed through a door. But Derek's made his position very clear. Nobody wants to cross him."

I exhale slowly.

"Sorry," she adds.

"No, it's fine. Thank you for telling me." I hang up, staring at the phone. This is ridiculous.

I work through the remaining listings, one after another. Every time I get the same response: no pets, no vacancies or flat-out refusals. Even the places far above my budget have suddenly vanished from the market. I even try stretching for a dingy terrace house. Still nothing.

Derek got there first.

Nobody wants to risk renting to the woman who crossed him. He's the head of the local rental association and must have started calling around the moment he slammed that window shut, no doubt emailing photos of the damaged door.

I'm stuck.

I drop my chin to my chest. I'll have to leave. There's no other choice. I need to move further out, maybe out of the area entirely.

Baylor snores, his fluffy body stretched across the back seat, oblivious to the fact our world is crumbling. I watch his fluffy chest rise and fall. I need to think. I need to find someone Derek hasn't reached yet. I am a good tenant. I have enough money for rent and a small deposit—not much, but enough.

The newspaper crinkles under my tight grip. I wish I could say this is a surprise, but it's the same rubbish in a different wrapper. It's like when Jay's parents fired me and smeared my reputation, preventing me from continuing my marketing career. That was my work before my life went to hell, and now no reputable business will hire me.

The only job I could get was delivering food—they don't care who you are as long as you turn up with the goods.

I bounce the phone off my knee, thinking. I have to dig deeper. There must be someone Derek hasn't reached. For my sake, for the sleeping dog in the back, I need to keep trying. Otherwise I'll become a statistic by the end of the week. Some nasty will prise us out of the vehicle like sardines in a tin.

They say the Human Sector is safe, but it isn't. Living here doesn't mean you're protected. Our borders are weak, our defences against the other sectors laughable. Everyone pretends it's normal to stay indoors after dark.

In our world, humans have evolved or devolved, depending on your view. 'Human derivatives' is the term everyone uses. Our DNA is still human, but with an added twist: fangs, claws, magic.

Some of us have a little extra, some a lot, and others hardly any at all. Pure humans—the original DNA strain—are vulnerable by comparison and nearly went extinct. Forty years ago, the government passed radical laws, granting autonomy to the derivatives and carving the country into sectors. Each species now governs its own.

I glance down at the newspaper. It's not just vampires, shifters or magic-users you have to worry about. It's the pure humans too. Sometimes it's the ones who smile at you in the morning, then lock you out in the afternoon.

Homeless.

We are homeless.

I let the misery wash over me, if only for a moment—no one's watching—and bitterness floods my thoughts. I'm nearly forty-one, and what do I have to show for it? I'm an embarrassment, and I'm... exhausted.

I'm so tired of it all.

Tired of scraping by, tired of never having anything solid to hold on to. Every year, every month, every bloody day, another piece of me wears away. It's like I'm nothing.

I want stability, a real job, and a place to call my own.

Love.

I wanted Amy's life.

Does that make me a bad person?

I was happy for her, but I was also jealous of her husband, her home and her happiness. And now? Now I feel guilty because I'm not jealous anymore. She's gone. Her life, her dreams, her future—gone.

It was all ripped away.

The deaths of Amy and Max have left me seething with hatred. Part of me knows it's wrong to condemn an entire group over one tragedy, but it's hard not to.

The vampires do whatever they like, and human laws do not protect us when we venture over their borders. We are second-class citizens in a world of monsters, and nobody cares.

This is hell. Because hell isn't fire, brimstone, a place of punishment for the wicked or unredeemed after death. Hell is here.

Baylor yawns, stretching his front paws and back legs at the same time like a starfish, and then he breaks wind. Loudly. The smell hits me immediately. It's vile. I gag. It's so bad I can *taste* it.

"Oh my god, Baylor." I slap a hand over my nose, fumbling to roll the window down.

He sneezes once, curls up tighter and promptly goes back to sleep, utterly unfazed by the chemical warfare he's unleashed.

I chuckle and turn my head, gulping in as much fresh air as possible. Even the exhaust fumes in the supermarket car park smell better than that. Trust Baylor to make me laugh. I close my eyes, inhale deeply and let the world blur at the edges. If I let the panic ebb, maybe I'll find some clarity and figure something out.

Baylor's steady snoring fills the car, oddly soothing. Each breath anchors me as I focus on that gentle rhythm.

Meditation isn't something I've ever been taught. I let the odd gift I have—whatever it is—guide me. I wouldn't call myself psychic, but there's... something inside me. This pull, this awareness, resonates like an unspoken command. A sense. A knowing. It sits between my chest and my gut, a gentle tug I've always felt.

Perhaps it's pattern recognition. A canny intuition. I've always been adept at picking up shifts in energy, sensing the emotional charge in a room. It's what made me so good at marketing—my ideas were always ahead of the curve.

Sometimes the urge to act builds so quickly that I respond before I realise what I'm doing. The older I get, the more often it happens, like the night Amy and Max went out. I had a bad feeling. I called her, but she didn't pick up. I never had the chance to warn her. Every day I wish I had tried harder. But I was there to scoop Baylor up from the aftermath.

I know the human brain is complex. I know magic exists—at least for some. Like every human, I've been tested, and I'm not magical. Still, I trust my instincts when they scream for others even if I have spent ten years ignoring them for myself. If that isn't magic, it's close enough.

Colours swirl behind my closed lids, ribbons of shimmering smoke in shifting hues. Lightning flashes through the darkness; energy coils twist as though trying to show me something. I don't resist. I let it wash over me.

And just like that, the panic slips away.

I open my eyes and glance at the newspaper. All the

suitable listings I've called are crossed out. A tiny ad in the far corner of the classifieds catches my eye. The text is so small it's difficult to read. **Room for rent. Pets welcome.** I initially dismissed it because it has no contact number, only an address.

I'm desperate enough to give it a go. I'm already in the car and have nothing to lose. I might as well check it out.

I enter the postcode, start the engine and drive out of the car park. Following the navigation system, I turn left. I drive southeast, towards the vampires.

The rain intensifies with every mile I drive towards the mystery accommodation. My fingers tap the steering wheel. I hope someone is home and that Derek hasn't reached them first. It's only about thirty minutes from the supermarket, yet I feel as though we have been on this road forever.

Beyond the tarmac stretches a barren scrubland, separating humans from vampires. I don't want to live any closer to those monsters. The nearer we get to the Vampire Sector, the more my nerves prickle.

The more it feels like I'm chasing the sun.

The dampness from my wet clothing keeps fogging up the windows, forcing me to squint. I fiddle with the vents to clear the windscreen. The last thing I need is to drive into a ditch. I follow the navigation's directions to turn right onto a narrow lane.

The road twists and turns through the thick trees and shrubs until the land opens, and a lone house appears through the downpour.

I ease to the kerb, my breath catching as I try to make out details.

Even with the pounding rain it looks quaint. Immaculate red brick with decorative flourishes, even the roof sports ornate ridge tiles, not a single crack or chip. The bay windows are perfect, their sash frames neat and straight, the glass gleaming. I'm no architect, but it seems Victorian, likely predating the road.

Who knows. It's not a farmhouse, yet here it stands alone. Odd. No neighbours, at least no human ones, as the Vampire Sector borders its back garden.

"Be a good boy. I won't be long," I tell Baylor, who's now wide awake. I crack the windows, grab my jacket from the passenger seat and jump out, tugging it on. The thudding rain drowns out my thoughts as it hammers my hood. I will worry about drying it later if all this goes to shit.

This house could be a stroke of luck.

The day is dull and dripping, yet the house is not. It stands solid and bright, as though it has been waiting for me. For a moment I dare to think this is where things finally change.

Then another thought intrudes—*this is too good to be true*. Perhaps someone placed a joke advert in the paper to tease the owners; that seems more likely than our being allowed to live here.

Water seeps into my shoes as I ignore Baylor's indignant howls at being left behind and walk along the pavement, peering around the back. A tall, solid brick wall encloses the rear garden, perfect for Baylor. Safe. Secure.

The naughty Husky will never escape it.

I make my way to the front of the house, slowing to a halt. The wooden gate unlatches itself with an unsettling, almost inviting creak.

Well, that's creepy.

It must have a faulty latch.

Despite the weather, the front garden remains eerily perfect: bright flowers unscathed by wind or rain, lawn trimmed with near-laser precision. As I look closer, I spot a subtle shimmer in the air. Something compels me to touch it, see if it's real or my imagination. I wiggle my fingers through it, and a warm buzzing settles over my skin.

Yes, there's magic here.

It's a ward.

A magic-user's house in the Human Sector right next to the vampires? It doesn't make sense. Some über-rich people use magic to keep their property safe, but those types wouldn't be renting out a room.

I eye the property with distrust, but my over-sensitive intuition—which should be screaming—is silent.

Well, I promised I'd be braver, so I take a deep breath, and without touching the creepy gate, step through the ward and start up the garden path.

The rain stops as though someone has turned off a tap. I glance back at the street. Water still pours from the sky, but not a single drop falls within the garden's bounds.

Wow. That is a powerful ward.

I halt on the front step and study the door. It's a deep teal, its stained-glass panels catching the dull daylight and scattering warm shards of red, gold and green. Bold shapes —diamonds and circles—glint like jewels set into wood.

I knock. My knuckles hardly graze the surface before the door swings inward, soundless, revealing a welcoming hallway floored with black-and-white chequered tiles. Coloured light pools on the tiles, as though inviting me inside. Ridiculously, I think this house might be my first glimpse of a true home. It stands solid and immaculate as if to say, *You are home now. Come in.*

"Hello?" I call softly. "I'm here about the room." My voice echoes, and the ward hums in response. I lean to the side, peering into the hall. An empty shoe rack sits off to one side, and a neatly polished staircase curves upwards.

The place seems old-fashioned, yet like the garden, shows no sign of wear. It is perfectly maintained.

That's when I realise the house itself is magical.

A wizard's house.

I stumble back. I have never seen one, few people have. I have only heard of them in mandatory magic lessons at school, and if my memory serves me correctly, they are pure magic, able to manipulate matter and relocate at will.

They have powers the Magic Sector doesn't talk about.

Legend says a wizard's house preserves its creator's soul.

They are sentient.

Why anyone would choose to become a house after death, I don't know. The idea rattles me. It's not as though they get a second chance. They are just... stuck. Watching. Waiting.

It's unsettling, like there's a sinister side to it. I shake off the thought and my overactive imagination.

I came here for a reason. If a magical house is willing to accept my troublemaking dog and me, I'd be mad not to give it a shot. I square my shoulders, lift my chin and step across the threshold.

The door closes behind me with a bang.

Chapter Four

My shoulders nearly meet my ears as fear spikes my pulse, but I force myself to breathe, relax and look around. Apart from the door slamming, nothing has changed.

The moment that thought crosses my mind, a stack of paperwork and a pen appear on the mahogany sideboard.

I stare at them.

Creeping closer, the words 'rental agreement' are written in fancy lettering at the top of the enchanted parchment, with both my name and Baylor's already written in. My hand trembles as I pick it up. It's a standard form, much like the one I signed with Derek four months ago—though Derek's document wasn't magic. If it had been, I wouldn't be homeless.

Magical documents are notoriously complex, but one thing's certain: you can't hide anything in them. That's why people hire paper mages—some of the scariest individuals you will ever encounter.

What they can do with a single sheet of paper is mind-boggling. In the business world, they are infamously ruthless—sign and fail to uphold it, and you are doomed. If it's *your* document and you cheat, the penalties are worse. Seeing this paperwork actually reassures me that the house isn't out to steal my soul. Everything seems in order.

The rent is higher than I was paying, but it includes utility bills, food for me and Baylor's pricey dog food. A good deal indeed. Now that I've recovered from my initial terror, I feel strangely... safe.

I have not felt safe for a very long time.

I'm still worried about living close to the Vampire Sector, but this place is powerful. The ward keeps the garden in bloom, untouched by wind and rain. If it can control the weather within its boundaries, it can ward off any rogue vampire who might fancy a Winifred-and-Baylor snack. I'm safer here than anywhere else in the country.

Relief hits so hard that for a second, I sway and have to close my eyes.

I haven't even seen the room. I need to calm down... but I can move in straightaway, all I need to do is sign. I pick up the pen and do it before the wizard's house can change its mind.

The rent is due now and then on the first of each month. I just place the money here, on the sideboard, and the house will handle the rest.

I count out the rent in cash, stacking the notes neatly. Both the money and the rental agreement vanish.

"May I choose a bedroom?" I ask the house, feeling

slightly foolish but wanting to be polite. The magic doesn't shove me outside, so I take that as a sign everything is all right. Not wishing to drip water everywhere, I hang my damp coat on the rack and slip off my shoes. I've decided to treat this house as though it's a person because, in a way, it is.

If I were stuck as a building, I'd want its occupants to be polite and kind. It must be a lonely existence.

Perhaps when the wizard first connected their soul the house was home to a family—their family. Then time passed, the family died, and the soul was left alone. Maybe that's why it wants to rent a room.

"I know how you feel," I whisper. And if speaking to a house also makes *me* feel less alone—much like chatting to Baylor—then so be it.

The stairs don't creak as I climb. The wooden bannister is warm under my fingers. At the landing, I find four open doors. A bathroom and three bedrooms. Two are the same size, the third is a smaller box room.

The bathroom is wonderful. A large, clawfoot tub sits prominently beneath the frosted window, while a spacious rainfall shower beckons me to wash the remains of this day away. I don't know how the house updates itself; it certainly didn't have these modern amenities when it was built. I might research it later to learn more.

The main bedroom faces the front garden. It's old-fashioned but lovely. The walls are covered in dainty, floral-patterned wallpaper adorned with small frames holding intricate, hand-drawn portraits of people time may have forgotten. I wonder if they are someone's loved ones. Memories.

Floral wallpaper and matching bedding... Normally I'd hate so many patterns, but I rather like them here.

In the corner stands a wooden wardrobe, its dark wood polished to a shine, beside a small dressing table with an oval mirror.

"It's so pretty," I say, deciding the front bedroom is my best option. "If it's all right with you, this room will be perfect."

I move to the window, push the curtains aside and peer out. Dusk is closing in; I need to hurry. I let the curtain drop.

"I need to fetch Baylor and bring my things inside."

I hurry downstairs, pull on my coat and shoes and dash to the car.

A white paw scrabbles at the window. I grimace. Behind the glass, Baylor's howls are sorrowful, and his blue eyes roll as though he's suffered hours alone—it hasn't even been twenty minutes.

"It's all right, it's all right," I say, grabbing his lead from my pocket, which I'd found earlier among my scattered belongings. I have a sinking feeling he will spring out of the car and flatten me. I take a deep breath, keeping the door closed on his grinning face.

He whines in protest.

"Wait. Sit." Tail wag. Bum wiggle. Baylor does not sit. "Sit," I repeat, firmer. He whines louder but eventually obeys. I don't quite fist-pump—it's a small accomplishment—but I'm proud of the progress.

I crack the door and clip the lead to his collar. "Staaaay." He stays. I open wider. "Staaaaay." He stays. I open a little more, and then I'm bowled over by a fluffy Husky launching at me.

I almost lose my footing but grab the door before we both hit the ground. He bounces, tugs, nudges; tug-tug again. The lead burns across my palm.

I shut the car, abandon the rest for now and let Baylor drag me towards our new home.

"You need to be good and respect this house," I warn. "No shenanigans, Baylor. I mean it, best behaviour." The gate swings open and Baylor hauls me to the front door, which opens for us.

"Thank you."

Inside, he bounds around sniffing everything. I keep an eye on his back end, praying he doesn't lift a leg against the furniture.

I cringe at what the house might think if he pees. "Please don't pee, Baylor." He's normally good indoors, but who knows how magic might affect him? Emotional peeing is a thing, I'm sure.

"Can we... um, use the back garden?" Another door creaks open, so I follow it, Baylor towing me into the kitchen.

The room is spacious, with high ceilings and large windows pouring in light. The chequered tile continues from the hall. A faint scent of wood and herbs lingers. Wooden cabinets painted soft cream line the walls, their oak grain still visible, with brass handles that catch the light. A porcelain sink with old-fashioned brass taps takes pride of place beneath a window overlooking the garden.

We reach the back door—it swings open—and step into a neat courtyard enclosed by brick walls.

I scan the cottage-style garden for anything Baylor might destroy. No plastic chairs, no wooden fencing, just solid brick he can't chew. The ward has kept the rain off here, too; the flagstones are dry. Baylor can play without getting filthy. I sigh with relief.

The flower borders are suspiciously bare: nothing but dark soil where green shoots should be. I narrow my eyes and mutter, "Did you strip the garden before we came out?"

A ripple of magic in the air feels like an answer.

Baylor watches me, ears pricked, tail wagging. "Be a good boy." I unclip his lead and he rockets away, still brimming with energy despite his earlier walk. He darts to a far corner, sniffing intently. He'll be there a while. "If he digs, I'll grab a shovel and fill it in."

Near the back door stands a metal bowl of water—courtesy of the house, apparently. I glance at it, then at the walls, gobsmacked. "Thank you. That's very thoughtful."

I hurry back through the kitchen, down the hall, and out to the car. It will take time to unpack, and I'm not keen on everything getting more soaked.

When I reach the car, I roll up the windows and freeze—the passenger seat and footwell are empty.

"Someone stole everything," I mutter, scanning the road. Then I see the boot is empty too. Did the house...? "That can't be possible. Right?" My eyes take in the silent road, landing on a new feature. Apparently, it might be possible. I shake my head, unable to believe what I'm seeing.

In the time it took to settle Baylor in the garden, the house has somehow sprouted a driveway. And a garage.

Compared with that, unpacking the vehicle is nothing.

I move the car onto the new drive, lock it and head inside, feeling dazed. Shrugging off my coat and shoes, I hurry upstairs to find, sure enough, the house has taken everything from the car and put it away.

It has put everything away exactly how I like it.

All my clothes are clean, dry and arranged in colour order, largest to smallest, and sorted by season. It's my odd little system.

The wizard's house has also replaced my makeup and hairdryer. I stare, speechless. My bottom lip wobbles. I'm not crying—I'm definitely not crying. I grab a tissue from the dresser, dab my eyes, then blow my nose.

"Thank you. That's really kind." I pat the wall. "Thank you so much."

I check the bathroom. Sure enough, everything is in place, hair products, soap, just as I like them.

"I'd better check on Baylor."

I head for the back garden, so hurried I forget my shoes, but the thoughtful magic stirs again, and a moment later they are waiting by the door. The kindness stuns me. An unfamiliar sensation. "Thank you again."

Baylor is still exploring. His tail wags when he spots me, and he flashes a big doggy grin.

I rest my head against the doorframe as the pressure in my chest finally eases. It has been a long time since either of us had something to smile about.

"You love the house and garden, buddy? I do too."

Chapter Five

A Week Later

I sit in the living room, watching while Baylor wrestles with a cushion. He lets out a low, grumbling growl and crawls across the dark green carpet on his belly, teeth gleaming as he nips at a tassel.

The cushion shoots into the air, twirls, then bops him on the bottom as it zips past and lands on the other side of the room.

"Huff-huff. Pffft," Baylor complains, his breath short and sharp. He notices me watching and grumbles again.

I raise my hands in mock surrender. "Hey, don't look at me. I do not control the house. You know better than to chew on the furnishings, buddy. That's not allowed."

I've been keeping score: wizard's house, ten; Baylor, nil.

A homemade treat materialises from thin air, hovering just above him. Baylor's nose twitches. Eyes wide, he tilts his head, watching it intently, tail swishing against the carpet. He leaps, snapping at it, but it's too high. A distressed whine escapes him.

The treat hovers in place.

Baylor circles it, moving cautiously. Then, as if guided by a silent command, he sits. The treat lowers, and with surprising gentleness, he opens his mouth. It is placed carefully inside, and he crunches it with delight, his tail spinning like a helicopter.

Another treat appears, and Baylor flops onto his tummy. Then another, and he rolls over smoothly. A fourth arrives, and he sits upright, offering his paw.

"What the…" I stare, mouth agape in disbelief. I don't believe what I'm seeing. Trained by a house in just one week. I just… can't.

The antique clock on the mantelpiece chimes softly, reminding me of my obligations. I glance at my mobile. The peaceful morning is over; it's time to work. Now that we live here, Baylor essentially has a full-time sitter, so I can concentrate on earning extra money and climbing out of this bottomless pit of bills.

Night-time delivery jobs pay nearly double, but they are tricky. Humans usually stay indoors after dark, out of reach of predators, which makes home delivery big business for anyone with a proper licence and a clean human background check. I refuse to work after dark. It isn't safe. So I'm stuck with the daylight gigs.

"So, you are sure you are all right with him?" I ask.

The living room door creaks in response.

I take that as confirmation. Over the past few days, I've become more attuned to the house, understanding how it communicates. "Okay, well, thank you. I will be back before it gets dark."

Baylor doesn't even notice as I slip out and jump in my car. I grin when I spot a lunchbox on the passenger seat, along with a glass bottle of juice. I take a quick peek inside to find a salad—celery, walnuts, and a dressing that smells divine—plus an apple and a banana.

I'm so grateful how the house is taking care of us. Moving here was the best decision I've ever made.

I head into the city.

Over time I've found a prime spot, a catchment area that covers six takeaways, several offices, and a cluster of homes. When business slows, I circle back, and the app feeds me a steady stream of quick jobs. By lunchtime the orders are rolling in; today promises to be productive.

As I wait at the pickup point for an order, a busy waiter hurries past. He nods at me in greeting, his white apron slightly askew. The place is buzzing. I have been avoiding collections here because it is Jay's mother's favourite restaurant. But today has been slow, and I cannot afford to be picky.

The air smells of garlic and savoury spices. Behind me comes the rhythmic clink of plates, the soft jingle of glasses, and the low hum of conversation, punctuated by bursts of laughter.

One familiar voice cuts through the noise. I tense, groan, and tilt my head back, silently pleading for divine intervention. Did thinking of her summon her? Of all the rotten luck, she has to be here. Why me?

"Samantha said, Peter—"

"Wait. Isn't that the woman who was dating your son?" Her friend's voice has the delighted tone of somebody who loves to gossip and enjoys being mean.

"Yes," the woman replies. "That is the hussy who broke his heart."

Hussy? Who is she calling a hussy? Not counting my conversations with Amy, I've never spoken ill of Jay, but it is getting harder to keep my mouth shut.

"The one who embezzled money from your company accounts?"

Oh, here we go.

I turn to face them, keeping my arms at my sides, relaxed. I want to fold them defensively across my chest, but I refuse to give in to the urge. Body language is everything in this situation, and I don't want her to think she's getting to me or that I'm scared. I give both women my best non-expression.

"Yes, that's her," she sneers, her blue eyes—so similar to her son's—narrowing with disdain as she assesses me. She casts a scornful glance at my casual clothes, her lips curling in distaste. My outfit can't compete with her immaculate designer suit and perfectly coiffed grey hair.

The urge to defend myself to this woman is almost overwhelming. *Come on, Fred, you no longer need to be polite.* "Are you still slandering me, Theresa?" The words spill out before I can stop them.

"Slander? It is not slander if it is true."

"Is it true?" I challenge. "Where's your evidence?" I raise my hands, tapping my wrists together to mimic handcuffs. "Where are the police? If I'm a thief, shouldn't I have been arrested? No one's knocking down my door, because it is not true. You are a liar."

"What Jay ever saw in you, short, fat—"

I stop listening. When I was younger, her venom might have broken me. But I'm not that sweet woman anymore.

Years of enduring her sharp tongue have hardened me, and now I'm confident in who I am. My sense of self can still wobble a bit, but I know my worth. Someone like her, who finds it acceptable to fat-shame, lie, and sabotage someone's career merely because they left her son, will never understand.

Her cruelty comes from weakness, not strength.

I stand a little straighter, as though a steel rod runs along my spine. Even though she's taller, I tilt my head so I'm looking down on her and tune back in.

"I am so glad Jay did not marry you." She turns to her friend and scoffs. "Could you imagine her in our family? Good God. Melissa, his fiancée, is so much more his equal—she's got a degree. She's smart."

I have a degree. I'm smart.

She must be disappointed that I'm not reacting the way she hoped. I already know about her precious son's wedding.

"And Melissa is an absolute marvel. They have been together for a year, and he knows she's the one—"

I freeze. What? A year?

They've been together for a year?

But... but I left him almost five months ago. He cheated on me? No—that can't be right.

Come on, Fred, stop being so naïve. Of course he did! He's a forty-four-year-old spoilt child who wants what he wants when he wants it. *You are not so observant now, are you?* my inner voice snarls. When it comes to Jay, I stopped listening to my screaming inner voice years ago. I thought I was perceptive; I even believed I had some supernatural gift. A gift? What a joke. There's nothing special about me.

How many other women did he cheat on me with?

Everything warps around me. My ears and nose feel blocked. The weight of her words crushes my chest, and the world distorts, as though I'm at the bottom of a swimming pool.

Don't cry. Don't cry. Please don't cry in front of this woman.

"After everything I did for him," I mumble. "I didn't think he would cheat."

"Pardon?" Jay's mum snarls. "Cheat? How can you cheat on a placeholder?"

Ouch.

"Don't you dare speak about my son." She strides forward, heels clicking on the tiles. With a sharp nail, she jabs my breastbone. "You." *Poke.* "Are." *Poke.* "Useless." *Poke.* "An embarrassment." *Poke.* "Not good enough for my son." *Poke.* "Of course he replaced you. What do they call it, Margaret?" She glances at her friend, who only gapes back at us.

"That's right," Theresa continues. "Monkey branching, that is the term. We did not have words like that in my day, but now it is everywhere. He kept you on a leash while he tested out his new fiancée." She smiles coldly. "Best decision he ever made, getting rid of you."

"I left him," I say quietly, my voice thick with the weight of it. Where she poked me, there's a sharp throb. When she jabs me again, I swat her hand away. I rub my chest, suddenly furious. "Do. Not. Touch. Me."

Behind the counter, my order's called. I turn away, grab the bag with a "thank you" and then get the heck out of there. I've got a job to do. Thanks to her, I'm not sitting in a fancy office somewhere, doing the work I trained for. I'll be damned if she's going to make me lose this job too.

"Don't you dare walk away from me!" Theresa screeches.

I pay her no mind and keep walking. Her voice rises behind me, but I don't listen. I leave the restaurant via the side door, hurry to my car, and in a daze, drive to drop off the order.

I'm so disappointed in myself for letting Theresa get under my skin. I don't even know why I care what that woman thinks. I should not have engaged; I should have ignored her. That's on me.

Why can't Jay and his awful mother stay out of my life?

When I was a kid, I read somewhere that when you date someone, it takes twice as long to get over them as the time you spent together. I do not want to be thinking about Jay for the next twenty years. In fact, I don't want to think about him at all, certainly not in twenty years, not in twenty minutes. That man is not living rent-free in my head.

Maybe Theresa is lying, but what if she's not? What if he did cheat on me? I could never understand how Jay could propose to another woman after only two months, but now... yeah, this makes more sense.

Amy always said Jay was a narcissistic twat.

I could easily waste hours trying to analyse what's going on in that man's head, but in the end, it's pointless. All I can do is judge him by his actions and how they make me feel. And the truth is, I don't like the person I become around him and his family.

And I need to stop giving these people power over me.

Whatever they think or feel has nothing to do with me.

My hands grip the steering wheel, knuckles whitening as I drive. Once the delivery's done, I mindlessly accept another job without even looking at it.

Half of me wants to RSVP 'yes' to his wedding, to go and watch him marry her. Marry Melissa. Perhaps that would give me what I need to truly move on. Healing, closure and the relief of knowing Jay and his mother are officially someone else's problem.

I plug the next delivery address into my navigation to realise I have made a *huge* mistake.

It's for the Vampire Sector.

I feel sick. "Oh bloody hell." I slap my hand against the dashboard hard enough to sting my palm. Why did I do that? Why did I accept delivery without looking? I can't believe I took a Vampire Sector order. "Fred, things happen for a reason," I mutter, trying to convince myself it will be all right.

I look out the window.

The sun's shining.

What could possibly go wrong? Besides, it's still three hours before nightfall. I've got plenty of time to get there and back. It will be fine. Vampires are daytime dead, and their fledglings, thralls and blood donors still need to eat regular food.

At least the drive is long, which means a huge delivery fee. I glance at my phone's map. The location is near the border, right at the edge. A quick in-and-out. And it's close to the wizard's house. Once I'm done, I can head home.

Yeah. It will be fine.

Chapter Six

A VAMPIRE DELIVERY on a random Friday evening. Brilliant. I can't believe I'm doing this, but cancelling the order would mark my record, and I can't risk that. I need this job. I don't want to add fuel to the fire—if Theresa ever discovers where I work, she will report me.

I would not put it past her—meddling is her favourite hobby. One pointed question to the staff at the restaurant would reveal I'm a delivery driver, not a customer. I must stay squeaky-clean, so I cannot refuse this job.

I collect the order from a high-end restaurant, probably the priciest delivery I will ever make. A stasis spell keeps the food piping hot, as though it has just left the kitchen. At least I needn't worry about the food getting cold. Expensive delivery, indeed.

To steady my nerves, I queue a motivational podcast. I

listen intently, nodding along to the podcaster as her soothing voice reminds me to master my destiny. Thirty minutes later—having learned I should give my nasty inner voice a name—I sail past the turn-off for home.

Moments after that, an enormous sign looms over the lanes: WARNING: YOU ARE ENTERING THE VAMPIRE SECTOR.

My heart skips a beat, and I immediately silence the podcast so I can concentrate. Unlike the Shifter Sector in the north and the Magic Sector in the southwest, there are no towering walls or imposing barricades here. The road widens into toll-style lanes, each fronted by an empty booth. A green light tells me I may proceed—humans entering the Vampire Sector need no papers.

The opposite carriageway is a different matter entirely, lined with guards and identification checks. As a licensed delivery driver, the electronic tag on the car will let me skip the queue on the way back.

The border is quiet now; just before sunset it will swarm with traffic. A glance at the clock tells me I have a shade over two hours of daylight. Plenty of time.

Behind me the checkpoint shrinks, and the tarmac grows silk-smooth. On each building, the windows glitter with UV-blocking glass. Everything is shinier here, almost too pristine. The farther I drive, the bigger the properties grow, and the owners' wealth becomes impossible to miss.

Vampires are territorial; they need space for their 'family.' They live in small groups, collectively known as Clans, each made up of a master vampire, lesser vampires, fledglings, thralls, donors, and daytime guards. Serving a Clan is —so they claim—an honour.

An honour to serve a corpse.

Vampires are the creepiest of all the derivatives. The vampire strain of DNA activates only once its host has drawn a final breath. Only death awakens the true magic in their blood. Reanimated, they remain unrotting yet undeniably dead, their existence revolving around an insatiable need for blood of the living.

They are parasites. Parasites still legally classed as human. *Human.* They fought for that designation, and who would dare deny a killing machine?

Even so, they are not all-powerful. At dawn, something in their magic flips, draining their strength and rendering them inert until nightfall. Perhaps daylight also recharges them—a surge their bodies cannot bear—so the magic in their blood shuts them down, like a remote-control car that has run out of power. This also means direct sunlight is fatal.

Fledglings are living vampires awaiting death. They are little more than marginally enhanced humans—sharper senses, greater speed—but nothing extraordinary. I am not even sure they drink blood. They do age and show some sensitivity to sunlight, yet once they die and their vampiric powers awaken, magic restores them to their biological prime. Perfect for hunting prey.

Thralls are long-term blood donors and servants. They begin as humans with trace amounts of vampiric DNA, but years of ritual bloodletting and blood magic transform them. Regular feedings—both the giving and receiving of their sire's blood—alter their chemistry until they exist halfway between human and vampire.

A thrall survives entirely at its vampire's whim. From

what I've read, they have no free will and must receive regular doses of their master's blood simply to stay alive.

A roadside sign jogs my memory: somewhere ahead stands a castle, residence of the Grand Master of the Vampirical Council, the ruler of the Sector, some say of the world.

A castle, how original. Right on cue, wrought-iron gates appear, opening onto a tunnel of trees and flanked by more armed guards than I saw at the border.

Yeah, vampires are scary.

Traffic thickens. Pedestrians bundle along in heavy coats despite the warm evening. Their blank stares unsettle me. Upscale shops, trees and bright flowerbeds frame the pavements like something from a glossy brochure. A lake shimmers to my left, complete with an orderly jogging track, while sleek apartment blocks rise to my right.

When the buildings start to cluster closer, the houses shrink, still immaculate but modest by comparison. My navigation chimes; I indicate and turn left onto the delivery street. Every garden is manicured to within an inch of its life. One home has its side gate ajar, rocking on its hinges with the breeze. Through the gap, I glimpse an enormous commercial bin. What on earth does a private house need with a monster bin like that?

I ease up to the address and nose the car against the kerb, engine ticking as it settles. The house has a beautiful oak porch. The beams are thick—probably as thick as my thigh—and most likely handmade. It's very pretty, with blue flowers twisting around it, and the front door is a cheerful yellow.

I grab the bag and jog up the path. A quick photo of

the yellow door proves I have delivered. Before I can knock, it flies open.

"Good afternoon." I don't make eye contact—I'm too busy fiddling with the app. *Why won't the photo upload?*

"Nice of you to turn up. What took you so long?" a man snarls.

"My apologies, sir," I reply, keeping my tone friendly, professional. I won't argue with someone who is 'hangry.' "The restaurant is on the other side of the border. A forty-minute drive. But please don't worry, the food is under a stasis spell, so it's still piping hot." I finally upload the delivery photo, then look up—and nearly forget to breathe.

My smile falters, and I stare, stunned.

Both hands brace against the doorframe, shoulders squared in challenge. He wears a black T-shirt that hints at the muscle beneath. Lower down, his thick thighs fill jeans, artfully torn at the knees, and black leather boots complete the whole 'I can kill you easily' vibe. He is so massive he fills the doorway; if he stood fully upright, he would tower above the lintel.

He clears his throat, dragging my attention back to him.

Violet-grey eyes, a silver hoop through his lower lip. On one side, sleek raven hair falls past his shoulders. The other is shaved and inked in intricate spirals that twist along his scalp, disappear behind his ear, and continue down his neck, wrapping around his muscular arm and hand in a stunning design.

In a world obsessed with conformity, he is walking defiance.

The man is... magnificent.

I scoff at myself. *Magnificent? Really? You are such a weirdo. Pull it together, Winifred. He is far too young.*

He scowls. He's furious and kind of scary.

Is he a thrall or simply a blood donor? I see no bite

marks, and I can't imagine him volunteering to be anyone's food. He's active in daylight, so he isn't a full vampire, yet the house behind him is dark and he is careful not to step into the sun.

A fledgling, then.

The bag is snatched from my hand. "No tip," he growls.

The venom in his voice snaps me out of my trance. I drop my gaze and shrug. What does he want me to say? "Thank you." I've been paid well to deliver the food—a smile would only seem patronising.

I give him a respectful nod. "Tipping isn't mandatory, sir. Enjoy your meal."

"Whatever." His forearms flex as he pushes his bulk backwards and kicks the door closed.

Wow. He nearly took off my nose.

I spin on my heels, then hustle back to the car. Beautiful, scary, and rude. I hope he doesn't file a complaint. At the street's end, a near-irresistible pull drags me left, towards the themed restaurant where Amy and Max ate their last meal.

I need to see it.

For weeks, I have pored over online maps, studying the street-view images obsessively, too afraid to set foot in the Vampire Sector itself. Now that I'm here, the urge to look in person is overwhelming.

According to the news reports, their car was still in the restaurant's car park when their bodies were found miles away. The restaurant insists they left on their own, and the police agree—yet something about the story feels wrong.

It will only take five minutes, I reason, *just a look-see.* But sunset is now an hour and thirty-five minutes away, and I can't risk cutting it that fine. I don't know the area nor its people.

I force myself to turn right.

Even as I drive away, my shoulder blades ache with the knowledge that the answers I want lie just behind me. Still, I've been here, made the delivery, and felt relatively safe; I can return when the time is right.

The checkpoint appears. My tag pings, the light flashes green, and I roll through without stopping. When my tyres cross into the Human Sector, relief floods me.

Five minutes later I step inside the front door of home, greeted by a rich, savoury aroma drifting from the kitchen. My stomach grumbles.

"Hi, honey, I'm home," I call, and the house's magic brushes my cheek in greeting.

How I wish I were a mage. I suspect the place would chatter nonstop to a true magic-user.

I toe off my shoes just as the back door bangs and Baylor barrels in from the garden, claws scrabbling for grip. "Hey, buddy. Had a good day? Been a good boy? I've missed you, yes, I have." I brace; my knees get the brunt of his frontal attack as he skids into me, and while he wiggles, I dig my fingers into his thick, smoke-grey ruff. "What a good boy." His eyes half-close in bliss.

Since we moved here, he's lighter, almost puppyish again, and I don't even care that he loves the house more than me.

The dining-room door creaks.

"Dinner's ready? Brilliant—give me a sec." I dart into

the kitchen, wash up, and hurry through to the dining room.

One place is laid at the far end of the long mahogany table. A high-backed chair glides out with a courteous scrape against the carpet, the house's silent maître d'. Tonight, it has gone healthy on me again, serving perfectly pink salmon, new potatoes, asparagus. It is glorious.

"Thank you, this looks amazing." A blur of fur flashes at the edge of my vision. "Baylor, no!" The shameless scavenger lunges for the plate, only to levitate clean off the floor. I snort as he drifts across the dining room back into the hall, paws pedalling air, and the house settles him just outside the now-warded threshold.

He flops with a melodramatic whine, nose millimetres from the magic, drool pattering onto the tiles.

I laugh. "Nice save," I tell the house as I tuck in. "Hope he was not too much bother today. Thank you again for looking after him."

Over the meal I recount my day, complete with Theresa's theatrics. My water glass trembles in its displeasure. "I know, she's awful. Jay did me a favour, really. Funny how the worst moments of our lives steer us onto the right path. Fate sure has a twisted sense of humour. His poor fiancée Melissa won't know what hit her. I'm grateful I don't have to endure another second of Theresa."

With a soft pop Jay's wedding invitation appears by my fork. Ivory lace, gold foil, obscenely thick card.

Oh no.

"Seriously?" I mutter. "Am I meant to RSVP 'no'? Can I not just pretend it never arrived?" I nudge it away.

A pen appears.

I groan and scrub my hand across my face. The wizard's house is so bossy. "He probably sent it to me to be mean, or as a warning. 'You left, look what I have done.' The whole thing feels like punishment. If I reply, am I not falling into a trap?"

Guessing at his motives is pointless. It was never about me; it has always been about him.

I know the house is right, and I know I've got to put this entire Jay saga to bed. I pick up the pen. I want to score into the card stock so hard that it leaves a hole. Instead, I carefully mark the box that says I regrettably decline the invite. "I guess I'll send that back to him on Monday," I grumble.

The invitation and the pen vanish in a blink.

"You can send it?" The mahogany sideboard's drawer jiggles a confirmation. "Oh. Okay, well, thank you." I have no idea of the extent of the wizard's house's power. It hurts my head even to imagine how the place works—its capabilities are astonishing.

"After I had that run-in with Theresa, I pressed *accept* on a delivery without looking and wound up in the Vampire Sector," I confess. The entire table rattles. "It was okay, I'm okay, I've seen worse creepy places on the other side of the city. The Vampire Sector, at least during the day, is not as bad as I thought." I nibble on the spear of asparagus. "I wanted to go to the restaurant—the one where Amy and Max went before they were murdered—ask some questions."

A fork appears out of nowhere and pokes me on the hand.

"Hey, ouch, no need to use weapons. I didn't go. It was

too close to dusk. But I wanted to. I want to go again. It just seems daft to drive all the way to the city when the Vampire Sector is basically in the back garden. I think, I think I might go back tomorrow, work the area and have a poke about."

I move my hand as the fork comes at me again. Inwardly, I smirk—the house is trying to train me like it does Baylor.

"I will be careful, I promise. I just want to... I don't know. I don't know what I can do. I'm a small cog in a very big machine, and there's nothing that I can do. Not against vampires, I know that, but for my own sanity, I need to at least try."

The fork wobbles; I slap my hand on it, trapping it against the table.

"I know, I know. Yeah. It's silly, I will not go." I lie. I snatch the rogue fork and my empty plate to take to the kitchen, but before I can move, they disappear, vanishing from my hands, the house unwilling to let me do the dishes. I know they will be back in their respective places later, washed and tucked neatly away.

I never have to lift a finger to clean; the house sees to everything. Every surface remains immaculate, and my clothes reappear in the wardrobe—washed, folded, and pressed. I love it.

Amy would have hated it. I smile, though the thought stings. Keeping her memory alive is important. I need to remember her because, as long as I do, she's not truly gone. You can't be truly dead if you are not forgotten.

Amy was an emotional cleaner. Whenever she was sad,

she'd clean. Mad? She'd clean. Happy? You guessed it, she would clean.

I can almost hear the battles she would have waged against a house that tidies itself: the housework wars.

"Are you up for watching a film?"

The television pops on in the living room, and the scent of popcorn wafts in. Movie night it is.

Chapter Seven

I was right about working in the Vampire Sector: almost no humans here deliver food, and the fees—even in daylight—are nearly double what I earn across the border. So why would I not work here? Less time on the road, less fuel, more money. Easy peasy.

This morning, instead of heading for the city, I turned towards the vampires.

Now I'm outside One Bite Won't Hurt, the 'themed bistro' where Amy and Max ate their last meal. Goosebumps pepper my arms. From the pavement, it looks more haunted house than haute cuisine, but the neon OPEN sign burns true to the website's promise of twenty-four-hour service.

After a long walk to tire Baylor out before work, I skipped breakfast, so at nearly eleven, a meal feels justified.

And if I have a quick chat with the staff about a very public murder, it's perfectly normal. Right?

I draw a shaky breath, wipe my damp palms on my jeans, and straighten my newly dubbed 'vampire-hunting' top—really just a black, sweat-wicking exercise shirt with long sleeves and a high neckline that hugs my throat. Fabric against my neck feels safer—who knows whether vampires study bare throats the way chocoholics size up a slab of cake.

Not that I plan to meet any vampires.

The bell over the door cackles like a Halloween toy, and I jump. Ahead, a host station shaped like chrome fangs guards the entrance, and behind it, the *pièce de résistance* dominates the room, a faux-blood fountain.

A wall of crimson liquid slides down smooth glass, backlit to suggest a pulsing vein, and the soft, rhythmic drip into the shallow pool below is oddly soothing. For a moment a charm thickens the air with a faint metallic tang, artificial yet disturbingly convincing, before the scent fades.

Velvet drapes and cobwebbed chandeliers complete the kitsch. Online photos never captured the full commitment. Amy, the horror buff, would have adored it.

A member of staff sweeps in, cape swirling, plastic fangs distorting her smile. The same dull glaze I noticed yesterday in others clouds her eyes. She looks exhausted. Perhaps life here does grind people down. I should head home—money isn't everything—but the truth matters more than comfort.

"Good morning. Welcome to One Bite Won't Hurt," she lisps around the fangs. "Table for one?"

"Yes, please. Are you still serving breakfast?"

"Certainly. This way." She leads me to a table at the

back—perfect for observing the room—then hands over a menu.

When she returns, I order the breakfast special.

The plate, when it comes, is pure theatre: scarlet beans, an egg moulded into fangs, sausages shaped as stakes, and a heap of crispy bat-wing bacon. All gimmick, yet perfectly cooked.

While I eat, I note the other diners. An elderly couple—mid-seventies, perhaps—sit hand in hand, giggling over their plates. Adorable. The sight makes me smile.

The waitress checks on them, then turns to me. My stomach dips. This is the perfect chance to ask my questions, but do I blurt them out or attempt something subtler?

She lingers beside my table. "Enjoying your meal?"

"Very much, thank you." I clear my throat. "If you have a moment, may I ask a few questions?" I flick my hair, leaning into the dizzy-blonde act.

She folds her arms, glancing about. "Sure. What's up?"

"I'm a delivery driver from the Human Sector." I jerk a thumb towards the border. "I had a drop-off here and like the area. Would you recommend living here? Is it safe?"

She exhales. "Pretty safe, just don't wander at night, but that's normal." Her laugh is brittle.

"Must you belong to a Clan to work?"

"Yeah. Apart from jobs like yours, everything's clan-owned," she says. "Big firms, corner shops, this restaurant."

"Oh, really. Which Clan owns it?"

"Clan Nocturna. I'm family."

"How does one join?"

"You look the type, and the vamps would love you."

She hesitates. "You would need a vampire's sponsorship, and most Clans aren't taking new members."

"Oh, okay, thanks for the info. So are you happy here?"

She drops her gaze. "It's... fine." Leaning closer, she lowers her voice. "The pay's good, the vampires are gorgeous, and being bitten"—she shivers—"is bliss. But they're sociopaths. Not human. Some try to care, but they don't. Do you care about a carrot? You might if it wilts, yet it's still food, and that's how they see us. They've evolved past us."

Her candour jolts me. I drop the act. I'm no good at game playing anyway.

"I lied. I'm here for answers. My friends Amy and Max Fisher were murdered four weeks ago."

"I remember." She wipes the table, hands trembling. "We closed while the police investigated. I'm sorry for your loss, but you shouldn't ask questions, not around here. Speak to the wrong people and you'll end up getting hurt, or worse, killed like your friends."

"Do you need help?" I whisper. The house has two spare bedrooms.

She shoots me a look of flat disgust. "I don't need rescuing."

Unnerved, I thank her, settle the bill, and add an oversized tip. With her warning echoing in my ears, I step outside and straight into a sheet of rain.

The downpour batters me as I dash across the car park and dive into the driver's seat, silently cursing my forgotten coat.

Instead of signing in and starting work, I pull up directions on my phone to where Amy and Max's bodies were found.

Whenever vampires kill, speculation follows. A loud, angry group called Human First publishes everything it can dig up. The members claim to seek justice, but they merely revel in pain. Still, thanks to them, I know the exact spot.

Rain drums on the windscreen as I drive. Reaching the location, I pull over. The area feels wrong. Why would Amy and Max have come here of all places?

The only explanation is memory magic: a vampire must have manipulated them into coming here.

I stare through the rain-slicked glass for five minutes. When the weather eases, I get out, kick at rocks, dandelions, and stubborn weeds. Hands on hips, I scan the ground. Nothing.

I expect a stain, a scrap of blood, something to mark the place where two remarkable people died. There is nothing. Not even a forlorn strip of police tape.

Ahead stands a derelict industrial building. I wander closer, but a sudden noise startles me. My nerves are shot; I feel silly and skittish. Low clouds roll back, heavy with more rain.

I dash to the car and slam the door. Coming here was pointless. I know there is nothing I can do—however much I wish otherwise. Common sense tells me to head back to the Human Sector. But I'm here now, and a day on double pay is hard to surrender. I open the delivery app, log in, and a cascade of orders fills the screen. I do not know the street names, yet the money is worth the learning curve.

I grind through job after job. The novelty breakfast

keeps me going, though the bacon leaves my tongue arid; I gulp a bottle of juice just to unglue my mouth.

By half-seven I accept one last run—back to the house with the yellow door. The pickup's nearby, so fifteen minutes later I'm cruising down the same road as yesterday. The rain has been off and on, with me avoiding the worst of it, yet the sky chooses that moment to split wide open.

I groan, but the door of number forty-two swings wide. He's seen me arrive, no chance to wait it out.

Grabbing the bag, I plunge into the deluge.

This evening I keep my phone tucked away until the final photo—no more rookie mistakes, unlike yesterday. I realise now how stupid and naïve I was to be fiddling with my phone while rocking up to a house in the Vampire Sector for the first time. I won't do that again.

Rain trickles down my face; a droplet clings to my nose. I shield the bag until I shuffle beneath the oak porch, and then it's in his grasp. His eyes—more violet than grey tonight—hold mine.

"Quicker this time," he notes.

I nod, shivering, not knowing what to say, frightened that I'll say something stupid or rude. My clothes cling—late Spring or not, the wind shaves ten degrees off and steals the warmth from my skin. Without taking my eyes off him, I pull out my phone to snap proof of delivery.

"Where's your coat?" He frowns, then reaches over his shoulder and hauls off his black hoodie in one fluid motion. The T-shirt beneath rides up, revealing a slab of abdominal muscle before it settles.

Bloody hell.

I glance away, then see nothing at all as he drops the hoodie over my head.

"Sir... please... you don't have to—" I mumble into the fabric.

"Arms."

I obey, robot-like. The sleeves swallow my hands, phone and all, and the garment hangs to my knees. Still warm from his body, it smells of musk, metal, and something darker... intoxicating. I stare up at him.

Satisfaction softens his expression: I'm warm, therefore acceptable.

A strange man.

"When do I bring this back?" I ask.

"Keep it. Next time, wear a coat." The door slams shut.

I flip up the hood, hurry down the path and clamber into the car. Who does that? Who gives a delivery driver their clothes?

I can't believe I just stood there, mouth agape, while he stripped and dressed me.

I shake my head and pluck at the fabric. A silver-stitched emblem stands out against the matte black: a bird, wings tucked, perched on a round shield. A single drop of blood gleams red at the tip of its beak.

Before starting the engine, keeping the hoodie in place, I wriggle out of my drenched top beneath. Much better. My jeans are still soaked, but I'm not about to peel those off.

I log out of the work app; it's time to go home.

The soft black fabric of the hoodie covers my fingers as I change gears. Like a lovesick teenager, I want to live in it, yet I refuse to cling to a stranger's clothes. I'll wash it and return it tomorrow.

Tomorrow. One more day working in the Vampire Sector won't hurt. Sunday is triple pay, and I don't have to wait for jobs. It will cover Baylor's recent mishaps.

I will keep my head down and my mouth shut. I have come to the very sensible conclusion that I can't solve Amy and Max's murders and would probably become the next victim.

If I die, where will Baylor go?

Relying on the house to take care of him would be selfish, and I don't want to leave the wizard's house alone. In the short time I've lived there, I've never felt safer. As daft as it sounds, the house is my friend, and Baylor is my fur baby now.

One more day, then I'll abandon vampire territory and concentrate on clearing my debts, the slow, sensible way, I promise myself.

A marketing job over here, safely beyond Theresa's reach, is tempting, but serving a vampire Clan is a step too far. Courier work is one thing, servitude to a master vampire is quite another.

Crossing the border, I toy with freelancing in the Human Sector under an anonymous company name. I cringe. The risk of losing everything is just too great. It would break my heart if I set up a company for Theresa to come along and ruin everything.

I know I shouldn't live my life based on fear, but the thought of losing everything again is paralysing.

I'm tired of being afraid.

Maybe I should go to the wedding... My heart skips.

Hang on, that's a great idea! If Jay truly thought I was a thief, would he invite me to his wedding?

No, he would not.

Would my attending publicly prove Theresa a liar?

Maybe.

I park, rush indoors and call, "House, do you think I should go to the wedding?" My words run together as I rush to explain my plan.

The invitation materialises on the sideboard.

"Brilliant, you didn't send it yet. Do you have any correction fluid?"

The tick beside *Regretfully decline* fades; '*Accept with pleasure*' is now marked. The house even selects beef for my main meal.

"Am I really doing this?" My voice trembles with fear and excitement. The thought makes me feel downright giddy. "Yes, I bloody well am. I will attend, wear a stunning dress, and meet Theresa's stare head-on." They will regret underestimating me.

I exhale a breath of determination tinged with maybe a little bit of madness.

Oh, my goodness, I'm going to my ex's wedding!

And I'm getting my life back.

Chapter Eight

The weather is glorious after yesterday's intermittent downpours; today is warm and sunny.

I'm working again and started early, so the day zips along. When a delivery for the yellow-door house appears, my heart lurches and I hit *accept* so fast I half-expect the phone to combust.

Day three. This is becoming a habit—one I'm going to miss.

Grinning like an idiot, I collect the order, try not to speed, and soon turn into the familiar street.

The freshly laundered hoodie is folded in a clear bag under my arm. At the door I knock and wait. Nothing. Another knock. Still nothing. Disappointed, I set the takeaway and the hoodie on the step, raise my phone for the proof-of-delivery photo—

The door swings open.

I beam—then freeze. The man in the doorway isn't *him*. A stranger stares back. My smile cracks; I hadn't realised how much I cared until this moment. Gosh, I'm a silly middle-aged woman. I need to go back to the Human Sector where I belong.

"I've got a tip for you," the stranger says, extending what looks like a wad of notes. His thumb hides most of it.

Something about his appearance is subtly wrong. His short, dark hair is combed with meticulous precision, every strand in place. Chalk-pale skin sets off lips so crimson they catch the eye whether you wish it or not. Dark grey eyes—flat and keen—are ringed with a disquieting burgundy hue, like dried blood.

My subconscious recognises the threat. Instinct screams *danger*. I step back from the porch and into the sunlight.

"No, that's quite all right, thank you. The fee's in the app. Enjoy your meal." I turn to go—

Pain explodes as he grabs my ponytail and drags me inside.

"What are you doing? Let go!" I claw at his wrist, trying to ease the burn in my scalp. "Let go!"

The beautiful man who gave me the clothes off his back to keep me warm yesterday would never have let this happen. Where is he? Why isn't he here to save me? Is he dead?

"Help! Help me!"

To shut me up, the stranger slams me against a wall. Once. Twice. The hand tangled in my hair slides to my throat, and a sharp fingernail pricks beneath my chin. He has claws.

"Look what you made me do," he growls, fangs bared. When he grabbed me, sunlight had touched his arm, the skin had blackened, and the truth hits me: a *vampire* awake in daylight.

I avert my eyes; strong vampires can steal your will if you meet their gaze. He doesn't bother. He wrenches my head to the side and sinks his teeth into my neck.

It hurts!

I strike out—my first punch ever—and his head jerks to the side. For a heartbeat, I think my hit will stop him. It does not. *Silly, Winifred.*

The only sound is obscene slurping.

The room whirls.

Then everything goes black.

Chapter Nine

I AWAKEN IN DARKNESS, lying on something lumpy that digs into my spine. It reeks of rot, making me gag. I slide my left arm out until my hand meets a wall; it thuds hollow under my palm. Plastic? A coffin? Have I died?

With my right hand, I touch my throat. Pain flares. The skin is ragged, but not bleeding. My mind flashes to the red mouth, the fangs... Oh God!

Feverish and leaden, I force myself upright, bang my head and feel the ceiling shift. Not a coffin. A bin. Memory sparks: the huge bins beside the houses. And now I realise what they are for. Not to store household rubbish, but to store bodies.

Body bins sitting casually next to their houses like our green compost bins.

Surely not. That can't be right—the authorities would notice mass killings. They must serve another purpose.

Yet the fact remains: I'm in a bin.

The vampire drank my blood and threw me away.

As my eyes adjust to the darkness, I see a limb. I'm not alone in this bin!

Heat floods my mind, emotion clawing its way up my throat. I feel this primal urge to scream. To scream and scream and scream. I clap a hand over my mouth.

Winifred, get a bloody grip. You are in a no-win situation—if you panic now, you really will be dead. Charging into the street, screaming for help, would be reckless. What if the day-walking vampire is still close?

But I want to go home.

I want to go home.

I have to get out!

I shove the lid a few inches and realise, with growing horror, that night has fallen. All the vampires are awake. I peer through the crack. A fence, a wide gate, the street beyond.

Fear mingles with numb resolve. I scramble over the rim, almost face-plant, then steady myself against the fence. The wood digs into my back as I edge to the gate. It isn't locked. I ease it open.

Silence—only distant traffic.

I slip through, closing the gate behind me. My car waits at the kerb. Keys are in my pocket; my phone is gone, probably lost when he grabbed my hair... I whimper. *Don't think about it, Winifred. Don't think about it now.* I fight the overwhelming urge to shrink into myself and crawl to the car.

Please, let no one see me.

Head high, keys ready in my hand, I walk the same path I skipped down earlier. My filthy hair hangs in a crooked ponytail; I shake it loose to cover the bite.

Inside the car I tremble. My clothes are intact, so he must have wanted only my blood. I should change my top, pull on a jacket to hide my neck, but fear pins me to the driver's seat. It takes every ounce of courage to start the engine.

Please, let no one see me.

My mind stays carefully blank as I drive. Eyes forward; nothing to see here. Nothing at all. At the border the tag chirps; the lane light flashes green. The tyres bump onto the rougher Human Sector road.

Five minutes later, I park and stagger to the front door.

The house shudders, doors rattling in panic. Frightened. The house is frightened.

"I'm all right," I rasp. A lie. The hospital would be sensible, but it's too late. I knew it when I crawled from the bin, when I felt the stillness in my chest.

I'm not breathing.

Kicking off my trainers, I head for the stairs, miss the first step and crash to my knees, terror ripping a sob from me. Hand to chest, no heartbeat.

The vampire killed me, yet I'm still here.

It's not possible. I was not a living vampire—the tests when I was fifteen proved that. I lack the necessary DNA.

I should be dead—or worse, mindless—yet my thoughts are clear. Newly dead vampires lose themselves for months, their minds dulled to nothing but hunger.

The hallway door creaks, and Baylor bounds out, tail

low. He halts, nostrils flaring, ears pinned flat, a thin whine escaping him.

Oh God. "Hi, buddy. It's okay, I know I smell funny, but it's just me." He slinks towards me. I sink my fingers into his fur. I can feel him. I can think.

I'm not mindless.

But I have no idea what I am.

I stay crumpled on the floor for so long that the house lifts me off the floor and carries me to my bedroom. Magic crackles over my skin, scrubbing away grime and knitting the torn flesh at my throat. Unseen hands guide me into my pyjamas.

Baylor hesitates in the doorway, most of his bulk still outside, panting in ragged bursts. I haven't seen him this anxious since Amy died. He whimpers, and I try to soothe him, but no sound comes out. I don't know what to say.

I sink into the mattress. "What about the windows?" I whisper. "What about sunlight?" Dawn is only a few short hours away.

A gentle pulse of magic strokes my cheek. *You will be safe,* it seems to say.

"Your wards can really stop it hurting me?" My voice is a croak.

Part of me almost doesn't care; let the sunlight take me. But the thought of burning like that vampire's arm—charred skin, living agony—terrifies me. I always pictured dying old and grey, holding the hand of someone I loved, not like this.

Not like this...

"I don't understand. I was tested. I'm a derivative mutt with traces of every creature's DNA. I barely carry any vampire, not enough for thrall status, let alone a full turning. How did this happen?"

I bury myself beneath the covers, hugging the pillow.

"I don't want to be a vampire."

Becoming a vampire is supposed to be a bureaucratic circus—licences, paperwork, permissions. Clearly, I'm a clerical error, a freak tossed in a bin like rubbish.

No one—least of all the vampire who treated me as a 'takeaway'—expected me to walk out alive... undead.

"I'm so frightened," I breathe. "How do I work like this? Do I keep delivering in the Vampire Sector and pretend I belong, or go back to the city and fake being human? What happens when I get hungry?" The idea of hurting anyone makes me shudder. I'd rather be dead. They hurt Amy, they hurt Max, they hurt me. I don't want to die, but I don't want to be this.

Magic fingers comb through my hair.

The mattress dips. Baylor climbs up and drapes himself across me like a weighted blanket. I wrap my arms around him—gently. Do I have super-strength now? I don't know.

Apparently vampires can cry. Tears slip hot and steady down my cheeks.

Just when I thought I was getting my life back, thought I'd turned a corner, the ground opened beneath me and dropped me even deeper.

I'm now so far down, I will never see the light.

Chapter Ten

I ping awake. Not the slow drift into morning. No, one moment I'm dreaming, the next I'm wide-eyed. Sunlight spills across the duvet; dust motes and stray tufts of fur cartwheel in the air, stirred by my breathing.

My breathing.

I am breathing!

And my heart is beating, pulse at my temples, a throb at the base of my throat that quickens as panic rises. I'm awake in daylight, not daytime dead. Did I dream it all?

What the heck is going on?

I tumble out of bed and stare into the dressing-table mirror. White scar tissue puckers my neck, proof the bite was real.

A vampire tore my throat open. I died—

No, none of that, Doris. I rename my inner voice as

recommended on my last podcast. Unless I want to be completely useless, rocking in the corner, I shove her dramatic monologue somewhere I can deal with later.

In my head, the version of myself I picture has always been twenty-something. I never imagine myself getting older, so sometimes seeing the ageing woman looking back from the mirror is a little bit of a shock. Now, however, the shock is greater still, because I look less like myself than I ever have.

My skin glows, and the face staring back is more refined. This is me, restored to my biological prime. Holiday glow—features sharpened yet somehow softened. Cheekbones defined. Pores erased. I prod my teeth with my tongue. I no longer look like myself, yet my teeth remain stubbornly human, and my body feels leaner, stronger.

I look like the best version of me.

I look like a vampire.

And I don't know how to feel about that.

Ageing is part of life. It's not always easy. As a woman, you see the fine lines creeping in, the small shifts in your body that don't reverse themselves. Still, at forty, I told myself I looked reasonably young. I think I did. Though I'm sure some teenager would glance my way and peg me as ancient.

But I didn't feel ancient. I felt like... me. A version of me who had grown into herself.

Age had not worn me down yet. Maybe that's confidence, or maybe it's survival. After Jay, I've had to rebuild. If nothing else, I'm grateful to be free of that. No more living under the weight of someone else's expectations.

But now I'll never age.

Not naturally. Not gradually. Not at all.

And in this world, that's not a blessing, it's a loss. Ageing is a gift not everyone gets. It means you are alive. Still changing. Still alive.

And I suppose... a part of me is grieving that.

I'm trying not to care what people think. I'm learning how to stand my ground. To stop being the victim in other people's stories and start being the lead in my own. And this—this... this frozen version of myself—is just another thing I need to learn how to carry.

I can do it. I just need to be brave. Again.

Yet the question remains—why am I breathing? Vampires are supposed to be corpses by day, so why am I buzzing with life? Is this what happens to them?

No. The proud creatures would trumpet a trick like this, not keep it secret. Whatever this is, it ties back to my turning. Or to something else having interfered, something like magic.

My knees go watery. Dizzy, I plop onto the bed.

"House?" my voice rasps. "Did your magic make me human?"

Floorboards creak, a breeze stirs, and then—static-thin, like a half-tuned radio—a soft, feminine voice.

I gape. "I can hear you!" I strain to catch every syllable. "You are quiet, but... did you say you gave me back my life? Does this mean I'm not a vampire any more?"

I... I have granted you a gift. While your kin sleep, you will be human until the sun sets, she says, clearer now. *The day is yours.*

Unbelievable. I'm still a vampire, yet half my life has

been restored—half fairy-tale curse, half miracle. I flop back on the mattress and stare at the ceiling in shock.

School wasn't kidding when they said wizard houses possessed uncharted power. To reverse vampire magic, even a little, is astonishing.

"Thank you for helping me." It's more than I ever dared hope for, even if, when the sun sets, my heart stops beating again.

Helplessly, I try to plan the rest of my strange life. "I can work in daylight," I breathe, hope sparking. "Be home before dark, stay hidden. No one needs to know." I pat my altered face. "If anyone asks, I'll claim Magic Sector cosmetic work." Not that I have friends or colleagues to notice.

No one cares.

House cares.

"This must have taken enormous power," I whisper. "What did it cost you? I don't want you hurt for my sake."

I'm all right, she whispers back. *You frightened me. I was worried. I did not want you to die, or see you in pain, and I didn't want you to be hunted by the vampires or to be forced to run away. I like having you both here.*

My eyes sting. "I thought of you as a friend even before this. Now I can hear you—truly hear you. What should I call you? 'House' feels rude."

No. The woman I was is gone, lost to time. I'm just a house.

"You are not *just* a house. You are my friend, and you saved me. You have saved me so many times. Thank you." I wipe my eyes. A large, fearful part of me wants to curl up, pretend this isn't happening, and hide in my room for ever.

Yet a small, louder, steadier part refuses to let the bad guys win.

I need to be practical. "I'll take a few days off, get used to this. A long walk with Baylor, then into the city for a new phone. Will the spell hold? I won't, er, burst into flames, will I? I'm not criticising, I'm just freaked out."

No need for fear. It will work, but be home before dark, unless you want the other vampires to discover what you are.

"I can manage that." I can do this.

I dress and whistle for Baylor. He bounds in from the garden, paws caked in soil—he's been digging again. Luckily, House always repairs the damage, filling in the holes before I even notice. One less mess to worry about.

I grab his lead and a cap with a peak, pulling it low to shade my face, just in case.

Then we step outside.

I feel safe inside the wards. It's everything beyond the gate that curdles my stomach. Baylor doesn't care. We are late for our walk and he's not shy about letting me know—awooing and yanking at the lead, eager to go. My hand trembles as I reach for the latch. Before I touch it, the gate swings open.

"Thank you."

You are welcome.

My heart skips a beat; it will take a while to get used to her voice in my head. "Can all vampires hear you?"

No. So far, only you—and other sentient things.

Wow, that must make for a lonely existence. Unsure how to respond, I remain silent as Baylor lunges forward, drags me across the boundary, and just like that, I'm out.

Sun on my face. Pavement underfoot. A newly made vampire, with a human beating heart.

Last night my world ended. This morning I'm outside because House gave me back the day.

I don't know what's coming. I've never felt this instinctively afraid. The vampire inside shrieks to retreat. But the other thing in me—the knowing that used to be a whisper—has risen to a clear voice. It says I'm safe. That I'm on the right path and that I can trust House. It says forward.

So I choose forward. Baylor at my knee, I turn the latch on my old life and let the sunlight find me.

Chapter Eleven

When night falls and I become... whatever I am now, I stand in the kitchen with a peach in my hand and stare at it.

What will it taste like? Sweet? Cardboard? Will it make me sick?

Will my fangs even work properly? Are they... straws? They snap out when I think of them, when I'm hungry or mad. I have prodded them with my tongue, even examined them with a hand mirror. There is nothing elegant or magical, just sharp teeth that extend like an overachieving canine.

I know vampire saliva is an anticoagulant; victims don't bleed out unless a vampire wants them to, and it seals punctures. Gross. Convenient. Both.

My fingers drift to my neck. Memory pricks. *No.*

Unless I absolutely must, I don't want to drink blood. But I can't deny I'm fascinated by the fangs and what else they can do.

Could I just... bite? My jaw feels stronger. I feel stronger.

Certain tests are essential after suddenly becoming undead. A peach seems a sensible start, even if fuzzy trichomes aren't exactly human skin.

I raise the peach and bite.

The peel yields with a soft *pop*. The taste is... dreadful. Dry, chalky ash, like a healthy-eating advert gone horribly wrong. Chewing feels like gnawing on a rubber stress ball. I make sure not to swallow. Horrified, I check the fruit, expecting grey rot, but the flesh is perfect—light yellow, glistening.

Still vile.

I bite again just to practise the fang action and lodge my right fang in the stone. After an undignified wriggle, I wrench free.

I carefully rinse out my mouth. Twice.

To distract myself from the lingering taste, I move to Experiment Two: strength. I eye the cast-iron oven. House probably doesn't *cook*, food simply appears. Still, it's hefty.

I crouch, hook my fingers under the lip, and lift.

It moves.

I raise it a few centimetres off the tiles.

What are you doing? House asks, voice cool but amused. *Put my oven down.*

"Sorry." I lower it gently, careful not to chip the floor, and rub my hands on my jeans. My fingertips look dented from the strain. Seconds later, the skin smooths, perfect again.

Interesting.

"Do we have any garlic?"

Why?

"Experiment Three: garlic."

You do know that's a myth, don't you? Same for holy water. Neither will hurt you. But if you must test your limits...

A clove appears in my palm.

"Thanks." I roll it between my fingers, then toss it in my mouth and give it an experimental chew. It's worse than the peach. I think anything I put in my mouth as a vampire is going to taste vile.

I clutch my throat, stagger dramatically, and gurgle.

Oh my gosh, Fred! Fred! Oh my gosh! House screams.

I crack and laugh. "Ugh, garlic's awful," I say, as House swears at me.

I turn on the tap again—nothing.

"Come on, that was funny."

Not remotely. I thought you were dying! I have put the water on timeout for lying.

"It wasn't a lie," I protest, grinning. "It was theatre."

Then take a bow.

"Please? It tastes horrific." I deploy my best puppy-dog eyes, stolen from Baylor, who is probably digging holes in the garden.

Water grudgingly flows. I rinse and spit.

"Thank you. Right, Experiment Four: chin-ups. I've always wanted to do proper ones. Like a soldier. Can you...?"

I can put a bar in the doorway.

"That would be perfect, thank you." A bar appears high enough that I have to stretch. I haul myself up. Easily. My chest clears the bar without effort.

"Yes! This is brilliant." After a hundred reps, I drop to the floor. Not hot. Not sweaty. I could get used to that.

What next? House asks, surprisingly patient.

"Experiment Five: skin. I want to cut my finger to see how strong my epidermis is."

You want to deliberately cut yourself?

"Yes."

A balanced throwing knife shimmers into existence. "Nice. Ooh, can I throw it after this?"

Experiment Six? Certainly. I'll prep a target.

"That's awesome, thank you." First, I press the blade to my fingertip. It's like trying to nick Kevlar or what I imagine Kevlar feels like. The edge barely dimples the skin.

If someone really tried, they could cut you, House notes.

I lean harder. A bead of blood wells—ruby bright—and seals again in two seconds.

"Handy," I murmur. "Now, the throwing knives."

The garage is set up.

I trot to the pedestrian door. The garage has become a miniature range, racks of knives gleaming under soft lights.

"This is great. Thank you. Don't judge me. I was rubbish at throwing as a kid." I flick my wrist. The knife spins, misses, and clatters. "Hm." Again. And again. Holding by the blade (probably stupid, but Kevlar fingers) gets me a stick... and a slow fall.

"Guess I need more force."

More force just bounces.

Throwing knives in real life is stupid, House says dryly. *The best way to lose a weapon. If it does not stick, someone throws it back.*

"Point taken." I tidy the knives.

I *should* try eating something else, but the peach and garlic have ruined me. Vampires boast they do not eat, claiming derivative superiority—so efficient, so tidy, unlike shifters and their meat mountain. Vampires can twist anything into a virtue.

Somewhere outside, Baylor yodels triumph at a freshly excavated hole. I smile despite myself.

"All right, Experiments Seven through Ten can wait."

Thank heavens, House mutters.

Chapter Twelve

One Month Later

It takes me a while to get used to my new undead life. During the day, I'm human and vulnerable. At night, I pretend my life has not changed.

Some activities are off the table: I cannot venture out at night, and no one can see me like this. To House's amusement, I still conduct odd little experiments at home. And at least I can still eat during the day.

Through awkward trial and error, we discovered I can eat normal food during daylight, but if I eat too close to sundown, say after six o'clock, I fall ill. My body needs time to digest before I 'die' for the night. I tried drinking tea—purely to see—and vomited it up at once. Food and drink are clearly out while I am vamped. Summer makes this routine manageable; winter's truncated days will be a nightmare.

The only thing I have not sampled is the red stuff. If I drink it, I truly am a vampire. I know it is so, yet convincing myself is another matter entirely. But of course, life doesn't work like that, and we have come to an impasse.

After the initial transformation, we hadn't expected my body to change. Vampires, at a genetic level, are immutable, but my human, daytime side is not, so the clashing magics throw a spanner in the works. I've lost a lot of weight.

Now we believe the vampire magic demands blood in my diet. Iron tablets don't help, so House—resourceful as ever—has procured some.

Tonight is Blood Test One.

I sit at the dining table and glower at a cup of blood. House makes it wobble, and the liquid swirls in sluggish circles.

"I don't want to drink it," I say, nose wrinkling. My fangs have dropped, giving me a faint lisp, which is irritating.

You have to, House says. *It'll keep you healthy, unless you would prefer to disappear into nothing or go on a wild rampage?*

"I don't want to rampage, but I don't want to drink that either."

Just drink it. Like a shot. Surely you have done shots before.

"How do you know about shots? Were you not born in the Victorian era?"

I might have been born in the late 1800s, but I am not completely dense, House huffs.

"I don't *shoot* anything that smells this vile. It's gross," I whine.

Doesn't matter, gross or not, if it keeps you alive.

I let my forehead thunk onto the table.

"The worst thing is the smell. It stinks of chemicals and slightly off, as though it's started to rot. Not exactly appetising." I shudder. I still reach home before dark, so I've no idea what people smell like to monster me. I do not *want* to know; it feels cannibalistic.

"Where did you get it?"

Silence.

"House. Where did you get the blood?"

My magic has tendrils I can extend a short distance, she replies, *allowing me to acquire small items unobtrusively. Most things I simply order and have delivered, but blood is different. The vampire courts keep a warehouse—I borrowed a couple of bags.*

"Borrowed? Righty-o. That's just great." House is stealing from the vampires now.

It's clean, O-negative, if that helps.

"No, it doesn't. So how do you order things?" I may be stalling, but I am curious.

My magic. I was a paper mage.

"A paper mage? Wow," I murmur. That explains the advertisement in the newspaper and the rental agreement. House was a scary badarse mage.

Now stop stalling and drink the blood.

Resigned, I lift the cup. Cold or warm, it will be thick and metallic. Eyes shut, I pretend it's tequila and throw it back. Copper sludge coats my throat; I gag but force it down. I can't even chase it with water—night body won't tolerate it.

No surge of energy follows. I sit, mildly nauseous, working my throat, trying not to vomit. After a few breaths the feeling subsides. I nod. "All right. That was... fine. I'm going to brush my teeth."

The cup vanishes.

"Thanks," I sigh, heading upstairs.

Soon I'll log on to the overnight customer-service job I picked up. One benefit of not needing sleep. My human self *rests* while the vampire *works*; between forms I'm effectively awake twenty-four hours a day.

Yet, astonishingly, boredom creeps in.

None of my motivational podcasts have ever covered *how to become a vampire*. Not one. There's no 'Five Steps to Reclaiming Your Power After Undeath.' No *Vampire for Dummies,* I checked.

After working for a few more hours, I log out of the system at two in the morning and stretch. I settle on the sofa, laptop balanced on my knees, and stare down the hallway towards the front door. Baylor snores at my feet, content and oblivious.

I need to move about. The thought has been looping in my head all night.

I need to move. I am going stir-crazy.

During the day I still do delivery runs, but at night, I am trapped, and where I once found comfort in the house's safety, the darkness now calls to me. I want to test my vampire abilities. Out here, in the middle of nowhere, it seems the perfect opportunity... but should I?

I know going outside at night is stupid. Dangerous. But

the blood I consumed sings in my veins, and the feeling is making me itchy and anxious.

I have got to move.

I spring up, grab a coat and shove on my trainers. "I'm going to stretch my legs." Then I slip outside and hurry down the garden path.

It's not safe, House murmurs behind me.

I ignore her.

I stand at the gate, hands on hips, scanning the silent road. Far off, traffic hums at the border. Otherwise, nothing. Stillness.

I walk this road with Baylor in daylight all the time, yet the darkness transforms it. The night feels alive. I can count on one hand the number of times I've been outside in the dark. The newness is intoxicating.

I roll my shoulders and start to jog. I've never been much for exercise, just enough to keep myself strong. I haven't gone for a proper run since school PE. But tonight feels different. Tonight, I feel strong.

Though I no longer need to breathe, I fall into the rhythm out of habit. My muscles don't burn or tire; they are powered by magic, not oxygen. Where once I would have been puffing after a minute, now the motion is effortless.

For an experiment, I hold my breath. My feet strike the road, steady and fast. I'm not even winded. My stride stays smooth, my lungs untroubled, but I inhale anyway—no point testing how long a human brain endures without oxygen.

I loop back towards the house, then halt, drawn by the scrubland beyond. In the distance, the Vampire Sector glows: buildings, towers, windows shining. When I was human, those lights were invisible. Now my night vision is crisp, as though binoculars are strapped to my face.

I glance at House, so close, then make a reckless choice. Instead of going inside, I veer into the grass. Cross-country. The ground is rocky, tufted with spiky weeds. Normally I would fear twisting an ankle, but tonight I am agile, my feet barely touching the ground. Wind whips my hair. It is exhilarating. This is—

This is *fun*.

I'm still grinning when I realise how far I have run. I have crossed the boundary, right to the very edge of the Vampire Sector.

A shout cracks the air. Guards. They must have seen me running.

Shit.

Chapter Thirteen

I flip up my hood, jam my hands into my pockets and saunter on, trying to look like I belong here. Just another harmless night-walker. Another shout, sharper this time. Fear knots my stomach.

Maybe they will mistake me for a teenager.

Maybe they will ignore me.

If they follow me, they will think I'm escaping—or spying—and I can't exactly explain what I am, can I? I must not lead them back to House.

"Oi! You!"

Boots thud closer. Voices bark orders. Panic bites. I keep walking.

Don't run.

Don't—

"You! Stop!" A hand clamps on my shoulder.

Instinct shatters into a single command: run!

I bolt. Not towards the safety of home, but away from it—deeper into the night—praying I have not made the worst mistake of my life.

The sector blurs past—lampposts stretch, shopfronts smear, parked cars stand frozen like statues.

I can run, truly run, and I do not tire.

But the guards can run too. They are older, stronger, more experienced. In vampire terms, I'm barely out of the cradle. I sense them gaining yet keep my gaze ahead, unwilling to lose momentum. A sharp *zip* whistles over my shoulder; sparks flare.

They are casting at me!

I fling myself around a corner and straight into a trap. A hulking guy with a vicious expression blocks the pavement. When I dodge left, a spell slams into my back. Heat spreads like viscous webbing, pinning my arms and legs together. Great.

"Little shit," he growls, striding closer.

"Why'd you run? It's past curfew, too close to dawn," says the second guard—the one who chased me.

"He's up to no good." The first man yanks down my hood. The tug pulls my blonde hair from its ponytail, and it tumbles around my shoulders. "Oh... *she's* up to no good."

They stare.

"Ma'am, what are you doing? You tripped the perimeter wards coming from the Human Sector."

I press my lips together.

"Silent, eh? We'll learn everything you're trying to hide when we speak to your Clan Master."

"At least she's not covered in blood," the big guard sniffs. "Not a speck."

"She's a lesser, barely more than a fledgling. She shouldn't be out alone," the second adds. He grips my arms, lifts, and I dangle as he marches with me to a van marked BORDER PATROL. He opens the back door and bundles me in. No rights are read; clearly, procedures differ here.

I sit, frozen with humiliation, while we drive for about five minutes. When the door finally opens, we are in a brightly lit underground car park. The same guard helps me out and carries me toward a set of steel doors.

Inside is a station much like those in human police dramas—fluorescent lights buzzing overhead, walls painted an uninspired grey, and plastic chairs bolted in neat rows. The air carries a faint tang of bleach and something metallic —old blood, perhaps, or magic.

A single austere desk spans the far wall, and the vampire manning it studies me over a monitor.

I force a half-smile, though I'm terrified. I need to get out of here before I turn human.

The snaring spell dissolves. Another guard seizes my wrist, slamming it onto the counter to expose the underside. "Is this a joke?" he snarls.

"She's not marked."

Not marked? What do they mean?

They gape as though I have two heads. I stay silent, but the custody vampire notes my confusion and softens.

"Every vampire bears a Clan sigil on the left wrist. Are you so young you have not been branded yet?"

"That's against our laws," the third guard states.

Uh-oh.

Staring at the desk, I tune out the guards' discussion about what they intend to do with me. I hadn't realised vampires were tagged on their wrists. There's no bluffing my way out of this. I've never been in trouble before, and now look at me, the first time I attempt to be a real vampire, I land myself in this mess.

Nice one, Fred.

A door bangs.

At once the voices fall silent. Footsteps cross the room. I keep my gaze lowered so I don't see the newcomer, but the guards' deference and the prickle of power at my back tell me whoever it is outranks them.

The sheer weight of the vampire's presence hammers at my senses, making my skin crawl. He is a magical powerhouse. I hunch lower. *I'm in so much trouble.*

"Sir, this vampire was running from the Human Sector across the scrubland," one guard reports. "She tripped the wards, and we apprehended her."

"Did she resist?"

"No, sir. She ran, but once spelled, she cooperated. She hasn't spoken, though—clearly frightened. The problem, sir, is that she's unmarked."

Fancy shoes step into my line of sight. Polished. Expensive.

"Look at me," the newcomer growls.

It takes every ounce of strength to raise my head.

Violet-grey eyes lock on to mine—eyes I recognise—and relief flickers through me. I had feared he might have been hurt after I was… killed. Yet he is alive—well, undead—and unmistakably in command.

He is a vampire.

So why was he awake during the day when we met?

There's no spark of recognition in those violet-grey eyes; to him I'm just a delivery driver, a speck in his world. He regards me without expression.

I try to return the stare. The ripped jeans and T-shirt are gone. He now wears a dark grey suit, so sharply tailored it seems sculpted to his frame, with a matching shirt and tie that deepen the violet of his eyes. His hair is plaited close to his scalp, and he still has the lip ring, which should make him look unprofessional, and yet it screams utterly him.

Not that I know this man—he's a stranger—but I think anything he wears, he will own it and wear with power. Half warrior, half billionaire tycoon.

"All right, gentlemen, I'll take it from here." He grips my elbow. "Lose the paperwork. She was never here."

"Sir? Do you know her?" the big guard asks.

One look silences him.

"Of course, sir," the custody officer says quickly. He claps his hands. "Bravo Team, daylight's coming. Lock everything down." The room empties.

My yellow-door vampire guides me through another doorway and down a long hallway, his hold surprisingly gentle. He steers me into a dark office, flicks on the lights, and settles me into an uncomfortable plastic chair. The office is small, almost suffocating, and I have no doubt this is where interrogations are held.

He searches his pockets, produces a compact device and presses a button; a faint ringing fills my ears. Magic blooms, hazing the walls, floor, door, and ceiling. Soundproofing, perhaps, or a privacy ward.

He makes a brief call. "I found her. I need a car at the station. Emergency Protocol One." Phone pocketed, he cups my chin, tilting my head to expose the scar on my neck.

"Who did this to you?" he snarls.

Chapter Fourteen

I GAPE at him as he towers over me. His body heat rolls across my skin, and a clean scent—musk, metal, and something darker, which my vampire senses now recognise as power—fills my lungs.

"You were human, and now you're not. So I'll ask again. Who did this to you?"

I can't believe he remembers who I am; his earlier blank expression fooled me completely.

His rage over my turning is palpable.

Yellow-door vampire releases my chin, grasps the back of the chair, and effortlessly spins it so that my shoulders thump against the table. Bracing his hands on either side of me, he leans in, caging me.

Oh my God. If my heart were beating, it would be racing.

Standing beside him, I feel tiny; nearly a foot and a half separates us. Seated, I might as well be curled on the floor.

"The spell gives us privacy," he says, his voice low yet vibrating with fury. "Winifred Crowsdale, answer my question. Who. Did. This. To. You?"

What the heck? "How do you know my name?"

I suppose that's the least of my problems. I'm trapped in a sealed room with an angry vampire. I won't mention my daylight escapades, but I can at least tell him how I was bitten. I lick my lips and—like a starving man—he tracks the motion.

His eyes darken to storm-grey. "Please answer my question."

"A man ordered a takeaway to your house," I rasp.

"When?"

"The day after you gave me your hoodie."

"That's impossible."

"*Impossible?*" Bitter heat rises in my voice. He did not just call me a liar.

"I'm not calling you a liar," he says, his eyes narrowing as though he can read my thoughts, "but no one should have been at that house."

"He answered the door in broad daylight. *Like you*, he was awake during the day."

A warning voice in my head whispers: *don't say too much*. This is dangerous ground, angry vampire, heavy magic, locked door—provoking him is a very bad idea.

"I'm telling you the truth. It was Sunday, the day after you lent me the hoodie. Someone placed a delivery at your address. I assumed it was you. I collected the food, returned your hoodie, and one of your friends decided I would make a good snack. He dragged me inside by my hair and tore out my throat. Shock and blood loss made me pass out or die, I'm not sure which." I awkwardly shrug.

"I woke up like this, in your body bin." My voice cracks. "You really are a bunch of sick bastards with no self-control. I'm surprised the human government hasn't wiped you out."

His expression darkens; a muscle ticks in his jaw. "Wipe us out? Are you forgetting *you* are a vampire?"

"Indeed. Your pal murdered me. Thanks for that."

"We're getting off track," he says tightly. "What did he look like?"

I describe everything I remember: his chalk-pale skin, crimson mouth, dark grey eyes, the way he caught sunlight and burned. His clothes, his stance, the tone of his voice and what happened next.

As I speak, a muscle jumps in his cheek. *He knows something.*

"How did you turn?"

"I have no idea."

He moves away from me and paces, rubbing the back of his neck. I use the lull to draw a deep breath.

"You are still so new," he says, glancing at me. "Still breathing. You have been an unregistered vampire with no clan for more than a month. How many bodies?"

"Bodies?" I echo, incredulous. "As in people? None. Do you think I'm out here murdering humans? I'm nothing like you or your friends." We lock eyes. I'm doing a dreadful job of reining in my temper. This isn't like me—I'm usually the one people walk over, not the one who fights back.

This beautiful man makes me feisty.

"It's less than an hour to dawn. I need to get you somewhere safe."

"I just want to pretend today never happened and go home."

"Where's home?"

"That is none of your business. I don't know you."

"I'm the only help you have got."

I grimace, ashamed of how I'm reacting. It's not *his* fault I was turned. I soften my tone. "I'm sorry, I'm not trying to be rude. I'm just... frightened. It's been a lot."

A knock interrupts. He opens the door a crack, speaks to someone, then closes it again, something small in his hand.

"Winifred, vampires aren't clanless. To survive, you must belong. There's no hiding and no running. You have managed so far, but time's up. Let me help. Let me take over now."

"Take over how?"

His phone rings. His shoulders tense, yet he ignores the call.

The weight of his undivided attention is on me. It's disconcerting—like I am standing in the presence of a god.

"I wish I could give you more time, but you have run out." He steps forward and looms over me. "Please forgive me. I won't let anything happen to you, and I *will not* let you fall into another clan's hands."

He blurs into motion. Gripping my left wrist, he flips it over and presses a small object against my skin.

A squeak escapes as burning pain shoots up my arm.

"Ow!"

Magic colours shimmer as a sigil sears crimson into my

flesh. A bird... a crow or a raven sits on a shield, blood dripping from its beak.

He pricks his thumb on a fang, dark blood welling, and smears it over the mark. "You are now a member of my clan," he says, calm and cold.

Ew, that's nice and hygienic, bloody vampires.

"It hurts."

"I know. It's for your protection."

I cradle my burning arm to my chest. "My protection? What about my consent?"

"There wasn't time." He extends a hand. "Come, I've arranged a safe house for you."

I'm so angry, my fangs are pricking my lip, but my intuition is screaming at me to go with him. For now. Numbly and feeling completely overwhelmed, I put my hand in his.

Power flows from his touch, flooding my fingers—my whole body.

What on earth is that? It didn't happen when the guards manhandled my wrist. It must be a vampire thing; he's that powerful. I try to pull my hand free, but his grip only tightens. He draws me through the station to the underground car park, where a blackened car waits.

"You are not taking me back to that house, are you?" Meaning the house where I died.

"No." That heat from his hand settles on my lower back. "Get in."

"Promise me."

His body goes rigid as he stares down at me. "On my honour. Now can we please go?"

I do as I'm told and slide over the leather seat. Panic

nips at me as we pull away. "What's your clan called? What is your name?"

He raises a brow. "You don't know?"

"No. I'm not part of your world. I've been calling you 'yellow-door guy' in my head."

He gives a short laugh. "Clan Blóðvakt," he says, the name rolling off his tongue. "My name is Valdarr. Valdarr Blóðvakt, Raven of the North."

Valdarr. The name is vaguely familiar, but I shake my head; I'm hardly fluent in vampire politics.

"Nothing? The Grand Master of the Vampires—does that mean anything?"

I swallow. "*You* are the Grand Master?"

"No," he says softly. "That would be the vampire who turned you. My father. I'm the heir."

"*Heir*? Heir to the Grand Master? So... the vampire who killed me is the Grand Master? Your father?"

He winces. "Yes."

This just keeps getting better and better. Why couldn't it have been some low-level vampire? Oh no, that would be far too easy.

"So are we, like... brother and sister now? Does this make us siblings?"

He looks as horrified as I feel. "No. We are *not* like brother and sister. Turning isn't... familial. You are simply a member of my clan."

"Your father's clan."

"No. *Mine*. I'm the master of my own clan. You wear my mark, and you will keep far away from my father. If the Grand Master learns about you, that you survived, he will kill you."

"He already tried. It didn't stick."

"Next time it will."

A silence stretches as we weave through the city.

"We will need to discuss what happened, how you survived. Have you ever given blood to a vampire, or taken vampire blood?"

"Not that I remember. Unless someone used that nasty mind trick on me. According to my recollection, I've neither given nor taken vampire blood."

I say nothing about House or her magic. Or what I am in the daylight. That is mine to protect, my sanctuary, my friend. Safeguarding House means safeguarding Baylor too, and I will never let anything happen to them. I promised. They both need me, and this overbearing vampire won't turn me into a liar, nor let me break my word to my family.

We reach the safe house.

The townhouse occupies a quiet street. Three storeys rise above a short flight of stone steps that lead to a glossy black front door fitted with a lion-headed brass knocker. Tall ground-floor windows, framed in white-painted wood, sit on sills dressed with window boxes overflowing with greenery.

Polished parquet floors glow honey-gold. The walls are wallpapered in silk, a hue of rich colours, like something from a luxury-design show. Every surface gleams; every piece of furniture is elegant, heavy, expensive. It's how I imagine a billionaire might live—if that billionaire were also a vampire.

Valdarr watches me take it all in. He doesn't rush. He seems to be waiting, perhaps for me to keel over and die for the day right in the middle of the floor. Then again, I've seen him awake during the day. I wonder whether his condition, like mine, springs from wizard magic, or something else, something older.

In the centre of the room, inlaid into the floor, lies a sigil: the original Clan Blóðvakt crest, I assume. It's more elaborate than the mark on my wrist. A silver bird perches on a Viking shield, bright red blood dripping from its beak. A ring of runes and carved words encircles it: BLÓÐVAKT – ÆRE FREMFOR ALT.

"The bird," I ask, "is it a raven or a crow?" I really should know, considering it's etched into my skin.

"A raven."

Right, he mentioned in the car that he is the Raven of the North.

"The writing is Elder Futhark," he continues, a hint of weariness ghosting his voice, "the oldest runic alphabet. *Blóðvakt – Ære fremfor alt* translates to *Blood Watch – Honour Above All*. But it's more than a motto; it's a soul-oath." He points to each rune in turn. "*Ansuz*—divine truth. *Ehwaz*—loyalty. *Othala*—ancestral duty. *Tiwaz*—sacred sacrifice."

"Oh." That's... a lot. I'll never remember it, let alone pronounce it.

He reaches for my hand again. "Dawn is close; I want you to feel safe while you sleep. Come." When our skin meets, power zips between us once more.

He leads me, not to a crypt, not to a basement, but upstairs.

"You will be perfectly secure. A ward strong enough to keep out enemies and the sun."

The room is beautiful. No windows, yet not claustrophobic. Warm lights, soft grey walls and creamy bedding, and the air smells faintly of cedar and old paper. A reading nook is tucked into the far corner. For something so secure, it feels comforting.

"I'm sorry," he says. "I have nothing for you to change into, but I'll make sure you have fresh clothes when you rise."

"It's all right." I try for casual. "I will be daytime dead in a few minutes."

He frowns.

Perhaps that's not the politically correct phrasing. I don't care. He practically kidnapped me.

"I'll see you at sunset." He moves to the door.

"Valdarr?" My voice is soft, almost sad; I will miss him when I escape. "I didn't like you stamping me with your clan mark, but I do appreciate your help. Thank you for rescuing me."

"Rest well, Winifred." He nods once, then steps back and shuts the door.

The lock engages with a deep metallic clunk. Bars slide into place top and bottom, turning the bedroom into a vault.

Safe or a cage. I'm not sure which.

I sit on the bed and scan the ceiling and walls—no cameras, no blinking lights. I don't have my phone, so I can't download an app to run a sweep for hidden tech. But I can't imagine Valdarr spying on me.

I wait.

The moment the sun rises, my heart stutters—a single, pathetic beat—then nothing.

I suck in a gasp, eyes fluttering shut. It doesn't hurt; it's merely strange. I roll my shoulders, then *whump*. The sleeping organ kicks in thudding sluggishly, then settles into something steady. Breath floods in and warmth chases through my limbs.

I wait for what feels like another thirty minutes. I listen. Silence.

Is Valdarr still awake like me, or does he sleep? Die for the day?

I creep from the bed, unlatching the reinforced door as quietly as possible and then tiptoe along the corridor, down the stairs.

The front door is locked tight, but in the main living room, a large bay window slides open soundlessly.

My heart pounds as I slip through. No alarms flare; the ward built to keep threats *out* and let occupants go doesn't fight me. After wrestling past the window boxes and their spiky greenery, I land gracelessly outside, my feet finally finding purchase on solid ground.

I run.

Except I'm human now, and running as a human?

Nought out of ten, would not recommend.

I huff, puff, and stumble. Within three minutes I'm wheezing and clutching a lamppost, desperate not to vomit. My legs are jelly; my face, beet-red. Eventually I recover and start walking. It's roughly six miles the long way round to avoid main roads and border cams.

Two hours later I'm home.

Baylor is delighted to see me.

House is not happy. *Where have you been?* she yells.

The gate swings open. Hot and sweaty, I shuffle

through. I take a single step toward the front door before it swings back and smacks me on the bum.

"Did you just... spank me?" I scowl, rubbing the spot.

She magics up a glass of water before I have even shut the door. I chug it; she replaces it with another. I drop onto the sofa, knee bouncing, and pour out the whole story.

She groans, swears, and scolds me six ways from Sunday, then asks what my Clan Master looked like in that suit.

I roll my eyes, smile and describe him in vivid detail.

We agree: no more nights out as a vampire. They'd find me. But no one is looking for the human delivery driver. Even if Valdarr knows my name, I should still be in the clear.

Chapter Fifteen

Three Weeks Later

It has been three weeks since the Vampire Sector debacle, and I have managed to avoid further fanged problems. I glance at my wrist. The raven's mark stares back. I suppose I shall always be tied to him, whether I like it or not.

I miss Valdarr, which is ridiculous. He's a stranger.

I wish I'd stayed longer, got to know him, learned more about the vampire part of me that still itches beneath the skin. I wonder what might have happened if I had asked questions, if I'd let him help instead of running.

Shamefully, I conducted some online stalking, 'research,' I told myself, on Valdarr and his clan.

It turns out I have been more of a shut-in than I

realised, because in vampire circles, Valdarr is a celebrity—an ancient one. Records place him founding the clan between 800 and 1050 CE. Over a thousand years old. My worry about being a 'cougar' is laughable; it is the other way around. He is practically prehistoric.

His father? Older still. And looking into their bloody and violent history, I do not want their attention—now or ever.

Still, I think about him far more than I should.

I'm certain there was a spark between us, yet it may be his enormous amount of power and nothing more than wishful thinking. After all, he is a beautiful thousand-year-old vampire, and if I'm honest, someone like me—someone not even good enough for Jay—could never be enough for Valdarr.

Yet he remembered me. Helped me. That counts for something, doesn't it?

Yet my intuition—the little voice that grows louder by the day—warns me that it is dangerous, and I believe it. His father, the Grand Master, killed me once; if he discovers I'm still walking around, what then?

My overactive imagination supplies lurid daydreams—vivid, brutal scenes in which he realises what I have become and ensures that my second death is permanent.

No bins. No miracles. Only pain.

It is almost as though I can see the future, a precognition that should be impossible. Every time it happens, I shut it down. I ought to speak to House about it, but it is easier to blame my misfiring brain, an effect of getting no proper rest.

I worry that my head will pop off from lack of sleep,

but I've adapted. Two months into this vampire business and I have found a new normal. I've been working, head down on deliveries in the Human Sector, then knuckling down to my online job at night. For once everything seems to be going... well.

I have even started a modest nest egg and feel more in control than I have for years.

I drink blood every other day, and we have discovered that 250 ml is the magic amount to keep my weight stable. It isn't about calories; if it were, I'd need litres of the stuff. It's about balance, about keeping the magic animating my undead body steady and strong. My bones are now covered in the perfect amount of lean muscle.

Today's problem? What to wear to the wedding.

You would think being turned into a creature of the night would excuse my absence. But no. I have to go. I need to rebuild my career. I need to show Theresa and her smug son that they didn't break me. That I'm still standing.

It's a win–win, provided I can scuttle out before sunset and avoid transforming during the family photos or worse, eating the guests.

From the hall, the giver of fur, filthy paws, and excessive slobbery kisses watches me with betrayal in his eyes. "Aroo, awww, awooo," Baylor lets out a series of long, theatrical howls from behind the warded door.

"Yes, yes, I know, you are abused," I tell him. "House and I are the worst, utter meanies for locking you out."

He sneezes.

"We will cuddle on the sofa in a few minutes, buddy. You will survive."

I turn back to my task. Three lovely dresses lie on the

bed. I'd love to claim I bought them, but I forgot the wedding was this weekend.

House procured them.

"I hope you didn't steal these," I say, eyeing the first option—a blood-red dress.

Don't be silly. I can manifest clothing.

"It is a beautiful colour—dark red, very elegant," I admit, "but not wedding-appropriate. I'm sure I read somewhere that red implies you have slept with the groom."

Which I have, obviously. We were together ten years. Everyone at the wedding will know, I don't need to underline it with crimson satin. Even if I do hate the groom and his mother, it's still not appropriate.

I turn to the second dress, a pale lemon. Lovely shape, great neckline, but... "Too pale. Under the wrong light it could look white. That's a whole other nightmare I don't need."

Then I examine the third dress and know instantly it's perfect.

Deep navy, with a high neckline and half-sleeves that reach the elbow, the fabric has enough weight to drape to a graceful midi length. The matching belt will cinch my waist, and the high neck will hide the scar tissue on my throat. I also have a couple of chunky bracelets that will cover my clan mark.

"This is the one," I murmur, picking it up. "Thank you, House, it's perfect."

You are welcome. It won't be awful.

I think she might be right.

"I have been thinking about your new name," I tease as I try on the dress. This has become a running joke between us. "Hannah, Harper, or Helen? You would definitely suit Harper. It's such a lovely name."

It is indeed, but considering only you and other soul-touched objects can hear me, I fail to see the point.

"I'm sorry, House."

Don't be. That dress fits as though it were made for you.

I straighten the sleeves and twist to see it in the mirror. House is right, it fits me perfectly, as though it were made for me—seamless, effortless, unfairly perfect.

Thanks to my vampire condition, I no longer need shapewear. All those little lumps and bumps I used to fret over? Gone—smoothed away as if they had never existed. My body has been... corrected, *edited*—a before-and-after photo without the diet, the effort, or the choice.

I should be thrilled; it's what I always wanted, isn't it?

Instead, I feel oddly hollow, as though the dress is hanging on someone else's body, a version of me who never had to fight for self-acceptance. A stranger in the mirror.

See? I told you it would be perfect.

"It is," I murmur, smoothing the fabric over my hips. "Thank you, House."

Tomorrow I will help with your hair and makeup. It'll take me seconds to make you presentable.

"Are you sure you can do that?" I grin. "I don't want to look like a Victorian ghost."

I know fashion. I know makeup. I'll make you look beautiful.

"Thanks. I appreciate it. If I do my makeup tomorrow, I'll no doubt poke my eye out. I'll be nervous. Frightened to death."

Oh, I know. But you will be fine.

"I wish you could come with me. I could take Baylor, put a bow on his collar?"

Absolutely not. You are not taking the pup. A pause. *Besides, it's going to be a gorgeous day. I've set up a paddling pool for him.*

Baylor loves water, so I can already picture it, and when House says paddling pool, she means swimming pool. The dog will have the time of his life, and honestly, it makes me want to stay home, sit in the shade, and watch him splash.

Sometimes doing the right thing really sucks.

But I need to attend this wedding. Jay doesn't get to rewrite the story and stroll away clean, and neither does his mother. I'm going, and I will clear my name.

I lounge on the sofa, my fingers buried in fluffy fur as I scroll through short video reels set to flashy music. Time slips, my vision blurs, the screen stutters—and... suddenly, I'm standing in the middle of a street.

Chapter Sixteen

What on earth is going on? How the heck did I end up here?

I spin, scanning the area. Across the road stands a clump of trees and a sign for WESTVIEW PARK. Nearby, a group of women in matching T-shirts emblazoned with 'Pink Ladies' shoulder leather bowling bags and chatter about today's lawn bowling competition.

On my side of the street, a mum pushes a pram—the tiniest baby curled inside—while a little boy of about four skips beside her, clutching the handle. His voice is bright and eager; he chatters about his new baby sister, words tumbling over one another in excitement. The mum looks exhausted, dark shadows under her eyes, yet she answers every question.

"Mummy, can Cathy come and play on the swings?"

"Not yet, sweetheart. She's too little, but soon you'll be playing on the swings together."

"Oh, can she watch?"

"Yes, she can watch you play."

Then the baby wails, a shrill, urgent cry. The mum bends to rearrange the blankets, murmuring comforts.

I notice the boy's grip loosening, one chubby finger at a time. His attention drifts. Across the road a fluffy dog trots out of the park, tail wagging, tongue lolling. The boy's eyes widen.

"Puppy," he whispers.

He steps forward, tiny shoes slapping the pavement.

There's a car parked to the left, another to the right. He squeezes through the narrow gap, hands outstretched.

"Puppy," he says again, louder this time, his hand stretching towards the dog.

"No!" I shout, panic surging.

I rush forward, instinct screaming at me to grab him, but my hand passes straight through. I can't touch him. I can't stop him!

He toddles farther, oblivious to danger. He giggles.

I hear it—the low hum of an engine. A car, coming fast. I see it before anyone else. It's seconds away; the driver cannot see him. My breath catches.

"Joshy! No!" his mother screams, finally looking up.

Time slows.

The car is almost on him.

He takes another step, still smiling at the dog.

I scream, but no one can see or hear me.

The car hits. The impact flips him into the air and his

small body twists, then crashes onto the road with a sickening thud.

The world erupts in screams—his mother, the bystanders—while I stand helpless, tears streaming down my face.

I jerk upright, gasping. *Oh heck.* Heart thudding, hands shaking, it takes a while to calm down. Baylor grumbles, touching his cold nose to my wrist. I'm still on the sofa in the living room, phone clutched tight in my hand. I haven't moved. I was scrolling...

I try to shake off the memory of an impact I didn't witness in real life. I try to ignore it, but I can't. Everything inside me screams that what I saw is real. A little boy. I can't ignore that.

What was the name of the park?

I grab my laptop and start frantically typing, fingers flying as I search. *Westview Park.* Yes, I think that's it. I close my eyes, and the scene re-forms, every detail crystal clear. It feels as though I'm still standing there. I have not forgotten a single thing. My vision memory is different: sharper, almost photographic.

I have the place, but I need the time. The Pink Ladies and their bowling competition... Another search—it's today.

"House!" She can hear me, obviously, but I can't seem to lower my voice. I'm panicking.

What is wrong?

"I had a vision. I was in a trance. I was scrolling on my phone, and suddenly I was standing in the street. It felt so real—a little boy was hit by a car." I give the details in a rush.

"I checked: the park is in the Vampire Sector. It's real, and the bowling competition is today."

I feel an overwhelming compulsion to save him.

"What's happening to me, House? Am I going mad?"

The reason you can hear me isn't my magic, it's that you are psychic, she replies. *You may always have had the gift, and the vampirism is amplifying it. It's rare—hardly spoken of—but some vampires are special. Do not worry, Fred, we will work it out.*

An emerging gift.

One that I've been doing my best to shut out for weeks.

"If it's real, I will need to go to the park and save that little boy."

I kiss Baylor on the crown of his head and leap up, heart pounding. I dash upstairs and throw on some clothes, nearly tripping as I shove on my trainers.

Tie your laces, House scolds.

"Right, right! I will!" I mutter, fumbling to knot them before grabbing my coat and bolting for the door.

I'm halfway down the path when I realise I've forgotten my keys. Spinning around, I see them hovering behind me. "Thanks, House," I say, breathless.

Be careful. Drive carefully. You won't save him if you have an accident.

"No, you are right," I reply, forcing myself to nod before sprinting to the car.

I pull out of the drive, gripping the wheel tight as I head for the Vampire Sector. My brain screams at me to go faster, but I have to be sensible. At the next stop, I slap the park's name into the navigation, then floor it as soon as the lights turn green.

I barely remember crossing the border. I follow the directions, skid to a halt outside the park and fling the car door open—I don't even switch off the engine.

I'm almost too late.

"He's going to get run over!" I yell, sprinting along the pavement. The mother turns at my shout, her scream piercing the air.

Without thinking, I do what I couldn't do before: I grab the little boy and yank him clear.

He wails, terrified.

I'm holding a child. A real child.

His dark-haired mother—her eyes the same green as his —snatches him from me, sobbing. "Thank you, thank you, he would've died."

The driver climbs out, pale and shaking. "I didn't see him. He came out of nowhere from behind that parked car. If you hadn't grabbed him... I—I would've killed him. I wouldn't have stopped in time."

My heart pounds. The vision was real.

"I think she's in shock," someone murmurs.

"I'm all right," I say faintly. "Just... glad he's safe."

I wave awkwardly and walk back to my car. I climb in, buckle up, and pull away—carefully, shakily.

A few streets on, out of sight, I stop and sit while my heart hammers.

The child is alive. He cried because I frightened him, not because he was hurt. The vision saved his life. Somehow, I ended up where I was needed.

That's... insane.

When I can face the road again, I drive to the end, turn around and head home.

Chapter Seventeen

I'M STILL COMPLETELY FREAKED out about yesterday—about rescuing that little boy.

If I hadn't been scrolling at that exact moment, if I had not slipped into a social-media trance, would he have died? I'm no superhero; I'm not anyone special. Yet what a thing to be able to do—visions of real life. I don't think I will be saving people every day, but it's as though this power needs me to believe it's real.

He would have died if I'd ignored that pull, that compulsion to go.

It's all so strange and terrifying.

House thinks I'm psychic, and it makes sense. I did have an odd little gift I had spent ten years ignoring before my life went to shit.

I won't ignore it again; I will try to learn about it even if it doesn't feel real. But for today, I need to set it aside, so I shove my phone into the glove compartment. I have a wedding to attend.

I park my car a street away from the venue and walk the rest of the distance. House has worked her fairy-godmother magic on me. She wasn't exaggerating when she promised to handle my hair and makeup. Flawless. Not overdone. Elegant.

I grip the fancy wrapped wedding gift as though it might bite me.

House and I spent *hours* weighing the options. We debated books, booze, bonsai trees, but in the end, we chose something that struck the perfect balance between polite and pointed.

A luxury candle in an elegant hand-blown glass jar. Scent: fresh linen and citrus. Name on the label: FRESH START. On the card I wrote:

Wishing you warmth, clarity, and a bright new beginning.
All the best,
Fred.

Amy would find the candle hilarious. I wish she were here. I wish House were flesh and blood. Instead, I'm alone, attending the wedding of my ex-boyfriend and the woman with whom he cheated.

Chin up, shoulders back. I can do this.

The hotel grounds are beautiful: sweeping lawns, immaculate flowerbeds, and a golden stone path without a weed in sight. I follow the clink of glasses, music, the murmur of voices, and a series of curated wedding signs pointing around the building to the rear terrace.

"Fred! Is that you?"

I turn to see Jay's father.

He approaches, takes my upper arms, and kisses my cheek.

"I'm so glad you came," he says, voice warm. "Are you all right? I've missed you." His glasses slip down his nose as he peers at me. Jay's father has always been a gentleman; I've never understood how he endures Theresa.

It still hurts that he never defended me against her slander, but why should he? I'm only his son's ex-partner. I was never family.

"Hi, Hamish," I reply, matching his smile.

"You look incredible. Being single suits you."

"Thank you. May I say you look extremely dapper in that suit?"

"Why thank you."

He guides me onto the patio: broad slabs of white stone framed by manicured gardens and the hotel's rear façade, where floor-to-ceiling doors stand wide open. Inside, a dining room glows in white and gold tones.

Small groups of guests chat over champagne flutes while waiting staff drift past with silver trays. Somewhere nearby, a string quartet threads the delicate hum of music through the laughter and conversation.

I spot the gift table, place mine among the others— white and gold boxes, tissue-stuffed bags with glittery bows. Mine blends in perfectly: classy, tasteful, not at all petty.

Not... *obviously*, anyway.

I feel eyes on me. Some curious, others confused, a few outright hostile. The stares range from *What's she doing here?* to *Wow, her 'magical makeover' is impressive.*

Yet there are smiles too, little nods of recognition from people I met during those ten long years. Old acquaintances wave as though we're still connected. I wave back and smile.

It's curious that none of our former friends are here. Perhaps Melissa planted her designer heel and struck them from the guest list. I still can't fathom why I'm here or why I came at all. The idea of reclaiming my career seems silly now.

"This is lovely," I say, my gaze snagging on the ceremony space: rows of white chairs flank a pale aisle and six flower-arched gateways. *Six*, as if one weren't enough. I'm so glad that this isn't my wedding day. Nothing says closure like attending your ex's wedding on your own birthday. *Cheers to me.*

"Melissa and Theresa worked very hard on all this," Hamish says with a small grimace, trying to hide behind his glass.

I smile and pat his hand. I'm simply glad to see a friendly face and secretly relieved security didn't toss me out at the gates. Perhaps that's the real reason why I didn't risk the hotel car park.

Hamish passes me a glass of orange juice, then steers me towards a knot of relatives.

"These are a few of Jay's cousins," he says. "Maristella, Tracy, Belinda and—"

"Oh, we've met," Maristella cuts in, eyes wide. "Ages ago, five years, I think?"

"Yes, I think so. Lovely to see you all." I smile politely.

"You look fantastic! Whatever you're doing, it's working," says Belinda. She and the others exchange one of those tight-lipped glances that says far more than intended.

"I can't believe you're here," Tracy blurts, then winces. "Oh, I don't mean that badly. I just mean... wow."

"You're incredibly brave," Belinda says.

"Incredibly beautiful," adds a new voice. "Hello, ladies."

A man steps into the circle with the confidence of someone who has never heard no. Dark hair, film star looks, and he knows it.

"I'm Charlie," he says, flashing a toothpaste-advert grin. "We haven't been introduced."

He offers his hand.

"Fred." I hesitate, but everyone is watching, so I accept.

Mistake.

He lifts my hand, and instead of a friendly shake, presses a kiss to the back of it. I keep my expression miraculously neutral, though the impulse to wipe away his spit is immediate. I step discreetly back.

"So," Charlie says with what he clearly thinks is a charming smirk, "bride or groom?"

"The groom," I reply, taking a healthy gulp of juice. I need alcohol for this. It's a shame that Jay's dad is on damage control.

"Fred dated Jay for a few years," Hamish supplies, trying to help.

Charlie's eyebrows rise. "He was punching above his weight, wasn't he?"

He laughs. I don't.

A deliberate cough sounds behind me.

I turn—and freeze.

Jay stands there, dressed in a dark grey tuxedo and fancy pocket square, a single white rose pinned to his lapel.

My heart does something awful and traitorous. Every muscle tightens, and I instinctively edge closer to Hamish.

Coming here was a very bad idea, my inner voice whispers.

I replay the night I chose to leave him. I see that woman cowering in the kitchen, silent after he caught her with his elbow in the hallway.

When I was younger, I would have pushed him back, told him off, said something. Instead, I swallowed every slight, every cruel word. Not once did I fight back, and the thought disgusts me.

When did I become so pathetic? It must have taken years, so many small moments that chipped away at my self-worth.

The woman I was would have never come here today.

Jay looms over me, and even in four-inch heels I still feel small, tiny, in fact, compared with him. His dishwater-blond hair brushes his collar, longer than it used to be; he has skipped yet another haircut. I wonder whether his mother has already berated Melissa, as she used to do with me, as though it were my fault he could never remember the appointment.

His gaze skims over me, and the smile falters into a frown.

"Fred, you're looking well. Very well."

Yes, I turned into a vampire a couple of months ago. No biggie. I focus on breathing slow, steady. No one must see that I am panicking.

Of course I knew I would meet him—it *is* his wedding—but part of me had hoped to float through unnoticed by him. No such luck.

"Yeah, you definitely traded down, pal," Charlie says, elbowing Jay in the ribs. "I can't believe you dated this girl, let her go, and she still turned up to your wedding. Burn." He wiggles his fingers, as though casting some smug 'bro hex.'

Jay does not rise to it.

"Nine years," he says, still staring at me. "We were together for nine years."

I shake my head. "Ten. You forgot the last one while you were cheating on me with Melissa. You must not have noticed I was still around."

Silence.

I can feel the attention of everyone within earshot. Did I *really* say that aloud?

I'm not sorry.

I came here for a reason, and these people are smart enough to add two and two together and realise my account makes far more sense than Theresa's 'I embezzled money from the company' excuse.

"Don't you think you had better get ready for your bride?" I ask, recovering quickly. "If you will excuse me."

I turn on my heel and walk—deliberately, gracefully—away. Behind one of the massive floral arches, thick with roses and baby's breath, I release a long sigh.

I hear Maristella mutter, "I want to be Fred when I grow up."

I cannot decide whether to scream or laugh.

The wedding co-ordinator begins ushering guests to their seats; the ceremony is about to start.

I remain hidden a moment longer, just long enough to collect myself.

Then I slip into an empty seat near the back. Hamish catches my eye and gives a jerky nod before taking his place by the altar.

A few minutes later Theresa sweeps in, every inch the mother of the groom. Her makeup is flawless, her hair artfully sculpted. Arm linked with Jay's, she marches past as though *she* were the bride.

I cannot hear her words, but I do not need to. She prods Hamish and Jay like dolls, straightens Hamish's tie and—judging by Jay's wince—yanks his hair while adjusting his collar.

Classic Theresa.

The string quartet strikes up the opening bars of Mendelssohn's *Wedding March*.

Everyone rises.

I have seen photographs of Melissa; she ought to be radiant on her special day. Instead, she stalks down the aisle with a scowl that could strip wallpaper, her father at her side, pretending nothing is amiss.

Then I spot it: her phone, wedged into the sweetheart neckline of her gem-studded gown, protruding between crystals like an afterthought. She has, quite literally, shoved a phone between her breasts, and no one mentions it.

Her scowl deepens when she sees me. She halts mid-aisle, rigid. Her father tugs her arm.

"You," she mouths.

The music continues; the quartet valiantly plays on.

After a few taut seconds her father murmurs to her and guides her forward. She moves again, reluctantly.

What was that about? I was invited. She has won: she is in the dress, at the altar, about to marry my ex. I am merely a quiet guest near the back, striving to keep my face unreadable, barely succeeding.

The ceremony proceeds. When the officiant reaches the familiar line—"If anyone objects to this marriage, speak now or forever hold your peace"—the atmosphere shifts.

It feels as though every head turns towards me.

The bride whips around and glares.

Theresa's stare drills into the side of my face, but I deny her the satisfaction. I lift my chin and picture Baylor splashing in his absurd paddling pool at home. I'm peaceful, happy, untouchable. They. Can't. Touch. Me.

The vows conclude; they kiss. It is done. Jay is married, and I am grateful it is not to me.

I remain long enough to watch them sign the register. Important, necessary. I have shown up, been seen and hopefully patched my reputation.

But I will not stay for cake.

Yes, I feel a little guilty about wasting a meal. But Melissa's dagger-eyes and the tension thick enough to cut with the wedding knife tell me it is time to leave. They ruined my life for a time, but I'm not about to ruin their wedding day.

I have my closure. I have made my point.

Time to go home.

I follow the golden stone path back towards my car.

"Winifred, wait!"

I stop.

Jay—of all people—strides after me. He is not with his

new bride, not being photographed, not cutting the cake. No, he is here, chasing me. I tense.

"Why are you leaving so soon?"

"Your wife looked furious," I reply coolly. "I thought it was time to go."

Before Theresa and Melissa decide to rip out my hair too.

He seizes my arm and steers me off the path, across the lawn, towards the side of the hotel.

"What are you doing?"

"You look so... beautiful. Incredible in fact."

"Jay, that's inappropriate." I wrench my arm free, skin crawling. "It is your wedding day. You should be with Melissa, not cornering me. This is wrong."

"I can't stop thinking about you." He steps closer. "I've missed you."

I step back. He advances again, and before I realise, I am boxed against the stone wall.

"When did you get so beautiful?" he murmurs. His breath reeks of whisky.

I plant my palms on his chest and push. "Jay, this isn't appropriate. Step back."

"But you're my girl."

"No, I'm not. I haven't been your girl for nearly seven months, and if we're honest, not for years. Melissa is your *wife*, and unlike you, I believe in commitment, in loyalty. I won't lower my standards—or my morals—for anyone, least of all you. Move back, now."

For one ridiculous moment I wish I had my vampire strength, my fangs.

Then—

Over Jay's shoulder I spot someone I never thought I

would see again, striding straight toward us. My mouth drops open, and a tiny squeak escapes me. *Oh my—*

"I think you'd better listen to the lady and step back before I make you," says a velvet voice that sends goosebumps along my arms.

And there he is. Valdarr.

He radiates quiet menace, standing in full sunlight, unfairly magnificent in another immaculate suit. The black ink wrapping down around his fingers makes him look lethal. He gives me a small nod and approaches with purposeful calm.

"Apologies I'm late," he says gently, then leans in and kisses my cheek. Soft, warm, familiar, as though we have done this a thousand times.

I stare, dumbfounded.

Jay stiffens. "Who the fuck are you?"

Oh my gosh, Jay did not just swear at my vampire! The thousand-year-old vampire wearing sunlight like a coat.

Valdarr steps between Jay and me, shielding me with his body.

"Her attachment to you is what made you special—you realise that, right? You should have counted your blessings and cherished her. She's no longer yours," he says, voice razor-sharp. "You are embarrassing yourself. Go back to your wife."

"I'm not gonna take advice from a punk with a lip ring."

Valdarr looks Jay up and down with open contempt, a slow, deliberate sneer curling his lips.

"Here's the advice from a 'punk with a lip ring': learn

the difference between *owning* and *honouring*. You tried the first. I'll be doing the second."

Wow. I have no idea what to say.

I simply stare at him. Valdarr. Standing here in the sun, dressing Jay down like an immortal knight in bespoke armour.

I don't care what happens tomorrow; right now, he is my hero.

Jay is equally speechless. His mouth opens and shuts like a fish on dry land.

Valdarr leans closer—he towers over Jay by at least eight inches—and murmurs something too soft for me to catch.

Whatever he says drains the colour from Jay's face.

"Come," Valdarr says, turning to me with effortless grace. "Let me walk you to your car."

He takes my elbow and guides me back to the path. We walk in silence.

I glance up at him. "What did you say to him?"

"Nothing important."

I falter. "I—I don't understand how you are here, in daylight, actually standing in the sun."

He wears a ring I have not seen before, a large ruby that hums with magic. Perhaps it is what keeps him safe from the sun.

"I'm a gifted old vampire," he replies, as though that explains everything. He pauses, raises a gentle hand, and brushes his thumb along my neck, just beneath my jaw, directly over my pulse. His brows knit. "What I don't understand... is why you are awake and *breathing*. I can hear your heartbeat."

I swallow. *Shit, I forgot about that.* I should offer him

some truth. "I don't know why I was turned, or how. I'm a vampire at night and... this during the day." I shrug, leaving certain details unspoken. "I have no explanation."

"I will help you discover what happened to you if you will do me a small favour. Keep your daytime humanity secret. Don't trust anyone; no one is safe."

I nod, ease out of his touch and resume walking. We remain quiet.

At the car he lifts the keys from my hand and opens the driver's door.

I hesitate. "You are not going to... take me?"

"No. I won't take you anywhere you do not wish to go."

My throat tightens. "Why did you come?"

"I'm your clan. I'm yours. And if we are honest, I've known where you were since the moment you ran from the safe house."

Oh. "You have people watching me?"

"Yes. You're a member of my clan living in the Human Sector, and we have protocols to follow."

My heart sinks. Oh no—Baylor, House...

"Don't panic," he says, offering a reassuring smile. "I'm not coming after you, your dog or your magical house. I'm glad you are somewhere safe."

He glances down, then back at me. "I learnt about the wedding from a background check. I came to ensure you were all right. I hadn't intended to interfere, but I couldn't allow his hands on you. You looked frightened."

"Thank you. I appreciate your help."

"Always."

He leans in again to hand back the keys, and when he

kisses my cheek this time, his lips brush perilously close to the corner of my mouth.

"Happy birthday. I will be seeing you soon, sunshine."

Dazed, I slide into the car. He closes the door with quiet finality.

He let me go.

He *let me go*, and he kept me safe.

I'm not wild about the idea of being followed by vampire servants... but right now? I can't *wait* to tell House what happened at the wedding.

I fasten my seat belt and pull away. A glance in the rearview mirror—he is gone.

After I change gear, my fingers graze the spot on my cheek where I can still feel the ghost of his lips.

Chapter Eighteen

I LIE on a lounger in the shade of a tree, watching Baylor splash in the pool like a toddler on a sugar high. When I arrived home, I changed and told House everything. She's now on red alert, scanning for anyone watching the house, checking and double-checking her wards. She hasn't found anyone—yet—but I can tell she is nervous, even if she won't admit it. She doesn't blame me.

I still blame myself.

The garden has expanded to accommodate the pool and what must be dozens of dog toys. All squeaky. All bright. All irresistible, judging by Baylor's dopey grin. This isn't a country for outdoor pools—our weather is chilly nine months of the year—but today the water glitters in the sun, neither chlorinated nor salted, simply water: pure and clear, kept immaculate by House's magic. Not even a fly dares touch its surface.

Baylor sprawls on the wide steps, chest-deep, tongue lolling as he pants with exhaustion.

I grab a towel. "Come on, it's time to get out."

He ignores me—of course he does—then dives for a floating T-bone steak toy.

"Baylor, it's time. Out."

He turns his back, tail wagging in open defiance, droplets flying.

"Don't ignore me," I say in my best mum voice.

He grumbles, circles back with the toy clenched in his teeth, and finally hauls himself out. I towel him down, muttering about dramatic huskies.

"Come on, buddy."

Inside, a flash of House's magic dries him instantly, and the damp towel vanishes from my hands, replaced by a mug of hot tea.

"Thanks."

Baylor flops onto the carpet with a huff. I sink into the sofa, clutch my tea and stare at the surface as though it might offer answers.

"I'm finding cold-turkey phone withdrawal really difficult."

You need to get to grips with this psychic gift, House reminds me again—probably the hundredth time since I got home.

"I know, but I'm scared."

You need to practise, she says gently. *There are still a few hours before dark.*

"What if I wander off again?"

I won't let you. You recognise the visions now. You can learn to control them. I've got you, Fred; nothing will happen.

She's right. If fate turns you into an undead seer, ignoring it can only make things worse. Besides, I always wanted to be special—here I am.

Yay.

Better to try now than spend the night brooding over the wedding or Valdarr and whatever he hissed at Jay.

"Okay."

I set the mug aside, run upstairs, grab my phone and return. Baylor is noisily licking his flank as though it owes him money.

"All right, everyone can hear you. Haven't you had enough of a bath for one day?"

He pauses to glare, then resumes.

"You will end up with a hairy tongue," I mutter, unlocking the phone.

I reopen the site, settle in and start scrolling. Nothing happens. I'm too tense, too aware.

Relax, House urges. *Trust me.*

Trust her? I do, and I do not want the power hijacking my brain. I keep scrolling, keep watching.

Ten minutes later it starts: a prickle behind my eyes, a shimmer, the sensation of slipping sideways without moving. This time, I let it happen, but I do not fall too deeply. I skim the surface. I'm aware now, and that helps.

The magic doesn't seize me, it flows, and I let the vision take me.

Chapter Nineteen

It's raining.

I stand in an alley behind what I think is a nightclub. The distant thud of bass pulses through the wall. Rain trickles from a broken gutter.

Check for details, Fred. Check for details.

I've read enough books—seen enough films—to know you look for clues, pay attention.

A bin stands nearby. A shiver twists my gut, but this one isn't a body bin, it's full of bottles and bar rubbish. Stamped on the side is the venue name: THE DOWNBEAT. I know it. It's a flashy nightclub in the Vampire Sector, fifteen minutes from my house and owned by Clan Nocturna—their crest blazes on the sign.

I jump when the back door bangs open, and a girl staggers out, heels wobbling and dress askew. A man follows, steady, composed, grinning. My nose wrinkles. He's a vampire; even in a vision, I feel his magic slither under my skin.

He props her against the wall.

She leans, blinking slowly. "I just need some fresh air," she slurs. "Can't feed you... my master won't like it. We're... doing paperwork... Thrall paperwork. I need to get home."

"I don't care," the vampire growls.

Then he bites her. No hesitation, no finesse.

I lurch forward. Panic blooms. I want to help—grab him, do something—but I catch myself. *Like the little boy, this is not happening now; I'm in a vision.* I can't intervene, only observe, hunt for a clue that will help.

Her heartbeat falters—slows.

When the little boy died, I'm sure I was thrown out of the vision then.

Hurry, Fred. Hurry.

I retreat, sprinting down the alley and into the street. Yes, I know this place. But what day is it? No newspapers, no posters; everyone's glued to their phones—useless.

A passerby finishes a message and locks his screen. The date and time flash up for a single, precious second: early hours tomorrow—1:38 a.m.

The vision tears away.

Chapter Twenty

I JOLT upright on the sofa, gasping.

Fred. Fred, are you all right?

"Yes," I manage. "But there's a girl—early hours tomorrow—who will be murdered by a vampire."

I pour out everything: The Downbeat, the rain, the time, the victim, the clan, the predator. My voice shakes, but I don't stop until it's all said.

"I must go out *tonight*." I groan. The words land like a dare. My heart thuds, loud and uneven, pounding in my throat.

Fear hardly covers it. I'm no fighter. I'm no gritty avenger with battle scars and brass knuckles. I've thrown exactly one punch in my life, and that was into a vampire's head while he murdered me. So, no, I'm not the punch-and-kick type.

But I'm not a coward either, and I won't let that girl die. I cannot imagine what might happen if I ignore the vision, the compulsion to act is almost overwhelming. These visions must matter. If she were meant to die, why show me? Someone—something—saved me; now it's my turn.

"I can save her, House." I stand, fists clenched. "Any idea how to stop a vampire?"

A few, she replies, deceptively casual. *Go into the kitchen.*

Baylor doesn't stir, flat on the carpet, snoring like a faulty motor. I frown and walk to the kitchen. A new internal door punctuates the far wall.

"Where did that come from?"

Oh, that, House says breezily, *is the armoury.*

"The what?"

Spells, enchantments, tools, things that go zap. You know, an armoury. I have been storing magic for years. I can alter the layout, and I thought a basement war room might be fun.

Is there nothing House cannot do? I stare, then turn the handle. The door creaks open—

I can't believe what I'm seeing.

No stairs. No basement steps.

A slide.

"You are joking. A slide?"

Stairs are boring, she says, amusement clear in her voice.

Despite my nerves, I laugh. "Last time I used a slide, I was ten. It was one of those old metal ones, hot from the sun, rivets digging into the backs of my legs. I burnt my arse and went home with bruises."

This one's smooth—and fun.

I don't hesitate. I sit, tip forward and whoosh. The slide

whirls me down in warm, magical speed; I laugh, hair whipping behind me. I land—miraculously graceful—on solid stone.

The room sprawls before me, softly lit by floating orbs. Shelves, cabinets, and racks gleam with unfamiliar weapons, shimmering bottles, and scrolls bound with silver twine. A workbench, a wardrobe. An armoury.

My mouth falls open. "Holy—"

Welcome to the good stuff, House says.

I don't know what to do with all the good stuff. The room is a maze of magic. I don't dare poke around in case something explodes. I shuffle forward, hand hovering over a glowing object shaped suspiciously like a gilded pineapple, when—

No! Don't touch that! House's shriek ricochets off the brick walls.

I screech and stagger back.

She giggles. *Giggles.*

"You are not funny." My heart does a frantic tap-dance and I fold my arms. "That's it! I'm not touching anything. Keep your creepy basement toys."

I spin to leave. I have no idea how I'm going to climb the slide, except it has vanished. In its place stands a flight of stairs.

I rub my forehead. "Of course there are stairs now. Why wouldn't there be?"

Come on, House says, ever so cheerily, *you want to save this girl? I've got just the thing.*

Something drifts from a top shelf and hovers in front of me. I squint at the floating, perfectly carved piece of wood.

If you are going vampire-hunting... you will need a stake.

"A stake? Really? Stabbing vampires is a myth. Humans don't have the strength to drive wood through a chest." As if I'm going to stab anybody.

Ah, House replies smoothly, *but you don't go through the ribs, you go up, underneath.*

I stare at the ceiling or wherever she's speaking from. "You have spent too long alone. I'm not sliding a sharp stick under anyone's ribs. I was thinking... a sticky spell, a binding charm, like the one they used on me when I was arrested. Something non-lethal that says, 'I'm brave and resourceful but also a decent human being.'"

You are no fun. Just touch it.

With a sigh I grasp the stake and concentrate. It's warm. Not room temperature, warm.

"Why is it warm?"

Magic. Slayer magic. A little soul-binding, too—

"Nope. Creepy." I let go and wave it away.

You live in a house powered by soul magic, House points out, voice softer now.

Oh no, now I've gone and hurt her feelings. "Oh no. I didn't mean you. You are not creepy, House. You're—you are brilliant. You are amazing. Just... wielding a dead vampire hunter's stick is a bit creep-flavoured."

It won't hurt you. It will guide you. Help you.

"And when I turn vampire, will it try to stab me?"

Don't be silly. Take her, just in case.

I wrinkle my nose at the thing. "Fine. But if it starts whispering in my pocket, I'm setting it on fire."

Deal.

I tuck the stake gingerly under my arm.

You said he had his back to you?

"Yes, but that might not be the case tonight. In the vision I wasn't physically there. My presence could change things. He will be able to scent me, hear me."

Things fly through the air and land with soft thuds on the long workbench in the centre of the room. I step closer and duck as one more thing sails over my head.

These, House says, *ought to knock a vampire out.* A handful of blue glass vials wiggle in place. *Throwing spells, non-lethal, enough to scramble his senses and drop him like a sack of potatoes. And this one*—a little spray bottle filled with something that looks like black goo—*will mask your scent and muffle your sound. It won't make you invisible, but it will make you hard to track.*

I grin. "Now, this is more like it. Thank you."

You are welcome. And you are still taking the stake.

"Of course I am," I mutter, though I have no intention of using it.

A satchel appears on the table, and everything drifts neatly inside.

There. Sorted, House says with satisfaction.

As I buckle the flap, House hums thoughtfully. *You should know that stake has a name.*

"A name?" I blink at it like it might blink back.

Beryl.

"*Beryl?*" I pause. "You are telling me this ancient vampire stabbing stick..."

Slaying artefact.

"The slaying artefact is called Beryl?"

She was a very angry Victorian lady, House says, smug. *Turns out, wrath and embroidery weren't enough, so she took up vampire hunting. Kept a stake in her knitting bag next to the crochet hooks. Slayed a hundred and seventeen vampires and one particularly rude reverend. When she died, her soul was bound to her favourite weapon. That one, right there.*

I stare at the polished wood. "A human soul in a stake." Magic-users are strange.

You must keep her out of sight. If anyone discovers her, she will end up in some magical laboratory. Beryl will be helpful. She hums when danger's near, buzzes if she dislikes someone, and comments on your posture.

"Brilliant," I mutter. "Just what I need, a Victorian ghost who doubles as an etiquette trainer."

The stake vibrates.

She likes you, thinks you have good hands.

"Well, I'm glad she's not judging my hemline." I shift the satchel onto my shoulder. "All right, I'd better have something to eat before I die for the night. I feel like Gizmo from *Gremlins*," I grumble. "The question is, what food *complements* vampire-hunting?"

That's obvious, House says with a laugh. *How about steak?*

This is going to be a very long night indeed.

Chapter Twenty-One

At midnight a thunderstorm rolls in, and by one a.m., rain is bouncing off the pavement. I sit in my car outside The Downbeat, waiting. I know I'm early, but I'd rather be early than late. Slipping out of the house required stealth. Valdarr's people may be watching, and I couldn't risk being stopped.

In hindsight, perhaps I should have looked for them, asked for help, passed on a message.

Why didn't I ask Valdarr for his number?

Even if I wanted to contact him, he's already grappling with my daylight humanity; adding psychic visions of future accidents and murders is too much. Who would believe a baby vampire muttering about being a seer?

None of this makes sense. I need proof. I need to know —without a shadow of a doubt—that I'm right, undeniable proof. Before I try to convince the heir to the vampire world, I need to convince myself.

And besides, I don't really know him. Yes, he was my hero today: he kept me safe, kissed my cheek. Almost charmed the pants off me. But that doesn't mean I trust him. His father killed me.

He's dangerous.

I'd be a fool to forget that.

I glance at the dashboard clock: thirty minutes to go.

I tug my collar wide and spray the scent-masking magic across my throat and shoulders. It smells as though ash and tomcat wee produced an unfortunate offspring in a compost heap. No wonder it renders me almost invisible—everyone's simply trying to escape the stench.

Raincoat on, spell satchel slung across my body, I step into the downpour. I move quickly, purposefully, knees knocking. If I were still human my heart would be pounding, but now it is silent. Vampire calm, one small perk.

The air reeks of urine, cheap perfume, and the sour stench of alcohol. After I check the alley, I wedge myself between the brickwork and a recessed doorway. Perfect: narrow enough to hide, angled enough to see. Rain smears the alley into greys and shadows. I watch. Time ticks on...

And then it happens.

Right on cue, the fire door bangs open. The vision unfolds, step by step. The girl staggers out, heels wobbling. The vampire follows, smiling a mouthful of teeth.

I grip the blue glass vial in my palm.

Wait—wait until he is distracted, until he feeds.

He sinks his fangs into her neck.

Now.

Dirty water splashes my calves as I sprint forward. I hurl the spell, and it strikes his head—more luck than aim, but it works. The glass shatters and the magic detonates like a second thunderclap.

He turns, jerks towards me, lips slick, hissing. Yet the spell acts fast: his eyes roll back and he collapses.

The girl stares at him, mouth agape, breathing in shuddering bursts.

"I'm not here to hurt you," I say, hands raised. "He was trying to drain you, and I had to stop it."

She sways. Blood snakes down her neck, soaking her blouse.

I hold my breath, then realise vampires still need air to speak. "Here." I press a packet of tissues into her hand. "Keep pressure on that."

Too dazed to argue, she obeys.

"We need to get you home. Were you out with friends?" Rule number one: if you go out together, you go home together. I don't mind playing taxi tonight.

She shakes her head. "Friends? No. I've just finished work." She points numbly at the door, blinking against the rain.

"All right. Can you walk?"

She nods once, slow and unsteady.

"Okay, come on, let's get you home."

I lead the girl out of the alley and onto the street. Passing vampires lift their heads, nostrils flaring at the scent of blood. I glare back—*Don't even think about it*—and bundle her into my car.

Inside, I crack a window to let the rain-washed air swirl through. Her blood lacks the chemical tang of bagged plasma, but it is hardly appealing. I drank extra before leaving the house, perhaps that is why hunger stays away.

She murmurs directions, voice thick and slurred, and fifteen minutes later we stop outside a tidy brick house—clipped hedges, warm porch light, picture-perfect vampire suburbia. I park and walk her to the door.

It opens before I can knock. A familiar face stares at us: the waitress from the vampire-themed restaurant, a member of Clan Nocturna.

"Crystal?" she gasps, catching the girl by the elbow. "Why are you home so late?"

"I caught a vampire feeding on her," I explain. "She's a little out of it."

The waitress narrows her eyes. "Wait... do I know you? Weren't you human?"

"Nope. You don't know me. Never seen me. Just glad she's safe. Bye." I flash an over-bright smile and retreat as though I have a train to catch.

I reach the car and stretch for the handle—

—only to be shoved from behind.

Pain detonates behind my eyes as my face smacks the side mirror. My skull rings; copper floods my mouth.

"You bit my thrall," snarls a male voice, angry and frankly idiotic.

"I *what*?" I gasp, ducking his next blow. More vampire speed than skill. "You absolute walnut. Smell her; I didn't bite anyone."

I duck again as he swings. "I dragged her away from a vampire behind The Downbeat, your clan's nightclub. I drove her home, that's all." Of course, no good deed goes unpunished.

He isn't listening. He lunges; I dodge, his hand snatching at me.

The spell bag slung across my body thumps my hip. With another burst of speed that surprises even me, I grab a vial, hurl it, and it smashes against his chest.

He stares at the spreading wet patch on his shirt, baffled.

"That's how I dealt with the vampire—the one who actually bit Crystal."

He sways, then drops to his knees.

"You are welcome," I add as he face-plants onto the tarmac. "Huh, I'm a badarse."

The stake slaps into my palm.

What the heck...

Reinforcements inbound, kid. Ditch the car and run.

The voice is not House's; it's sharp, female, unfamiliar, and coming from the stake.

One downed vampire becomes four more, gliding from porches and rooflines. They circle, fangs bared.

"You killed Ian," one of them snarls.

I can see why they would think that, what with him not breathing and all. But the vampire is asleep.

"Beryl?" I whisper.

Yes. Welcome to the party. Now move your undead arse!

I run. Rain lashes my face; my coat snaps behind me. The street blurs.

This is bad, very bad. I am running from vampires. Again. The border police caught me quickly last time, but perhaps—just perhaps—I can outrun this lot.

A spell slams between my shoulder blades, pitching me into a bin. Glass bottles clatter and smash; the plastic shell bounces across the pavement. My legs turn heavy, useless.

Not again.

I'm a pathetic excuse for a vampire.

The man who accused me of killing Ian steps towards me. He smiles—all teeth and promises of pain.

Yeah, it's not a nice smile.

A door swings open to my left. A woman steps out, with dark hair and eyes of liquid silver that glow in the gloom.

Beast shine.

She's a shapeshifter.

A cricket bat dangles loosely from her hand; she twirls it like a sabre.

"What's going on here?" Her tone is flat, unimpressed.

"Nothing for you to worry about," my accuser replies. "It's a vampire matter. Go back inside."

The shifter huffs, raising the bat. Her silver gaze narrows. "What I see," she says, pointing the bat at him, "is five male blood derivatives circling one woman."

"Five?" I mumble.

She flicks the bat upward. I follow the gesture and spot a vampire perched on the roof above me. If she hadn't appeared, he'd have pounced.

"Go back inside," the vampire repeats.

She bares her teeth in something that isn't quite a smile. "Those aren't the words," she murmurs. "'Go back inside, Alpha's mate'—*that's* what you're looking for." Mockery drips from every syllable as she settles into a batting stance. "Nope. Don't think I will. I rather fancy using your heads as cricket balls."

I gulp. "Thank you, but you can't take on all these vampires for me. No one else needs to be hurt."

She ignores me. The vampires do something odd: they retreat from her.

What am I missing?

It's not just the bat, Beryl murmurs. *She moves like a fighter, and look, she has company.*

I sense them, the heavy, predatory aura of shifters sliding from the shadows, dozens strong, watching and waiting.

Oh.

That would do it.

The vampire thug meets my eyes. "We'll see you soon, baby rogue." Then the lot of them melt into the night.

My knees give way and I flop onto the pavement—straight into a puddle. I don't care.

"What are you doing?" A deep male voice booms from the doorway. Bright light spills out, masking his features. "Where did you get that cricket bat? Tell me you didn't. Lark, that was in the glass case. It's *signed*!"

Lark's silver eyes widen. She mouths *oops*, tucks the bat beneath one arm, and crouches beside me.

"That hex is nasty. Want help stripping it?"

A shifter removing a spell? Suspicion coils, but my instincts say trust her. I nod.

Lark extends her hand, fingers waggling. Something tugs inside me, behind my shoulder blades, as though a layer of skin peels away. It doesn't hurt, just unsettling, like peeling off a face mask in one smooth pull.

Moments later the weight vanishes and feeling floods back into my legs.

"Thank you," I croak.

"Glad to help." Lark rocks back on her heels, studying me. "Are you all right? Need anything?"

"I'm fine. Just a misunderstanding."

Her gaze drops to Beryl.

Panic flickers. I tighten my grip on the stake and scramble upright on shaky legs. I don't wait.

I run.

"Let her go," Lark says softly behind me.

I don't look back. Guilt churns, but I push it aside. Too many shifters. Too many unknowns.

What am I going to do now? I have never been in trouble before, and now I'm stuck in the Vampire Sector. I just want to go home. I can't cross the scrubland because of the magic, and the border guards would spot me in seconds, and I cannot go through the checkpoint without my car.

I'm trapped.

I need my car. I can't believe this is happening.

"Thank you for helping me." I slow to a fast walk and slide the stake into my coat pocket.

I did it for House; she would have been upset if you had died.

"Whatever the reason, thank you. When daylight comes," I mutter, "I will have to go back for my car, if they haven't chopped it into pieces. Have you any idea what I should do, Beryl?"

Oh, now you ask me? she snaps, all snippy indignation. *I thought if I spoke while I was in your pocket, you would set me on fire.*

I groan. "Did I say that? I'm sorry. I'm really sorry, Beryl, but I need your help. Running from shifters and vampires is all new to me; a few months ago, I was an ordinary human." I straighten instinctively while she grumbles—like a very cross grandmother—about rude people.

I hurry back to the nightclub alley, back to that same stupid doorway. It's the only place I think of that's quiet. I sit on the damp threshold, coat wrapped tight, and spray the stinky magic again in case any vampires or shifters come searching. Pressed into the shadows, I close my eyes and try to relax.

Daylight takes forever.

At last the sky brightens. My heart begins to beat; my legs feel heavy as I leave my doorway and walk the now empty streets. I'm wet, cold, and miserable by the time I reach the car—but there it is, untouched.

"Beryl, can you check whether the car's been tampered with?"

No. What do you think I am? A crime-scene investigator? I don't do magic scans. I'm not House. I stab and kill; that's the gig. She sniffs loudly, sulkily.

"Oh. Right. Thanks anyway."

I climb in, peel off the soaked coat and pull on a warmer top, not caring if anyone sees my sports bra.

The traffic at the border is heavier than usual. Vehicles inch through the pre-approved lane ahead, just enough of a pause for my gaze to drift to the noticeboard beside the booth.

I freeze.

My photograph.

A photo of me taken from outside Crystal's house.

My mouth goes dry; my hands tremble. "Oh no. Oh no,

no, no. This is bad—really bad. Clan Nocturna reported me. Beryl, I'm on a wanted poster."

Congratulations. How exciting.

"It's not exciting. It's lethal! What do I do, what do I do? It's not just border posters. I will have made the news as they publicly issue all the kill-on-sight warrants." I slap a hand over my mouth. "Theresa and Jay will see that. They will tell the vampires who I am." My voice breaks as I mutter through my fingers. "I'm doomed. So doomed. All that effort at the wedding to convince people I wasn't a thief. I think people finally believed I was decent. Now I will never get my life back. How the heck am I going to pay rent?"

It's dreadful, Beryl agrees.

"Who am I kidding? Rent? I can't pay rent if I'm dead. I will never get past the border. The guards will drag me from the car and kill me." Panic slams into me, and I'm about to do something stupid, like jump out of the car, when Beryl zaps me. Pain shoots up my arm like an electric shock, and I yelp.

Calm down, she says flatly. *Stay relaxed.*

The lane light turns green.

They are looking for a vampire, not a human delivery driver. They have not identified me yet, otherwise my delivery clearance would be cancelled.

All right, drive. Nice and steady. Beryl continues to coach me, half calm, half sarcastic. I breathe, keep exactly to the speed limit and make no sudden moves.

At last, our driveway.

The garage door rises, and I roll the car inside, safely out of sight from the street. When it thuds shut, I stay behind the wheel, clutching Beryl, then burst into tears.

House's magic scoops me from the garage and tucks my weeping self into bed. I hardly use it for anything but lying down these days.

"I'm rubbish," I mumble into Baylor's soft fur as he snuggles into me. "No hero. Everything I touch just... just unravels."

Did you save the girl?

"Yes, yes, I did. But then I needed saving. I'm nothing like Lark."

Lark? You met Lark? Dark hair, silver eyes?

I nod. "Yes. She's a shifter and really nice."

I hear the smile in House's voice. *I'm glad she helped. Did she seem all right? Healthy, happy?*

I lift my head. "You know her?"

Yes, she is my friend.

"She saved me, told the vampires she's the Alpha's mate. A bloke in the doorway—could not see his face and did not catch his name—was giving her grief about using a signed cricket bat. He sounded more amused than angry. She was so confident; all the shifters took her lead."

Wonderful. I'm so happy she saved you. Good news at last. Her story is for another day, though. Sleep.

"I don't sleep," I mumble.

Yet with House stroking my hair as though I were a child, I sleep—no dreams, just a head-first plunge into exhaustion.

Chapter Twenty-Two

I must be out for sixteen hours, perhaps more, before House wakes me.

Fred... Fred, wake up.

My eyes snap open. It's dark. I slept the entire day away.

"Did you magic me to sleep?" I grumble.

House ignores my question. *The warrant was issued by Clan Nocturna and approved by the Grand Master. He knows you are alive.*

"Oh." My stomach flips. "That's... really bad."

And there are strangers outside the wards. Not Valdarr's lot. I doubt they are here for a chat. House's tone tightens. *They are wearing tactical gear; I think they mean to attack.*

"Attack?" My voice shrinks. "But... but your wards—"

Oh, we're letting them in, Beryl says brightly from the bedside table.

"I'm sorry, what?" Sleeping must have made me delirious. "Let them in? The hit squad?"

Yes, House replies. *They think this place has a flimsy ward. We will open the door, then be rid of them.*

"Be rid of?" My voice leaps two octaves.

Don't fret, House purrs. *Everything will be fine. We will deal with this in-house.*

"Famous last words," I mutter.

Privately I'm screaming *Where is Valdarr?* Unfair, given it's not his duty to protect me. Yet it's only natural, as he's the only vampire I know. But I don't need a man to protect me when I have House, Beryl, and Baylor. Plus, I'm a vampire.

I slide out of bed and dress in a hurry. "Baylor!" I call.

No response.

"Baylor! Baylor!" He must be sulking after no walk today. Claws clatter on the stairs. A moment later, he creeps into the room and disappears under the bed. Poor boy, he knows something's wrong.

I drop to my knees. "It's okay, buddy. House, Beryl, and I are going to deal with the naughty vampires."

Deal with—I wonder what that will entail.

Baylor lets out a soft, uncertain "awoo."

"It's okay. What a good boy. Brave pup. I'll be back soon. Stay here, nice and safe." I stroke his head, kiss his nose, then leave and lock the bedroom door.

"House, if we handle these vampires, what about the next lot? We can't fight the whole country. With a kill order, everyone's involved, even the human government. Perhaps I should just... leave. I have no job, no rent money.

I'm a burden and I'm putting you at risk." I pause on the stairs.

That doesn't matter. When have I ever needed money? Stay as long as you like. You and Baylor are family.

"I'm not a charity case. I can't take advantage of you."

Then we will move. I'll fold myself.

"Move? Fold yourself? So the rumours about wizards' houses are true—you can move?"

My feet hit the hallway floor and I grab my trainers from the shoe rack.

Oh yes. Didn't you know? I can pick myself up and go anywhere. I try to stay in this country, but I do not have to. I don't even need to stay on this continent. We could choose somewhere warm.

"You would... take us with you?"

Of course. It costs power, and I have not been rooted here a full year, but it's doable. If we are careful, *they will take a while to find us. I have been bouncing around for more than a century.*

"Wow."

Get ready—they are about to breach, House whispers.

Beryl slaps into my palm.

"What do I do?" I hiss.

We're up. Let's go.

"But... what do I do?"

You are bait, kid. Suck it up.

I edge away from the front door, keeping clear of the windows. My back meets the wall; from here I can see both the living room and the kitchen. My whole body trembles.

Beryl tuts. *Typical. If you want something done properly, you have got to do it yourself.*

She launches from my hand, hovering before me, the point of the stake angled outward, ready to fight.

Everything happens at once.

The bay window in the living room shatters—glass exploding inward like a spray of diamonds that tinkles across the floor. At the same moment, the back door blows off its hinges, and smoke floods the hall.

I hold my breath, but my eyes sting.

The vampires are here.

There are four of them. Two surge in at the rear, two claw through the broken window like creatures from a horror film. Black combat gear swirled with grey, goggles, and ghost-pale faces in the moonlight.

They see me immediately.

"Team One to command: target is in the house. Target has been sighted. Confirm execution order," growls the smaller female.

If I could press myself deeper into the wall, I would. I stay motionless, palms flat against the wallpaper. My only hope is House and Beryl. Yet beneath the fear runs a grim certainty: *this is futile*.

Boots crunch closer. Weapons rise, so many weapons, all trained on me. My heart is silent, but dread coils around its useless husk.

"Order confirmed," crackles a voice in their earpieces. "Take her out."

"No," I whisper—though nothing escapes: throat glued, body locked. I am a rabbit before wolves. Before vampires.

Then Beryl moves.

I shut my eyes; I cannot watch. If that makes me a

coward, so be it. I will not see how I die. I brace for bullet or blade.

Nothing comes.

Instead, laughter—Beryl's wicked, gleeful cackle. Groans follow, then screams, and the wet squelch of tearing flesh.

Hands over my ears, I hunch smaller. Warm blood splatters my face, slides down my cheeks, drips from my wrists. I sink to my knees, curling into the corner.

Thud.

Thud.

Thud.

Bodies.

A scented breeze—rosemary and cool air—eddies through the hall. Smoke thins, the copper stench fades, and I open my eyes to watch as the shattered glass lifts from the floor, swirling upward to slot itself neatly back into place. The window is whole again.

The living room is immaculate. No smoke. No blood. No trace of the four vampires who came to kill me.

My hands are red, sticky. My hair feels matted. Bits of vampire are tangled in it.

I gag.

Then House's magic washes over me, warm as a gentle wind. Tingling my skin—and just like that—I'm clean again.

It's all right, House whispers. *It's done.*

That was such fun, Beryl giggles.

She flips lazily around the living room, and my gaze snags on something in the centre of the coffee table: an earpiece.

It squawks to life.

"Team One, do you have confirmation of the kill?"

I don't need to ask why it's still here; House and Beryl clearly want me to do something.

"They really were the bad guys, right? And we're the good guys—even though we... killed them?"

You didn't kill anyone, Beryl says, her tone suddenly prim. *That was all me. You are perfectly innocent.*

I nod slowly, twisting my hands. "But they won't see it that way, will they? They will think it was me. Neither of you is here, and conveniently, I'm the only one who can hear you. That's the very definition of insanity, isn't it?" I swallow hard. "Hearing voices."

The vampire who murdered you sent a hit squad, House says gently. *We are the good guys, Fred. You can trust that.*

I close my eyes for a second, then nod again. "All right, what do I do with that?"

Tell them not to try again, Beryl suggests sweetly.

"Okay."

I step forward and pick up the earpiece. The smooth, black plastic is cold in my palm. A tiny button on the side must unmute the mic.

I press it, take a deep breath, and release my nerves—my fear—and channel my inner vampire.

"Your people are dead," I say, voice cold and steady. "Do not come here again. All further attempts will be met with the same lethal force."

Static hisses, followed by a sharp voice. "Who is this?"

I don't answer; the message has been delivered.

I crush the device in my fist—plastic and metal grinding

together—then open my fingers. House's magic sweeps the shattered pieces away.

Come on. You have not eaten today. You release the pup, and I will warm some O-negative. Thought you might like it hot tonight.

I coax Baylor out from under the bed, drink the warm blood—still disgusting—then spend an hour in the shower, scrubbing until my fingers prune, convinced I still have chunks of people in my hair.

I never thought I'd end up like this.

I didn't do anything, not really—I hid in the corner with my eyes closed—yet I feel responsible. I *am* responsible. They only came because of me. How many centuries of knowledge have I just erased?

There's that 'live by the sword, die by the sword' nonsense, and no, they weren't innocent. I understand that. But I'm just a normal woman: vampire by night, human by day, talking to soul-magic-infused objects, dead people... and I'm sad my life has come to this.

I doubt my continued existence is worth the lives of four others, but it's done now, too late to undo. For someone who won't even swat a fly, who rescues spiders with a glass and paper, this is hard to process.

I wonder whether the switch will ever flick—the one that would allow the vampire inside me to let the world burn. What did the waitress say? "Vampires are sociopaths." Will it get easier if I stop caring?

I curl up on the sofa, listening to a podcast on trauma recovery while Beryl—apparently a permanent fixture—grumbles about modern psychology. I ignore her.

Night turns to day. Baylor, still grumpy after yesterday's

non-walk, plays in the garden. I push toast around my plate, not hungry.

At around ten a.m., they come again. This time, not the vampires. No, now it's the other derivatives' turn.

First, police cars block both ends of the street. Thirty minutes later, people from the Magic Sector arrive: wizards, witches, mages.

I peek through the bedroom curtains, and I spot one man, tall, with white-blond hair, arguing animatedly with the group. He points straight at House.

"This isn't good," I whisper.

No, it is not, House replies. *I presume the Ministry of Magic sent them. The handsome one with the white-blond hair is Lander Kane, a Council member.*

"Can they breach your wards?"

If Lander Kane helps them... perhaps. His magic is very strong.

"Can we move before they try?"

Silence.

She's keeping something from me.

"Could you fold yourself without me?" I wait a couple of heartbeats. "It's me, isn't it? If Baylor and I weren't here, you would have gone already. We are interfering with the magic. You need more power to take us with you."

She doesn't answer.

And that is answer enough.

Chapter Twenty-Three

After the first hour of my hypervigilance, House magics a dining-room chair into the bedroom so I can sit. Baylor leans against my leg, pressing his full weight into me and whining softly. I stroke his thick fur, murmuring in a sing-song voice, trying to calm us both.

Whatever they are planning will be bad.

I consider slipping into a vision to see whether it might help, but no, House already has enough on her plate without dragging me back from psychic wanderings while we are under siege. To go outside now would be suicide.

And what would that say about everything House has risked for me?

This is my fault. The thought loops like a broken record. I brought this mess to her door. I put us here.

Outside, the magic-users inscribe an intricate circle

around House's wards. Nearly three hours pass before they finish. I resist the urge to pace from window to window like a caged animal. House is watching everything; my panicked peeking would achieve nothing but sweat.

At about three in the afternoon, they take their places. Thirteen of them, each standing on a precise point of the design they have created.

Without signal or cue, they begin to chant.

Their voices rise and fall together, rhythmic and exact, like a metronome striking inside my skull. The words are unfamiliar, ancient, and powerful. The language of magic makes pressure build behind my eyes; a headache blooms.

I cannot understand what they are saying.

House surely does, yet she has fallen silent—probably preparing, calculating, ready to fight or move us.

The chanting swells to a crescendo; the circle flares. A line of white fire ignites and begins to rotate around them, growing so bright I have to squint and turn away.

Only then do I notice a faint, shimmering strand of magic hanging in front of my face—thread-thin, almost invisible, just millimetres from my skin.

They have breached the wards.

I gasp.

A glance out of the window confirms my fear: the circle has altered. It is no longer just a circle. It has become a pentagram. Thin magical lines now criss-cross the centre, slicing straight through House's wards.

I reach out, fingertip hovering from the strand. The air buzzes. A sharp spark zaps my skin.

Don't touch it, House whispers.

I snatch my hand away and scan the room for more

threads, but for now there is only the one. I shove the chair aside and retreat.

"This is really bad," I murmur.

Yes, House agrees.

A deep, unnatural vibration rolls through the floorboards. The walls quiver; furniture lurches out of place. The bed judders a foot across the room.

Afraid the flying furniture might injure Baylor, I clip his lead to his collar. "Come on, buddy, let's go downstairs." My voice shakes, yet he obeys—tail low, ears flat—pressing against my leg as we hurry down the stairs.

We take up a new position in the living room.

"Is there anything in the basement we can use? Anything at all? I want to help. I want to fight for you." My words tumble out in a rush.

No. There's nothing you can do, Beryl says gently, floating at my side.

"I'm so sorry, Beryl. This is my fault."

Hush, no, it's not, kid. Sooner or later it was bound to happen. House has been running a long time. We both have.

A flicker of hope sparks. "Look!" I cry. My nose almost touches the window. "The circle is fading!"

One wizard collapses—then a witch, then another—each dropping to their knees, clutching their heads. All thirteen are not powerful enough to beat House. The circle dims as more of the magic-users falter; the pentagram sputters, its perfect symmetry breaking.

"We might actually win this!" My voice cracks with hope.

But just as the circle begins to crumble and I dare to

breathe, movement catches my eye. Lander Kane steps forward.

No.

He is neither chanting nor part of the original thirteen. His face remains calm; his white-blond hair lies perfectly still despite the wind whipping around him. His gaze fixes on House, and for the first time since this ordeal began, cold fear crawls up my spine.

"House..." I whisper.

I see him.

He is trying something different.

Lander raises both hands: the fingers of his left hand splay wide while, in his right, he brandishes a wand. Nothing happens at first. I count to five, then the remaining lines of magic pulse once, twice, then twist together like rope.

And the blond mage's feet leave the ground. He floats.

His power pours into the fading circle, which flares back to life. The pentagram reforms. Brighter, tighter.

The floor beneath me vibrates harder than before. Baylor whines and presses tighter against my legs.

House groans. Not aloud, but through the very bones of her structure. I feel her struggle. Her strain.

Cracks spider across the walls; deep fissures race from skirting board to ceiling. The bay window—repaired only last night—cracks under the strain, a spiderweb of fractures zig-zagging across the glass.

I tug Baylor away from the window.

In the kitchen, I hear the mended back door splinter once more, wood groaning as magic claws at House.

The living room furniture crumples as though made of

sand. Everything vanishes as House pulls all her magic into her defence.

House is falling apart.

"Stop it! Lander Kane, stop. It's hurting her! You are hurting her! Please, stop!"

He does not stop. Perhaps he cannot hear me. The floating mage's eyes have turned completely white.

"House, I'm killing you. Our being here is killing you. It's my turn to protect you. Fold, move. Go now. You need to save yourself."

No. I won't leave you.

I do the only thing I can. "I love you. I will find you. Thank you for being my friend."

With Baylor pinned to my side, we rush to the front door, I fling it open, and run into the front garden—straight into the pentagram's magic. It scorches my skin, but Baylor, being non-magical, is unharmed.

Tiles tumble from the roof—one, then another. House is literally breaking apart before my eyes.

"House, you must go. Go now!"

Maybe she can't. I whip around and glare at the floating mage. Snatching up a piece of broken tile, I hurl it at him. It strikes him square in the chest.

"Leave her alone! Leave her alone!" I scream, advancing, desperate to shatter his white-eyed concentration.

Baylor snarls and clamps onto his trouser leg, yanking. "Good boy, Baylor, get him." I'm heading for pet-parent hell. "Please, please give us the strength to help my friend," I beg the universe. We pull with everything we have. The sleeping vampire in me growls and—

Lander falls. His bulk knocks us both to the ground just as the chimney crashes into the back garden.

His magic sputters.

In that moment House folds; she disappears—garden, walls, everything—leaving only a patch of rubbish-strewn scrubland.

She's gone. She's safe.

I scramble upright and check Baylor. My brave dog hasn't a scratch. Then I spot the bag, stuffed with my vital documents, two sets of favourite clothes and a small pack of dog food to keep Baylor going for a few days. Beryl. The stake remains utterly still, but I can feel the faint warmth of her magic pressing against my hand.

The bag also bulges with cash—undoubtedly every pound of rent I ever paid.

A sob wrenches from my throat. "House," I whisper, "please, please, please be safe."

"Well," Lander says, his voice silky and dangerous, "you're quite the stubborn little problem, aren't you, Winifred?" The mage rises, dusting off his trousers. He glares at his wand, broken, whether from the fall or my interference with his magic, and then turns that glare on me. "You broke my wand."

"Good." I glare back. "Why did you have to hurt her?"

"Her?"

"House. Why did you have to hurt her? She hadn't harmed anyone—she only ever kept people safe."

"She was harbouring a criminal."

I draw a tight, angry breath. "I'm no more a criminal than you. You are the one behaving like a monster."

His head tilts as he studies me from head to toe. "What I want to know," he says, pocketing the wand's remains, "is why you're not daytime dead. Baby vampire—yet you are"—he glances at the sun—"alive."

"I'm not a vampire. I'm human. You lot attacked my home and for what? You think I'm a vampire? Spoiler alert, you got it wrong."

"You were a vampire last night."

"Was I?"

"We have photographs, evidence."

"Do you? Did I bite anyone? Or did I see a girl in trouble and give her a lift home?"

He spreads his hands. "Well, as you can see—"

I lift my palms. "I'm no vampire." *Not at the moment,* I mentally mumble.

Baylor whines, pressing against me. He sniffs the bag and stares up at me, his eyes sad. I stroke his ears to soothe him. He's going to take the loss of House hard.

We both are.

"We'll have to sort this out," the mage says, beckoning to the police. Two officers stride over.

"Winifred Crowsdale, would you come with us, miss? We need to speak to you."

"Of course. May I bring my bag?"

The officer eyes it. "What's inside?"

"Clothes, phone, a book for when you leave me in a windowless room for hours, nothing illegal."

The mage narrows his eyes, then nods. "Let her bring it. We'll search it at the station."

I scoop up the bag, careful not to jostle Beryl.

"The dog." The officer reaches for Baylor's lead.

"What? No—can't he come with me? He has separation anxiety, and he will eat strange things if unsupervised. Please?"

"Sorry, Ms Crowsdale. It's procedure."

We have an undignified tug-of-war over the lead. I know I'm lucky they didn't shoot me when I went for Lander, and I know I should let go, but... he's my pup, I'm the only person he's got.

"He'll be well cared for."

My lip wobbles.

Only when Lander Kane chuckles nastily do I loosen my grip. My cheeks burn with equal parts mortification and fury.

Baylor whines as an animal-control handler takes him to a van.

"It's all right, buddy," I call softly. "You will be fine. Be a good boy, I will come for you as soon as I can." My voice cracks.

The officer steers me to the waiting car, hand hovering near my elbow as though I might bolt.

The mage watches each step, eyes sharp. "You're clever," he murmurs so only I hear. "But you can't lie your way out of this forever. The Grand Master himself issued your warrant."

My stomach knots, yet I keep my tone bland. "If the Grand Master is so eager to speak to me, he can do it himself."

The mage smiles. "Oh, he will. Sooner than you think."

The car door slams behind me, severing my last glimpse of the empty plot and the van holding Baylor.

I decide I loathe Lander-bloody-Kane, but I must admit

the mage is right—I can pretend to be human only until nightfall.

Crap.

Chapter Twenty-Four

They don't cuff me, and in a small mercy, Lander isn't allowed inside. After they search my bag—Beryl, thank heaven, nowhere in sight—I'm led through processing.

"That's a lot of cash," the custody sergeant remarks.

"Yes, well, idiots from the Magic Sector came and blew up my house. I grabbed what I could."

The bag and contents are sealed in a plastic evidence pouch, and I'm escorted to an interview room. It's much like the ones in the Vampire Sector: grey on grey, four plastic chairs, one grubby table, a single camera blinking red in the corner. No dramatic mirrored glass, alas.

"Would you like a drink?"

"No, thank you." Warm tea would be lovely, but with sunset approaching I'd rather not vomit mid-transformation.

The questioning begins. We circle my identity, my history, my supposed humanity and 'alleged association with derivatives.' I stick to my human story: paperwork, licences, nothing to hide. The human officers grow ever more perplexed as I stick stubbornly to my pre-vampire story. Their brows knit deeper. I can almost hear: *Why is everybody interested in her if she's just a delivery driver?*

At last they leave me alone.

Exhaustion presses down. I worry the police are stalling, dragging matters out so they can hand me over to the Grand Master's people. Even Lander threatened as much.

Soon my heart will stop, my lungs will still, my fangs will nudge forward and if I'm not careful they will know exactly what I am. If I keep breathing, blinking, doing all the human things, perhaps I can fool them?

Yeah, until the vampires come.

I worry about Baylor, another mum lost, another home gone. Tears sting, but I blink them away. Everything will be fine once I collect him.

It has to be.

A scrape at the door captures my attention. The handle shifts; the door creaks open. No one stands there. Beryl hovers out of the camera's view in the corridor.

"What are you doing?" I murmur, lips barely moving. Microphones are unforgiving.

Come on. I'm breaking you out.

"You are what? What if someone sees you?" I promised House to keep her out of sight. Nevertheless, I glide into the corridor. I have no real choice: either sit here and wait for the baddies to drag me to my final death, or trust Beryl and escape.

My bag, still sealed, sits conveniently nearby.

"How did you manage that?" I scoop it up.

Magic, obviously. Not as if I have thumbs. This way.

She zips ahead, corridors deserted. It's nearly nightfall—even the police support staff don't like to be out at night. Left, right, up one flight, right again. We slip into an untidy office. Papers litter every surface; filing cabinets gape. Two mugs of congealed coffee sit abandoned.

Window, Beryl taps the glass.

It's a long drop. Twenty feet at least.

"You want me to jump?"

Look at the sky, any minute now you will turn into a bloodsucker.

My heart gives its final beat. One last thud and silence. Dreadfully familiar.

"For Baylor," I mutter. I rip the evidence pouch off, slip it into an overflowing bin, open the window and drop the bag outside. Rather than jump, I wriggle forward on my stomach, swing a leg over the sill, grip the window frame, and dangle, probing with my toes for the top edge of the window below. *Just like the chin-up experiment, I will be fine.*

Beryl prods my foot.

"Stop poking."

Well, hurry up. You are going to get caught. We still need to fetch the dog.

Her next nudge helps guide my feet. It's difficult as I'm so petite. I drop one and a half levels—eight feet left—when strong hands clamp my waist. I yelp as I'm lifted down and against a broad, iron-hard chest.

Musk, metal, and power. I know by scent.

"What are you doing, sunshine?" Valdarr's voice is velvet amusement in my ear. "I arrange your release, and I find you escaping through a window like a burglar. Are you hurt?"

He turns me to face him, his tattooed fingers gentle as he cups my cheek.

"I'm fine." I search surreptitiously for Beryl. Mercifully, she has hidden and refrained from stabbing him. I will take that as a win.

"I'll need to make calls to explain your 'exit.' Come, Baylor awaits."

"Baylor?"

"I collected him from Animal Control before they closed. He's in the car, doubtless chewing something expensive. Shall we?"

He hefts the bag and gestures towards the car park.

"What? You have rescued Baylor?" I blurt, a surge of love for this man flooding my chest. "Thank you so much." Relief washes through me—my buddy is safe.

Valdarr guides me to the same black, UV-armoured car we used earlier, its tinted windows beaded with drizzle, the engine idling. The driver has his arms wrapped protectively around the headrest to shield it from Baylor's teeth, but all that's forgotten the moment the door opens.

Baylor spots me and lets out a joyous howl, his whole body vibrating as he dances across the back seat. I wince when his claws scrape the leather. I dive into the car and wrap my arms around him. I lavish him with kisses as he wriggles.

"I missed you too, buddy, so much. Have—" *kiss* "you —" *kiss* "been—" *kiss* "a good boy for Valdarr? I hope you haven't bitten anyone. No biting people, even when Mummy says so. I was wrong to ask you to nip the nasty mage. We won't do that again."

A familiar chuckle interrupts.

I glance up and freeze. Lander is standing outside the car, watching us. Instinctively I shove Baylor behind me, arms spread wide to block him.

"What is *he* doing here?" I growl.

"You never told me she's so adorable. After that display, I could even forgive her for breaking my wand," Lander says, patting Valdarr's shoulder as though they are old friends.

My stomach drops. "What is going on? Are you friends with him?" I shoot Valdarr a sharp, disappointed glare.

"Hero to zero in three seconds, tough crowd," Lander says smoothly. "Look, love, I'm not a bad guy. I was doing my job. There's a warrant for your arrest, and that house has caused problems for years."

"Name one thing she's done wrong." I don't wait for his answer. "Nothing. House has done nothing wrong. Admit you are a horrible person."

"She interfered with a shifter's turning, and with you." His gaze hardens. "Why do you think you're human by day, yet clearly of the fanged persuasion now? She meddled; you were never meant to turn."

"It wasn't her fault I woke up in a body bin," I snap, voice trembling but firm. "I was just doing my job delivering food. I did not plan to become someone's dinner."

"Yes, and her magic both forced and disrupted the transformation," he replies, stepping closer. "If you hadn't been living there, you'd have died that night. No resurrection, no partial turn. The house interfered, and that's illegal."

I open my mouth to argue, but no words come.

Lander presses the advantage, voice soft now, almost gentle. "I've reviewed your records. You don't carry enough vampire DNA for a proper turning. The house tampered with the magic, as she has before. She crossed the line."

"I don't believe you. You... you threatened me, told me the Grand Master was coming for me."

"That wasn't a threat; it was a warning," he says evenly. "I was trying to keep you alive."

"Alive? You just said if it were up to you, I'd be dead. Make up your mind." I shake my head and rest a hand on Baylor's back. He presses against my leg, ears pinned, eyes locked on Lander. A low growl rumbles in his chest.

"If he moves closer, bite him," I mumble.

Baylor huffs, as if in agreement.

"House is my friend, and I won't hear you malign her, especially when you do not know her side of the story. You attacked her. You are the villain here."

"I beg to differ." Lander leans back and he smiles, hands sliding into his pockets.

Smug twat.

"I was doing my job." The warmth drains from his tone; hard edges emerge. "There was a warrant signed by the Council and countersigned by the Grand Master. When magic repeatedly alters derivative biology without sanction, it becomes a threat."

There he is. I wasn't buying this 'Mr Nice Guy' act.

My vampire tugs him away from the car. "Lander, can

you tidy up Fred's exit? She escaped custody through a second-storey window."

"Of course."

They exchange hearty handshakes that set my teeth on edge. I cannot blame Valdarr for keeping the peace—it is the sensible course—but I do not have to like it. Baylor whines; I draw him closer, whispering, "Shh, it's all right."

Valdarr slides into the car.

"I'm sorry I was rude to your friend," I murmur, staring out of the window. "I just detest that man. He hurt my friend, and I do not trust him."

"I understand."

I realise, as I sit in his luxury car, that I have nowhere to go. My only transport vanished with House, and I have no idea what to do next. In my haste to reach Baylor, I jumped in without thinking, and now I must find a dignified way to leave.

I clear my throat. "Thank you again for your help. We'd better be on our way." I reach for the door handle.

"Last night, I didn't abandon you. I was there when the assassin teams attacked. My father sent six teams to kill you."

"Six? I saw only Team One—" Oh...

"I didn't leave you unprotected," he goes on. "I trusted the house's wards. I never imagined she would invite them inside."

I do the math: six teams with four vampires, Beryl handled one, which means Valdarr faced the other five. Twenty assassins.

A chill runs through me. "Thank you," I whisper, throat tight. "I'm sorry you had to do that." My thumb traces the sigil on my wrist. Baylor licks my hand, sensing my spiralling thoughts. The mark means little to me, but I suspect a great deal to Valdarr. "Your father won't stop, will he?"

"I'm the heir, that gives me some leverage. I have convinced him not to pursue you publicly. The wanted notice and the kill warrant have been withdrawn. But..." He hesitates. "My father is actively hunting you. Your turning raises questions he can ill afford to answer, and Clan Nocturna still isn't pleased."

"Oh."

"Fred, I realise this is sudden, and we haven't discussed relocation, but you are homeless and actively targeted. It would be safest to stay at the clan house for the time being, if you agree."

Something is bound to go wrong. Still, what choice do I have? I must trust it will work out.

"Okay."

"Okay." Valdarr signals the driver, and we leave the car park.

"About Clan Nocturna—"

"I saved that girl. I didn't attack her."

"I know. The area's CCTV showed everything. We apprehended the vampire and he confessed."

His violet-grey eyes narrow. "What I can't fathom is how you knew she was in danger. You arrived, waited for the exact moment she needed help, as if you knew what would happen. Why, Fred?"

I shift, worrying one fang with my tongue. "Well... besides the daytime-human issue, I, um—think I might be psychic?" It comes out like a question.

It sounds absurd even to me.

"I've always had strong intuition," I begin. "More than a gut feeling. Years ago, my friend Sara was fretting over her boyfriend. I advised her to leave him and concentrate on herself, certain she would soon meet the love of her life, someone she had always overlooked. Eighteen months later she met her childhood friend again, fell in love, married, two children."

I rub my eyes. "Life got messy. Jay disliked her, so we drifted." She wasn't the only friend he disliked, and I stopped listening to my intuition after Mum died. Had I paid attention to that inner voice, I'd never have wasted ten years with him.

"But you see the pattern: I've always had a weird little gift—it's hard to explain; I don't understand it myself." I wave my phone. "A few weeks after I was turned, I suffered vivid daydreams of your father finding and hurting me. When I forced them away, the magic changed: while scrolling, I drifted into a vision of a boy about to be hit by a car, so I went and saved him. Later, I tested the gift again and had the vision of Crystal being bitten, killed—"

He cuts in, "So you decided that going to the Vampire Sector to rescue her was a good idea?"

"House knew what I was planning, and I had that knockout potion. B—" I stop myself just in time from mentioning Beryl's help. I'm hopeless at lying. I recount the whole story—the Clan Nocturna fiasco, meeting Lark, everything—and it sounds even more absurd aloud.

"You have had an eventful few days," he says finally.

"Mm."

"Shall I ask my contacts about your house? Make sure she's safe?"

My head snaps up. "Would you... would you do that? I'd be so grateful." Tears sting.

"Of course."

We cross the border into the Vampire Sector and drive for another forty-five minutes. Beyond a pair of massive gates and a power-heavy ward, the stone drive crunches beneath the tyres as the car slows. The driver deposits us at the foot of a broad flight of stone steps leading to an oak front door, then pulls away without a word.

I tighten my grip on Baylor's lead, staring up at the imposing façade. What if Baylor chews through this beautiful place? Without House, an unfamiliar weight settles in my stomach. I hope Valdarr can discover something about her. I pray she is safe. Staying away is probably the best protection I can give her for now.

What if I don't belong here at all? Half the time, I'm a tasty human snack.

"Is being awake during the day common among vampires?" I ask.

"No, only the very old—my father, me, and a few members of our clan. I wake around midday, and with each passing century the time I remain immobilised grows shorter. You saw the ring?" I nod. "That artefact is exceedingly rare, not many can walk in the sun."

Carrying my bag, he offers a reassuring smile.

If my heart still beat, it might skip—when he smiles, he is almost painfully handsome.

We climb the steps. The door swings open before we reach it, and a vampire steps out into the darkness.

Chapter Twenty-Five

He's a slim vampire with dark hair styled in a perfect '90s boy-band curtain cut. A single hoop earring gleams in his left ear, and a medallion bearing the Clan Blóðvakt crest rests against a sharply pressed shirt. He blocks the threshold like an overworked PA guarding a CEO.

"My liege, there's a lot to get through," he says, eyes fixed on a tablet. The stylus hovers, ready. "Meeting with the shifters at—"

"James," Valdarr interrupts, "I'd like you to meet Winifred."

Black eyes snap to mine.

"Hi, James," I say, forcing a friendly smile.

He clips the stylus to the tablet, tucks the device under one arm, and offers his hand. "Ah, you're the woman I've heard so much about. The newest member of our clan. A pleasure."

"Pleased to meet you." I barely graze his fingers before he pulls away.

Valdarr steps inside, missing the moment when James whips out a bottle of hand sanitiser and douses himself. He scrubs like I've infected him. Perhaps it's germs—or dogs. I give him the benefit of the doubt.

Still rubbing his hands, James follows Valdarr. His voice drops just low enough for only my vampire ears. "You won't be here long." The look he throws over his shoulder drips contempt.

Ah, so not OCD. Pure dislike.

Fine. I respond with a pleasant, vapid smile, leaning into the dizzy-blonde persona people expect. I've lived under that stare before. I give him nothing to use against me. I won't be broken or manipulated this time.

We enter a sleek, modern office: charcoal walls, low bookcases, a single steel desk with a matte surface and no clutter save for a slim laptop. A muted abstract painting hangs opposite the windows, and recessed lighting casts a soft glow.

Valdarr gestures to a chrome and leather chair opposite the desk. I dutifully sit, noting all the exits, while James remains standing, tablet poised.

Baylor sniffs, turns in a tight circle—about a hundred times—and finally flops down with a dramatic sigh, eyeing James's skinny ankles like chew toys.

I've created a monster.

"Do you need anything?" James asks, all sugary charm. "O-negative? B-positive? Warm? Chilled? Dog treats?"

"We are fine, thank you."

"James, is Fred's suite ready?" Valdarr asks.

"Yes, my liege."

"Excellent. All right, Fred. Let's go over the clan rules."

Rules?

James clears his throat. "Clan Blóðvakt: Primary Laws of Conduct. One. Loyalty to the Grand Master. Every member shall offer unwavering allegiance to the Grand Master and his appointed heirs. Defiance constitutes treason and will be punished accordingly."

I nod slowly. Unwavering allegiance to the vampire who killed me. Don't commit treason. Got it.

"Two. Obedience to the liege." James flicks a glance at Valdarr. "That would be your host. His orders are binding. No exceptions."

Valdarr looks bored; James looks smug like he lives for this shit.

"Three. Secrecy above all. Clan affairs must remain hidden from the other derivatives. Breaches, accidental or otherwise, carry… consequences."

No need to spell them out.

"Four. Blood control and consent. Feeding must be consensual and discreet. No rogue turnings, no public spectacles, no draining humans."

I keep my face blank.

"Five. Territorial respect. Do not cross into other clans' lands without explicit permission."

That sounds relevant. Note to self: no wandering. No knocking on Clan Nocturna's door with a bleeding thrall. No wonder they were so mad.

"Six. No magic without authority. All magical artefacts,

abilities, or anomalies must be registered with the Council. Unsanctioned use may result in exile."

My stomach tightens. Beryl. And I'm a walking, talking anomaly. At this point, what I haven't done seems more relevant. Perhaps I should have received a Do's and Don'ts brochure the day he branded me. Unaware of these rules, I have been breaking them as though it were a sport.

"Seven. Conflict resolution. Duels require authorisation; grievances must be filed formally. Street fights and assassination attempts are frowned upon." James glares.

Baylor gives a soft growl, which I mask with a cough.

"Eight. Allies and beasts. Human servants, thralls, pets, enchanted objects, all are the legal responsibility of their keeper. Misbehaviour will be punished accordingly."

I nod at Baylor. "He's very well behaved," I say sweetly.

"Nine. Curfew and conduct. All members must remain within assigned quarters during daylight. Surveillance ensures safety *and* compliance."

I glance at Valdarr; he avoids my eye.

"Ten. Final death protocol. Any member who breaks the law will be summoned to the Hall of Silence for trial. If found guilty, ritual execution follows. Formal blade, open and public ceremony."

I nod. "Cheery."

James snaps the tablet shut. "We are quite civilised when rules are followed."

Valdarr leans forward, softening the mood. "It's a lot, I know. But don't worry. I'll walk you through the important bits. Just don't burn anything down and don't kill anyone."

"*Again,*" James mutters under his breath.

Baylor stands and stretches, positioning himself

between James and me. He doesn't growl this time, but he stares with unwavering focus. A silent warning.

I reach down and ruffle his ears, never breaking James's gaze. "I'll remember the rules."

And I'm sure they will trip me up sooner or later.

Especially with James, after his oh-so-friendly welcome, watching for the smallest infraction to see my head lobbed off.

But panicking now won't help. I nod, smile like a dutiful little vampire, and follow Valdarr down the hallway to my suite.

We pass striking pieces of modern art, abstract shapes in blood-red or void-black. Baylor's claws click across polished parquet, then tap-tap on marble.

Valdarr stops before a heavy oak door. "This is you."

He enters first, setting my bag on the dressing table. The suite could be in a luxury hotel with its polished mahogany, deep blue velvet upholstery, warm lamplight. I unclasp Baylor's lead; he circles, sniffs, then flops beside me with a huff.

"I'll let you settle in." He smiles—almost shy—and leaves, closing the door behind him. The suite has a vault door, like the one in the townhouse. It must be a safety feature in all his properties.

Ah, young love, Beryl sings as she zips out of the bag. *He likes you.*

I scowl. "He does not, he only pities me." Huge difference.

Chapter Twenty-Six

The suite is beautiful, clearly designed for human guests. Floor-to-ceiling windows and a glass door overlook a walled courtyard paved with broad slabs and dotted with oversized planters. If I can beg some mulch from the gardener, I could create a discreet loo for Baylor.

Alongside a tiny kitchen that boasts a fully stocked fridge, there's a dining table with four chairs, and a bedroom with a king-size mattress that felt like a cloud when I tested it. Valdarr has even arranged a wardrobe of designer clothes, each piece tailored to fit as though made for me. In one corner, a book-nook cradles a deep-seated chair and footstool.

I select a book with a worn leather binding and settle into the chair. I dare not risk my phone in case scrolling triggers another vision, especially when I'm in no position to help anyone. If it happens, I need someone beside me to stop me doing something dangerous or simply stupid.

I miss House. I miss my home.

As dawn breaks, my heart gives its first sleepy thud. Baylor, however, still refuses to use the courtyard—the flagstones clearly fail his Husky standards—so he resorts to the frantic I-need-a-pee shuffle, whining for emphasis. Reluctantly, I clip on his lead. I'm supposed to stay indoors during daylight, but his needs must take precedence. Breaking rule number nine.

I'm coming with you, Beryl announces.

"All right." I slide her into a back pocket. "Can you see from there?"

I don't have eyes, she grumbles. *I sense things.*

We sneak through silent corridors—Baylor knows the way—and reach the front door, where two guards stand post.

Oh. No.

Why didn't I think of this? Of course there would be daytime security, not just the ward. Now I've broken the promise I made at the wedding. Valdarr asked me to keep my daytime humanity secret, and by flouncing out the front door I've ruined everything.

Perhaps they will think I'm a blood donor or a thrall?

"Ms Crowsdale," one says, nodding. I grimace. "I'm Lee, and this is Oscar. We're part of the day team. I understand you know the rules, but—"

"I do," I interrupt. "Baylor needs the loo. Promise we will be quick."

Lee smiles at Baylor's increasingly frantic dancing.

"Today should be fine. I'll clear it with the Heir tonight. I'm sure he'll allow you anything."

Odd remark. I thank him and slip outside. Once clear of the guards, I unclip Baylor. He sniffs everything, circling me a dozen times before disappearing entirely.

"Baylor!"

Ten frantic minutes later I find him head-first in a burrow, soil flying.

"What would you do if you caught a rabbit?" I mutter, clipping his lead. "Naughty boy."

We wander further, marvelling at the sheer size of the estate, until a couple of figures lurking ahead stop me cold. Wrong clothes—matte black swirled with grey, *black-and-grey tactical gear*, exactly like the vampire assassins from the night before.

Not Valdarr's people.

Human assassins.

Beryl snaps out of my pocket. *We have a problem.*

"Tell me something I don't know," I whisper, backing away as Baylor growls.

I hurry away.

Where are you going? she demands. *You are a member of this clan. Stop them!*

I glance behind me, and Beryl hovers like an impatient wasp.

"Me?" I whisper back, pointing at my chest. "What do you think I can do? Security is here for that. We can warn them, walk to the gate and use the radio—"

If those humans are here, then the security people at the gate are already dead. I will take the heavy lifting; you just stay with me. I'm not leaving you on your own. You will get into trouble, she mutters.

"I thought you were a vampire hunter. Why would you protect vampires from humans?"

I hunt the bad ones. Those men work for even worse vampires. Attacking during the day isn't a fair fight. It is wrong. And what if they kill your *vampire, strike when he can't defend himself? How tragic would that be?*

A protective spark flares hot in my chest. They will not hurt my vampire. My stomach churns. I'm no fighter, yet Beryl seems confident enough for both of us.

Baylor pads silently at my side, shoulder brushing my leg, tense and alert.

We creep along a hedgerow. I try to tread lightly, but every step crackles. Even Baylor seems to side-eye me. The louder I try *not* to be, the more I sound like a baby elephant.

"Not helpful," I hiss when another twig snaps.

We round a corner and spot the same two men.

Beryl slaps into my palm. *There are cameras. I'm sorry about this, kid. Follow my lead.*

Before I can ask what she means—or even protest—she yanks my arm, and I stumble forward. "What?" Heat lances down my spine. My fingers go numb. Something ancient slips in behind my eyes and *clicks* into place. The strength that floods me is not my own.

Oh no. No, no, no. I did not sign up for this—

BAYLOR FREEZES in the bushes with a soft whine; only his eyes track us warily. *Bloody hell, is she controlling my dog, too?*

The two human assassins—hardened killers, armed to the teeth—advance. One hefts a serrated black knife.

Beryl does not care.

She's doing this because of the estate's CCTV, desperate to keep her secret, and the assassins' body-cams leave no room for subtlety. Every movement is sure and brutal. My body flips, reacting before I can think. I feel possessed. With my body moving like a marionette, I surge forward as she taps my dormant vampire magic. Every movement is sure and brutal.

Strike, pivot, drive. I feel the wood punch armour, hear ribs crack, taste copper spray. I try to resist, to yank the control back, but fighting her while she fights them will get me killed. With sheer horror ringing in my mind, I let go and ride it out.

Her magic is brutal. They never stand a chance.

When it is over, I'm shaking, sticky with blood. She does not release me, instead, she yanks us toward the next pair... and the next.

My mind screams; my body obeys.

I cling to a mental corner and count breaths.

At last I pin the final intruder. Beryl, lodged beneath his chin, bites into his neck.

"Who sent you?" she demands through my mouth.

"Clan Nocturna," he rasps. "The clan and the Grand Master are coming for you. Your lover can't save you. He can't protect you."

He mutters some random words; a tattoo on his collarbone flares. His mouth contorts, and then he starts to choke.

A suicide spell, Beryl murmurs, finally letting me go.

I roll away and, still on the ground, scramble backwards on my bottom, watching as he disintegrates into ash.

"Horrible," I breathe.

They ensure no one can be captured, Beryl replies.

"That's not the only horrible thing, Beryl. What were you thinking? Why did you do that? Override me?" My voice cracks; I'm trembling.

People had died, and no matter their allegiance, the weight of it presses on me. I have killed, whether Beryl guided my hand or not. To keep her secret, she used me without asking. I'm complicit.

"Have you ever been used without your consent? I promised to keep your secret, but using me like that... that was wrong, Beryl."

Tears blur my vision; nausea churns. My fingers tug at the grass, restless and sore, and my palm throbs from gripping the wood too tightly.

"I thought we were friends."

We are friends. But it was the only way to save your life. Now quit your moaning, get up, and dust yourself off. We need to clear the rest of the estate.

Shock settles in like ice.

Together we scour the grounds—Beryl sensing, steering; me stumbling—until she's certain no assassins remain.

I move in a daze.

For the first time, I wonder if misery with Jay might have been safer than all this magic.

Chapter Twenty-Seven

I sink onto the front steps, soaked in blood. I don't dare go inside. I will track gore everywhere, and I don't want to leave in case we have missed someone. I know they were the bad people, but...

I can't stop trembling.

Time passes. The blood dries on my skin and flakes away. Shock pins me to the step. Near midday, Beryl clamps to my palm and goes still.

The front door opens.

"Fred?" Valdarr says gently.

I lift my eyes. He stands just inside the threshold, careful to stay away from the light. He isn't wearing his protective ring.

"Hey," I croak.

"Are you all right?"

No. "I broke Rule Nine, curfew and conduct, and probably Rule Seven, conflict resolution. Baylor hates the courtyard stones; he needed the toilet. We went out; Lee cleared it. We stumbled on intruders. They overwhelmed your day security." I point—hand shaking—at the fallen forms beyond the hedges. "Lee and—" I flap my hands helplessly. "Oh gosh. I can't remember his name."

"Oscar," Valdarr supplies quietly.

"Oscar. They are gone. All of them. I checked. They fought hard, took some attackers with them, but in the end…" I swallow. "They wore the same gear as the clan hit squad from the other night. You must recognise it."

"Come on," he says softly. "Let's get you cleaned up."

I stare into the garden. "What if they come back?"

"They won't. When the time check was missed, extra security was dispatched. A full squadron is on the grounds now; they will take care of the fallen. Come inside."

"But I'm so dirty," I whisper.

"Come on." He adds the magic words: "Baylor looks hungry and thirsty. Come on, sunshine."

I rise, walking up the steps on leaden legs. My bones ache. He takes my hand, pulls me into his arms, and gives me the biggest hug.

"You are safe now."

"I was so frightened that they would hurt you." I cling to him. "At least I didn't burn anything down. I'm so sorry I broke all your rules."

He lifts me and carries me through the house into my suite.

"The windows!" I gasp.

"All the glass is safe within my properties; the sun can't

hurt me." He sets me on the bathroom mat, grabs a towel, and turns on the shower. "Get clean. I'll leave clothes outside the door and feed Baylor. It's the stuff from your bag, right?"

"Yes. Thank you."

"No bother." Valdarr kisses me on the top of the head and closes the door.

Under the hot water, I sob until the water runs clear and my fingers prune.

Squeaky-clean and dressed, I emerge to find he's made pancakes, cut fresh strawberries, and on the table is syrup. He nudges a glass of orange juice towards me.

"I presume you eat during the day?"

"Yes, thanks," I say, though I'm not sure I can eat—I simply don't want to be rude. For him this is an ordinary day: fighting for his life, killing assassins—just another routine. None of it feels real. I sit, pick up a fork, and my hand trembles. "But nothing within four hours of sunset—otherwise I feel a bit sick when I... die for the night. Did you make these yourself?"

"Of course. Is this all right? I can make you something else."

I just stare at the plate.

"What? Did you think a vampire couldn't cook? I have human friends," he says, leaning against the counter, arms and ankles crossed, studying me.

"No, of course not. I'd never question your culinary skills." I take a small bite. The pancake is perfectly fluffy, but it clings to the roof of my mouth. "This is lovely. Thank you," I rasp. The pancake is now stuck at the back of my throat. I take a big gulp of orange juice.

"I reviewed the security footage while you showered."

Talk about multitasking.

Worried I will break the glass, I set it down carefully and try a little bit of fruit.

"Nothing I say can truly express how much I regret what happened today. Not having adequate daytime security put you at risk, but you dealt with the problem and saved my life."

The piece of strawberry lodges in my throat as fear clamps around it. I cough and lay my fork aside. "Your room must have one of those vault doors. I bet you were perfectly safe." My leg bounces; my knee knocks the underside of the table, and the plates jump. The orange juice splashes. "They wouldn't have come if it weren't for me. The fighting... I did nothing. It was—"

The orange juice spreads like blood.

I shake my head. "I can't do this. I can't lie. I cannot pretend I'm all right. I'm not." I stand, searching for a cloth. "I need to wipe the table."

Valdarr is suddenly there, standing in front of me.

"I'm so sorry, Fred. You are in shock. I didn't think... I've been a vampire so long I forget what it's like to be human and vulnerable."

"They all died," I hiccup, the words splintering out of me. "Not just your people, but the assassins. They all died, and there was blood, and Ber—" I choke on her name.

My instincts kick in, and I realise I must betray Beryl.

Valdarr must know I carry a sentient stake powerful enough to override my will. I don't want any secrets between us. I am already pushing my luck with the rule-breaking and the trouble I have brought to his home, and I need to start being honest.

It is not my secret to give, but, noble intentions aside, Beryl frightens me. I cannot deal with her on my own.

"It was Beryl," I say softly. "Beryl is... the stake—she's sentient. She used me, took over. It wasn't really me doing all that killing. I don't know how to fight. I'm not... I'm not a murderer. I help people; I don't kill them."

Sobs rip through me; my chest burns as though scalded.

Valdarr sits, lifts me effortlessly into his lap and rocks me gently. His fingers comb through my wet hair, soothing.

"Today I missed my old life. Even the boring parts, the safety I once took for granted. I left because Jay was horrible, but look what's happened since. Everything I touch goes wrong!" The words tumble out in a wail I can't swallow. "You must think I'm the worst person alive." The worst friend.

"You are incredible," he whispers into my hair. "You have done nothing wrong. You are safe. I'm here."

"I'm sorry," I sob, tears and snot soaking his shirt.

Then I really throw Beryl more under the bus. "It was Beryl's idea. I meant to run, but she said they would strike while you were vulnerable. Then she jumped into my hand and took over. I tried to fight her, but... I thought it was safer to let her do her thing. I messed up. She did it for the right reasons. I know that sounds bad, yet she's a good person. She only possessed me to keep everyone safe, and because of the cameras. Still, when I close my eyes, I see their faces..."

All I see is blood.

"I can help," he murmurs. "Something to ease the trauma. Do you understand compulsion?"

I nod against his chest. "I understand the concept."

"Good," he says, kissing the top of my head. "I'm an elder—ancient—so I can use a delicate form of compulsion. I won't erase the memories; that ends badly. But I can cushion them, make them feel old. Instead of reliving them from hours ago, they will feel years distant. You will still feel sorrow and anger, but the sharpness will fade. Will you let me?"

"Yes," I whisper. "Please."

"Okay, sunshine."

He wipes my face with the hem of his shirt. I sniff and laugh weakly. "I'm making such a mess of you."

"What's a bit of snot between clan mates?" he teases with a soft smile. "Ready?"

"Yes. Please."

He lifts my chin. "Look into my eyes." His power flows over me—warm, safe—like sinking into sun-lit water. "Tell me what happened today, from the start."

I do: talking to Lee, the rabbit, Beryl taking over, the stabbing, the tattooed assassin and his suicide spell. Every detail. As I speak, the memories soften—still vivid, but no longer raw. The edges blur, leaving only a distant ache.

When the compulsion lifts, I'm staring into his violet eyes.

"I hope I never have to ask you to do that again," I say, throat raw, eyes burning. I must look a mess. I have never been a pretty crier, but Valdarr gazes at me as though I'm precious. Nobody's ever looked at me like that before. It's an unsettling but lovely feeling.

"It's all right," he murmurs. "I hope I never have to, either. But you will be okay. I know you will."

"Thank you," I whisper.

"Now, where's your Beryl?" he asks.

I don't want to leave his arms—I could stay there forever—but I slip from his hold and fetch her from the bathroom.

She lies inert in my hands, and I am worried. The moment Valdarr opened the front door, she shut down, and her wood is now unnervingly cool. I may still be angry, still hurt, yet I will not let him touch her. Instead, while I outline her history—Victorian slayer, soul-bound stake, the armoury, recent escapades—I settle her on a cushion in the sun so she is comfortable. A hardwood stake hardly needs comfort, but I cannot help myself; House would have approved.

Valdarr listens. When I finish, fury flickers—not with me, but for me.

"Do you think she will retaliate? Do you feel safe?"

"Beryl is bloodthirsty, but she has strong morals. Her first instinct was to protect you from our attackers; she wouldn't hurt us. Even after I dobbed her in."

We are both quiet while I return to the table, eat and wrestle with my guilt.

I had to tell him.

"What I want to know," I say, "is how the assassins bypassed the wards and the guards."

"Someone let them in," he murmurs. "I will discover who betrayed us. I have called a clan meeting for tonight—you will meet everyone."

"Oh." I swallow. "All right."

Chapter Twenty-Eight

This evening I'll meet the entire clan of vampires. Does *entire* mean only the vampires, or everyone—blood donors, thralls, fledglings? How many souls does Valdarr command? And will they hate me as much as James does?

I'm old—and wise—enough to know I don't need to be liked; life seldom works that way. I'm also not foolish enough to feel calm about stepping into a room full of vampires.

I brew lemon tea with honey, settle in the book nook, and listen to a podcast on healing—sadly, it offers no advice on being used by a sentient, vampire-hunting stake to kill humans.

My stomach flips when I glance up and catch Baylor staring at the wall, confusion on his furry face. He is waiting for a treat that will never come. He doesn't understand that

House is gone—that normal buildings don't brush his fur and cuddle him. They don't conjure doggy treats and swimming pools just because it's a warm day.

Oh, how I miss you. So much. I wish I could find you.

I go and raid the fridge for a treat and find some thin slices of ham and almost lose the tips of my fingers as Baylor gobbles them down.

Beryl lies inert on the sofa.

The day crawls until the sun finally dips, and about thirty minutes after nightfall, a knock sounds at my door.

A statuesque woman stands on the threshold, dark skin, liquid-brown eyes, and the kind of unhurried poise most people reserve for red carpets. She wears simple workout gear but carries it as though it were haute couture.

For one foolish moment I wonder if she might be Valdarr's girlfriend, then scold myself for caring.

"Simone," she says, offering her hand.

"Fred."

"It's lovely to meet you, Fred."

Baylor sniffs her cautiously. She presents the back of her hand.

"I don't really like dogs," she says matter-of-factly, giving him a perfunctory pat. "Where I come from, dogs hunt or guard; you don't keep them as pets."

Baylor's ears tilt, unsure what to make of her, but he behaves. I scratch behind them. "Good boy."

Simone's smile is feline. "The security cameras caught how you dispatched those assassins. Brave work. You fight remarkably well, so I thought I'd introduce myself before tonight's meeting and while our liege is busy."

If only she knew it wasn't exactly me.

She tilts her head. "Fancy a workout? I know you're newly turned, but you're a day-walker! I've never met anyone with your gift before, so you must be special. Dispatching the humans today must have been dull; they break so easily. Have you had a proper play with your powers yet?"

"Er... no, not really. And I haven't met many vampires." Unless running from them counts.

"Wonderful—exciting!" She claps once and strides to my wardrobe as though we are lifelong friends. Workout clothes fly my way. "Go and change. The others will be hours yet; we've plenty of time."

"Oh. All right." I hesitate. "Are we allowed?"

She shrugs. "Who's stopping us?"

Moments later, I follow her through the house to a moonlit room with floor-to-ceiling windows opening onto a patio. Beyond them, a sleek glass annexe houses an illuminated indoor pool. Vampires, it seems, live well.

Weights and strange matte-black machines are arranged with military neatness. The air smells of cedar and lemon polish. In the centre lies a sparring circle: dark wood inlaid with runes. No soft blue mats here. I wonder whether a vampire body even bruises.

We stretch. Simone moves like water; I mimic her easily —this body feels engineered for efficiency—even if my brain hasn't caught up.

"Right," she says, shaking out her hands, the faintest smirk on her lips. "Show me what you've got."

"I thought we were just working out." I glance at the equipment. "I've never really—"

"Never?" She raises a brow. "In the security footage you

handled that stake like an expert. Don't tell me that was beginner's luck."

"It might have been." I grimace.

"Only one way to find out." She gives the universal *fight me* gesture.

I have no idea what she wants me to do. I reach for her wrist, but she slips away, frowning. "Again."

I lunge—clumsily—and this time she doesn't merely dodge, she hooks her hip and sweeps my leg out from under me. The world tilts. Floorboards connect with my face. My nose blazes.

"Ow! Bloody hell—"

Simone hauls me up, one hand on my elbow, the other patting my shoulder. "Sorry. My bad. Let's try it slower." She places my hand on her wrist. "See this grip? Thumb here, fingers here. Now hold, don't just... flap at me."

We drill it, over and over. My grip is either too loose or too tight. Once, I nearly wrench her shoulder out of its socket; I'm still not great with this vampire strength. Patiently, she corrects me until my muscles remember before my brain does.

"Good," she says, stepping back. "Now, punching."

I tap the reinforced bag; it barely moves. She snorts.

"Honestly? It's like you've never thrown a punch in your life. Lucky for you, I'm a brilliant teacher." Her fist cracks into the bag like a gunshot. "Power comes from your hips. Twist through. Punch *through* the target, not *at* it. Again."

I try.

She rolls her eyes, steps behind me, adjusts my stance—

wider—then nudges my elbow. "Plant your feet. Feel that? Now pivot your hip. There. Better."

I punch again; a satisfying thud echoes. My knuckles don't even twinge. I grin.

"Better," she concedes. "Now: jab, cross, knee, shin."

"All of that?" I splutter.

She grins. "You'll thank me later."

We drill the sequence—jab, cross, knee, shin—again and again. At first I'm all elbows and hesitation, but a rhythm emerges. I'm not fast or smooth, yet at least I'm no longer mortifying.

At last she steps back, looking thoughtful rather than impressed.

Perhaps she expected the stake-wielding whirlwind puppeteered by Beryl and instead found... me.

I excuse myself to prepare for the meeting. When I leave, I notice Simone on her phone, her voice low and her expression unreadable. I file the moment away, no point in borrowing trouble.

Choosing clothes for the clan meeting takes forever, but in the end, I pull on jeans and a soft jumper—casual, comfortable, nothing that screams I'm trying too hard.

Baylor stays in the bedroom; I lock the door, pocket the key, and follow the voices down the hall.

Six vampires wait in the drawing room: Valdarr, Simone, James, and three I haven't met. No human security, no blood donors.

The drawing room is a study in clean lines and sharp edges, with slate-grey walls, dark carpet, and a deep, angular charcoal sofa encircling a minimalist glass table. A bookcase spans one wall. Above the fireplace hangs the original Blóð-vakt crest; I recognise it at once from the safe house floor.

Beside Simone stands a mountain of a man—easily six foot six and just as broad—with thick auburn sideburns, a ruddy complexion and a rolling laugh that makes everyone smile—even my tense shoulders drop.

If I weren't half-terrified, I'd probably laugh with him.

By the hearth leans a pale blond man in jeans and a T-shirt, green eyes sweeping the room with quiet intensity.

The last newcomer—tall, spare, wary—keeps to the shadows near the bookcase.

My foot scrapes the door frame and every head swivels towards me.

"Ah, here she is," James snarls.

It takes everything not to run away. I hate confrontation.

"Do you have to be so horrible, James?" Simone says. Did I catch a faint sneer on James's name? I store the thought for later. She smiles and offers a friendly wave; the others nod polite greetings.

I step in. *Fred walks into a room full of vampires*—it sounds like the start of a bad joke.

"It's been centuries since we've met a day-walker," rumbles the red-haired giant. "Not one who doesn't use magic, anyway. I'm Ralph." He takes my hand—firm yet gentle—and gives it a single respectful shake.

"Hi, Ralph."

The blond man follows suit. "Tony. Thank you for keeping our liege safe today."

"Hi, Tony."

Bookcase Guy remains silent.

Valdarr studies his people with controlled intensity. I suspect he'll intervene if anything escalates, yet for now—his expression carefully blank—he seems willing to let me speak and stand up for myself.

Simone winks at Valdarr. "I can't believe you bagged the clan a day-walker. Not all of us are lucky enough to own magic jewellery. When I rise, I spend the remaining hours trapped behind wards unless I fancy bursting into flames."

She must think I'm confused, because she answers the question I haven't asked. "The older a vampire is, the less we need to sleep during the day. Many of us rest until early afternoon and can sometimes be woken, though we're a little groggy. Younger vampires—under a couple of hundred years—sleep right through daylight. Valdarr, being over a thousand, can rise just before noon. I'm more of a four-in-the-afternoon type myself, even in winter. The Grand Master doesn't need to sleep at all. However, we're all still deathly allergic to sunlight. Unlike you."

I shiver. The Grand Master does not need to sleep at all. Crikey.

"We've all seen the footage," Tony says. "I've compiled every good angle—soundtrack optional—if anyone's curious."

"I watched the CCTV. She's awkward," James snaps. "She's young, it was pure luck. How old were you when you were turned, Fred?"

"James, it doesn't matter how old she was when she was turned; when she's a talented day-walker," Ralph muses.

Valdarr gestures to the sofa, and we sit. "Drinks, anyone?"

I half expect human donors to file in, throats bared, but

Valdarr fetches bagged blood himself and pours it into crystal glasses.

Simone catches my puzzled look. "We don't feed directly from humans," she explains, hands folded on her knees. "James keeps volunteers at his estate up the road, but the rest of us prefer bagged blood; it's simpler, safer. We are peaceful monsters."

"We were peaceful," Ralph adds, "until Clan Nocturna and our Grand Master interfered. I can't believe they sent human assassins. Do they even realise Winifred is a rare, valuable day-walker?"

"Why does everyone keep saying that? She's not a day-walker," James bites back. "During daylight Fred's human."

Tony's mouth drops open.

"Human? I don't understand. Did something go wrong with the turning?" Ralph asks.

I shrug. "I have no idea."

I hardly understand House's magic myself; how can I explain it to a room full of vampires? A small part of me still hopes the Grand Master turned me—conventionally, however impossible—rather than leaving me a freak. Then guilt bites: House saved my life. As I told Lander, without her interference I would be dead.

The excitement in the room fades, and they all watch me as though I'm some strange, new creature.

Six pairs of eyes swing to Valdarr.

He sighs, pain etched across his face. "The Grand Master killed her—he meant to drain her—and we believe magic was responsible for Fred's turning. The Ministry of Magic thinks the wizard's house she lived in altered the process. Fred died, he disposed of the body, yet the sentient house's magic revived her and held her in suspension. She rose as a vampire, drove home, and at dawn the house completed the spell. Fred is human by day, vampire by night."

"Fairy-tale stuff," Simone breathes. "Serious magic. Can we see this wizard's house?"

"It's already moved," Valdarr says. "The Ministry of Magic botched an attempt to contain it. Lander Kane tried to chain the house to the site, seize control, and Fred—by all accounts—knocked him flat and broke his wand."

Simone shoots me a wicked grin.

Tony leans forward, his gaze sharpening. "About the humans you killed today—do you need to talk? Was it your first time?"

"Hardly," James hisses. "She murdered a team of assassins and didn't even let them crawl home; conveniently, the bodies vanished with the house."

"If we are pointing fingers, James, I took out twenty of those same assassins," Valdarr says.

"To protect her." James jabs a trembling finger at me.

"Have you got a problem with our youngest, James?" Tony asks cautiously.

"Yes, I have."

"James," Valdarr growls, handing around glasses of blood. I take mine with a mumbled "thanks," try not to grimace, and swirl the thick liquid, giving my restless fingers something to do.

"No! I will not be silenced. I have the right to speak my truth."

"Oh, great. Here we go," Simone mutters.

"After offering your blood, you lacked the decency to

stay dead, thereby embarrassing our esteemed Grand Master. You seduced his heir, bit a claimed thrall, spelled a master vampire, murdered Clan Nocturna vampires when they retaliated, attacked a Ministry of Magic councillor—causing an incident—and your actions provoked today's assault on our peaceful clan, killing honest security staff and endangering our liege." He scowls at Simone. "That was hardly brave work. My advice is to drag Winifred to the Hall of Silence, put her on trial, and be rid of the problem."

Off with her head.

"When you put it like that, it *does* sound bad," I mumble, then laugh, low and humourless. Who would have thought mousy Winifred would cause such a stink?

Chapter Twenty-Nine

James opens his mouth to reply, but the man who has been propping up the bookshelves glides forward first. Even at a glance he radiates danger. He has dark hair and skin, is leaner and shorter than Valdarr, yet moves with the predatory ease of a seasoned fighter. Anyone with half an instinct would mark him as lethal.

"James, you're being unreasonable," he says, voice cool. "Do you really think I'd let anyone near our liege without running a full background check?"

"But, Harrison—"

"Do not interrupt me." His tone could frost glass. "You're acting like a child forcing a square peg into a round hole until the corners snap off. You can't twist the facts to suit yourself." He folds himself into a chair, leaning forward.

Simone mirrors him; she's now wearing a smug smile.

"Besides, you are upsetting our liege."

Now that Harrison has pointed it out, Valdarr's expression is rigid. His jaw is clenched so hard he must be grinding his teeth down to nubs.

"Explain, youngest," Harrison orders. "Start at the beginning." His dark-blue gaze pins me. "Tell the truth, we'll know if you lie. What happened the day you met the Grand Master?"

I glance at Valdarr for help.

"It will be okay," he says gently.

I nod, throat tight. "All right. I was making Sunday deliveries. Food orders. One was for a house with a yellow door: Valdarr's. It was about four o'clock, broad daylight. I knocked, left the takeaway, and returned a hoodie Valdarr had lent me the day before when I'd been soaked in the rain. The door opened as I was leaving. A vampire I didn't know took the food, grabbed me by the hair, and dragged me inside."

I swallow and rub the scar tissue on my throat.

"He pinned me to the wall and bit me. I told him to stop. I never gave permission to take my blood." I draw a breath. "I woke up in the bin, drove home, and the next morning my heart was beating, my lungs working. But at sundown the vampire magic kicked in—I died again. That's how it's been ever since."

I set the glass down and tap the rim to steady myself.

"I did my best to ignore the vampire thing; I was scared. I kept working days in the Human Sector and nights from home doing customer service shifts." I never gave notice, just disappeared. I'll have to email them. *Focus, Fred.* "I started losing weight, and House and I thought blood might help."

"The house? You can talk to a house? That's utter bullshit, the girl is barmy." James throws his hands in the air and laughs.

"James." Harrison growls. "Ignore him, please continue."

"I drank blood for the first time about a month after I was turned, and a few hours later, it felt as though I were crawling out of my skin."

"How did you get the blood?" Harrison interrupts.

"From House. The wizard's house can *take* things—she sourced bags from a vampire warehouse."

"Bagged blood?"

"Yes, only bags. I've never bitten anyone." I shoot James a glare. "I had so much energy that night, I ran down the road to test my abilities. It was amazing, but I lost track of myself. House sat near scrubland on the edge of the Vampire Sector. Looking for varied footing—or maybe guided by instinct—I crossed into vampire territory. Border patrol caught me, and they took me to their station, and Valdarr rescued me and brought me to a safe house, but by morning, I was human again. I was worried he might discover my strange condition, and I had Baylor and House to think about. So I jumped out of a window and went back home."

"Baylor?"

I manage a small smile. "Baylor's my dog."

He nods. "When did you meet Clan Nocturna?"

"I met a member of their clan while searching for

answers about my friend Amy and her husband, Max. They were killed after dining at One Bite Won't Hurt—"

"See? Poking around where she's not wanted," James mutters.

"But I didn't meet the clan vampires until—um—I stopped a vampire from killing Crystal, one of their thralls. I drove her home."

"She went into their territory without permission," James pipes up again.

"She didn't know," Simone tuts, elbowing him.

I start to explain the visions—how it all began—but something stops me. I pause.

I can't.

My instincts scream at me to keep the visions between Valdarr and me. So I shut my mouth—mid-sentence. He raises an eyebrow. I shake my head. He probably won't like my keeping this from the clan, yet I have to trust my power, and right now it isn't happy.

Maybe it's the clan.

Maybe it's James.

Maybe it's something else entirely.

I don't know. But I do know one thing—I can't tell them about the visions. Not yet.

"Why bother saving the girl?" Simone asks, leaning forward. She sips her drink, chin in hand, eyes intent.

"Because it was the right thing to do. Not helping her felt wrong."

She nods.

"You all believe this crap?" James sneers.

Harrison ignores him and presses on. "And then?"

"I drove Crystal home and made sure she was safe, but a

Clan Nocturna vampire started shouting that I had bitten her. I told him to check the wound—it wasn't mine. I'd rescued her, not attacked her. He wouldn't listen. I threw a knock-out spell at him. The other vampires blocked my car, chased me, and that's when some shifters stepped in and saved me."

They all stare at me.

Ah, right.

"Shifters?" James scoffs. "So now we've got shifters in the mix as well. Any other derivatives you've forgotten to mention? Did you stab them too?"

"No, I did not," I snap, reaching for my glass. My mouth is dry, so I take a gulp of blood—then grimace at what I've done.

To my surprise, it doesn't taste awful. The blood has no taste of chemicals; this is different, fresher. Some spell must keep it that way. Whatever it is, it works—it's... pleasant. I hum into the glass, then set it down. No point guzzling while everyone looks at me as though I'm the biggest monster in the room.

"So... the shifters were kind," I continue. "They let me go. Their Alpha's mate removed a spell Clan Nocturna had thrown at me, and I went home. Then I learned there was a warrant for my arrest. They had declared me rogue and told everyone to watch for me. And then... assassins attacked."

"And you killed them," James says sharply.

"No. The—" I stop; I can't say Beryl's name. "The wizard's house stopped them," I say at last. "The house... killed them." Mentally, I apologise to House.

"She's lying," James snarls.

I raise my hands. "Fine. House didn't kill them, and

neither did I. But I'm not telling you who did. I promised. Valdarr knows. You'll have to trust him—it wasn't *me*. Even if it had been, they were assassins."

"Lying, bitc—"

"James. I will not tell you again." Harrison growls.

"Yes, leave her alone," Simone says. "Whether she stabbed them or not is hardly the point, is it? Gods, you are such a dick."

I clear my throat. "The following morning, the Ministry of Magic attacked House. Valdarr rescued Baylor and me from the humans, and now I'm here. You all know what happened today."

Silence settles over the room. "I can leave, if you would prefer," I add more quietly. "If you think I'm unsafe to be around, I understand."

"You are not leaving, and James, you are not making this into a problem. Let it go," Valdarr says firmly. Then, to my interrogator, "Did Fred lie?"

"No. Apart from protecting her mystery friend, everything she's said is true and matches my inquiries. And today she acted in the clan's defence."

"I'm glad we're all on the same page," Ralph says.

Valdarr clears his throat. "Now, we need to discuss something else... something personal." There is a shift in the room. An alert stillness to him. "My mate."

"What?" Simone blurts. "You've found your mate? A true mate? A *fated* mate?"

"There hasn't been one in generations," Tony mutters.

"I know," Valdarr replies. "I'm more surprised than anyone."

He's staring straight at me.

Why is he staring at me?

Now everyone's staring at me.

I shift in my seat. "What's a fated mate? I mean, I've read enough fiction to guess, but..."

"It's like a soulmate," Simone says, eyes wide.

"Exactly like a soulmate," Valdarr confirms. Then softly, almost reverently, "Only rarer. Stronger. Permanent."

My mouth goes dry.

He doesn't say it, not yet. But the way he's looking at me—

Then he gives me one of those beautiful smiles that steals my breath. "You are my fated mate, Fred. You. Are. Mine."

The table erupts. Everyone shouts at once.

Chapter Thirty

"Is this a joke?" James and I say in unison.

I glance at him, then back at Valdarr, cheeks burning. No one has ever declared anything like this about me, with that level of certainty. It must be a joke. Why would he want me? I am hardly 'fated mate' material.

"I don't understand," I mumble. "I don't believe you."

Valdarr doesn't blink. His voice is low and steady. "When I told your ex I was going to cherish you, I meant it." He draws a breath. "I intended to take my time—to let you feel safe, wanted, to learn about you and to let you learn me, to court you properly." He hesitates. "But, unfortunately... we have run out of time."

James hurls his cup at the wall. "This is bullshit!" Glass shatters; blood spatters the slate-grey paint.

I flinch.

"Oh, now you've done it," Simone murmurs, fingertips resting against her cheek.

James lunges—

—and vanishes.

Harrison intercepts him mid-stride, lifts him as if he weighs nothing, and pins him to the far wall. Was he going to hurt me? Probably.

Valdarr steps in front of me and growls.

He seems even larger. His shoulders roll forward, muscles tense, and his top lip curls to bare sharp, gleaming fangs. For the first time he looks every inch the vampire.

"You dare attack my mate—after I have claimed her!" he roars.

Harrison whispers something sharp into James's ear, seizes him by the scruff and drags him out without a word. The others raise their hands, take a collective step back, and file out of the room.

Valdarr's chest rises and falls in quick, shallow bursts—as if he is hyperventilating, furious.

Yet I am not afraid; I feel fiercely protected.

I slide from behind the table and move towards him. His hand snaps out—not roughly—and captures my wrist in a gentle grip. He lifts it to his face, not to his mouth but to his nose. The sensitive skin tingles as he inhales, slowly, as though my scent is the only thing anchoring him.

His eyes flash violet. I gasp.

He lowers his gaze and breathes again, slower, calmer. The hand that holds mine is careful, even as his nails lengthen into black claws. His thumb strokes my skin in a whisper-light caress meant to soothe.

"My apologies," he says at last, his voice gravel-rough.

"He will not do that again. No one will ever speak to you with disrespect again."

"It's fine," I manage—though it isn't. "He is allowed his opinions."

"It is *not* fine, sunshine." He shakes his head and closes his eyes. "I feel as though I'm losing my mind. Everybody wants to disrespect and hurt you." This situation is hurting him. He visibly shrinks before my eyes.

"Not everyone," I say, keeping James's name to myself. No need to poke the upset vampire. "The rest of your clan have been kind and welcoming."

"I'm so sorry. I don't know what's happening, my life isn't usually so dramatic."

"None of this is your fault."

He releases my wrist slowly, as if prising himself away.

I tuck my hand against my chest, still feeling the warmth of his touch, the ghost of claws, the memory of breath on my skin.

"Will he be all right?" I ask. I do not want Harrison or Valdarr to pop James's head off.

"He will live," Valdarr says. "James is... protective. Paranoid, after a hard life. Usually we humour him, but this time we can't. He just can't be near you for a while. It isn't safe. I'm not safe."

That's not exactly reassuring. "I'm sorry. I never meant to make your clan fight. What does 'fated mate' even mean?" I ask softly. "How is it possible?"

His expression gentles. "I knew you were my mate the first day I met you."

"What?" I sit back down with a thud. "When you slammed the door in my face?"

He smiles. "Strange, isn't it? I felt the bond lock in place, and I panicked—worried I'd frightened you, terrified I'd never see you again... and just as terrified that I would. Humans are fragile. I'd never steal your life or your humanity. Even if we had tried to be together, you would never have turned—no genetic marker, I checked. I planned to watch from afar, keep you safe, let you live. I never wanted *this* for you. Then, at the station, when I learned what my father had done to you, everything changed."

"So you didn't want me when I was human, but now I'm some human-slash-vampire hybrid, you are interested?"

"I will always want you," he says firmly. He reaches across the table and squeezes my hand. "My feelings do not dictate yours. We can take our time. No pressure. If you don't want this, I will get you, Baylor, and when we find her, House, out of the country, somewhere safe. You have options, Fred. You are in control; you decide."

I exhale. "You are fated to me, but do you even like me? I'm not in your league."

He moves so fast I barely register it—one moment across the table, the next beside me, cupping my jaw, thumb smoothing my cheek.

"You, Winifred Crowsdale, are perfection. My sunshine in the dark. Don't speak of yourself like that again." His voice drops. "I would crawl miles on my belly for a glimpse of those blue eyes."

Words fail me.

Valdarr leans in and brushes a kiss, an almost achingly tender kiss, against the corner of my mouth.

All I need do is turn my head, yet I freeze.

Men like him do not choose women like me; the moment feels too unreal.

It feels like a lie.

"We will go slowly," he murmurs. "If you want me, I will move heaven and earth to prove I'm worthy of your time—that includes protecting you from my father."

He pauses. "So far, I've done a dreadful job. My father is not a good man. I have avoided politics for centuries, but now he's targeted you. If we move too soon, we risk war; if we wait and build support among the other clans, we stand a chance."

I have no words, so I stay silent.

"I have spoken with the shifters," he continues. "You impressed the Alpha's mate; she wants to help. But you are an unregistered turning, and there's the Clan Nocturna mess. First, we must face the Council. If we survive a public trial, we might have a chance."

"We?"

"Sunshine," he says softly, "I know you don't believe me. To you, I'm just a vampire who's barged into your life with a homicidal father and a pile of problems." His voice falters, then steadies. "I know it is sudden, and you don't feel the bond—you weren't born a vampire. But I don't care."

He kisses the tip of my nose.

"I do not care if it's one-sided. I have enough love for both of us, and I will do everything in my power to make you happy."

His eyes hold mine, steady and raw.

"So when I say we will survive the trial, I mean it. I do not want to live in a world without you."

I stare at him with disbelief. Not because I doubt everything—well, perhaps a little—but because no one has ever said anything like this to me.

I have never been anyone's first choice.

He says he doesn't mind if it's one-sided, that he has enough love for both of us. Somehow, that makes it worse. It's too much—too kind, too certain—and I'm not used to people being certain about me.

I don't know how to stand in the light of someone's love without squinting, without bracing for it to turn or disappear.

For it not to hurt.

He wants to make me happy, to wait, to try—and something tired, old, and frightened inside me wants to cry at the thought. I've lived too long where love arrived with conditions, came quietly, left loudly, and only after I shrank myself small enough to be tolerated.

I do not know how to accept what he is offering.

Not yet. Perhaps not ever. But the thing that scares me most is that part of me wants to. Wants to try. Wants to believe him. Wants to be his. I have no idea what to do with that.

I pull away and clear my throat, though it emerges as a squeak. My hands fuss with the hem of my sleeve. "Well," I say after a beat too long, "that's... a lot."

Smooth, Fred. Very smooth.

"I mean, most men buy you dinner or say you have nice boobs, not declare eternal devotion and a shared survival pact."

I risk a glance. He hasn't moved, watching me as though I'm the sun and he hasn't seen daylight in years.

"Look, I'm not saying I don't appreciate the sentiment. I'm just... I'm not very good at this. Whatever this is." I gesture between us. "And, honestly, I'm still processing the whole trial-slash-potential-death thing, never mind the soulmate situation."

A breath, then I quietly add, "But thank you. For saying it, for meaning it."

I can't give him more than that. Not now.

But he knows it isn't a no.

Valdarr smiles.

"Sunshine," he murmurs, "if I wanted declarations in return, I wouldn't have offered mine first." He lifts one shoulder in a half-shrug. "Personally, I think that was rather romantic—very poetic. Survival pacts are terribly in at the moment."

I huff a laugh before I can stop myself.

"And for the record," he adds, violet eyes dancing, "I do like your boobs, but I thought I should lead with the undying devotion."

I shake my head, yet I'm smiling now.

My smile fades. "Where will this public trial be?"

"The Hall of Silence."

"Oh, James will love that," I mutter, swallowing. I take another sip of blood and dab my lips. "Very well, let us deal with that first, then your father. I shall do what I can to help."

"It will be dangerous, Fred."

"Then I will try to remain alive and useful."

"I will protect you with my life," he says. "So will the clan."

"Even James?" I arch a brow. "When do we go?"

"Tomorrow night."

"So soon? Anything I should read? Prepare?"

"No. If you sound rehearsed, they will notice. Just be yourself."

I nod. "All right." Great. "I want to help," I say, mustering courage. "Perhaps I could attempt a vision with your help?"

"Very well. As long as you are safe, we can try."

"Yes, let's try."

We return to my suite—my phone is there, anyway—and I settle on the sofa. Valdarr hovers until I pat the cushion beside me.

"Come on," I say. "Sit."

He does, and I fiddle with my phone. "This will look odd," I warn, "but I need to watch reels."

"Watching videos sends you into a trance?" He sounds surprised.

"I do not know why it works, but it may take a while."

"In that case, get comfortable."

Thirty minutes pass—nothing. I huff in frustration.

He pats his lap. "Lie here."

Placing a cushion across his thighs, he guides me down until my head rests on it. My cheeks burn. He strokes my hair, rhythmic, soothing, exactly as House once did. With his other hand he lifts mine, tilting the phone towards my face. I take the hint and resume scrolling.

From the corner of my eye, I see Baylor belly-crawl closer. Valdarr's free hand disappears into his fur. I grin and concentrate.

His fingers in my hair, the mindless flick of videos—together they work.

Just before the vision takes me, I do something new: I focus. Rather than begging the universe for anything, I fix on Valdarr and tomorrow night, clinging to one sharp command—*protect him*.

Astonishingly, it works.

I am outside the house. Three cars wait while the clan prepares to leave. Seeing *vision me* is jarring—I look nothing like the middle-aged human I once was. I force my attention to Valdarr.

Everyone climbs into the cars. I remain behind, unable to follow. I try not to think of our destination, instead, I focus on the danger ahead.

The vision wavers, reforms at a junction. *Wow, that's a weird sensation.* Our car enters the crossroads, and another vehicle hurtles from the opposite side and smashes into us. Through shattered glass, I see the moment of impact—Valdarr folds himself around me, shielding me.

The vision snaps back. I am ejected, gasping.

He must have... he must have died.

For me.

Are you all right?" Valdarr asks.

No. But I drag in two breaths and croak, "Yes. How long was I out?"

"Around forty seconds."

Forty seconds? The vision had felt more like an hour. Vision time clearly doesn't match real time. I could spend hours—days even—inside a vision, and only moments might pass in the real world.

I remind myself I have never attempted this as a vampire. Perhaps the vampire side of me is stronger, sharper and better equipped for psychic work. Maybe. I don't know. I only know I must cling to what I learn and pray it will be enough.

"I need to try again."

Determination pulls me under. Vision me is alert: she urges the driver to divert before the crash site, and the car takes a different route.

That is when it strikes me— how perilous this meddling might be. Vision me now knows what I know. I have altered the future.

A spell slams into the car, killing everyone inside. I am ripped away.

I go back in.

I ignore the vehicles and hop through moments like turning pages, checking every turn, every street, hunting the safest path.

Fear sharpens my memory.

Again. And again. Close calls. Ambushes. More spells.

I keep going.

At last—after several failures and one narrow escape—we reach the Council chambers *unscathed*.

We step inside—

—and that is when the true ordeal begins.

Chapter Thirty-One

Last night's back-to-back visions were anything but healthy. After dozens of attempts I ended up glassy-eyed and shaking, nearly unconscious, until Valdarr—quite rightly—put his foot down.

Strangely, I was grateful for my vampire half. Had I attempted them while being human, and forced that many visions into a single sitting, I would have fried my brain. The undead part kept me going... until it could not.

Now we stand in the heart of the Vampire Sector.

The district is ultra-modern, almost science-fiction, with technology I have never seen; I half-expect hover-cars to zip past. It feels as though I have stepped into *Back to the Future*.

We pause before an immense block of black glass.

The Hall of Silence.

My anxiety spikes. I have never been this frightened—not for myself so much as for Valdarr, for the clan who took me in, for anyone who might pay the price of my existence. One misstep and it is not only my head on the block; I might make a mistake that has my vampire killed.

"Are you all right? You're looking a little peaky," Simone says.

"Fine, thanks," I lie, forcing a weak smile.

I am anything but fine.

We are about to enter the Hall of Silence, a building full of vampires who believe I am a rogue, and I'm going to face the Head Vampire who actively wants me dead. No pressure.

Valdarr stands beside me like a silent sentinel.

I have not told him what I discovered in the visions; fear stayed my tongue. I also have a sneaky suspicion that the power wouldn't let me. If he had known, he might have reacted differently and changed something. It does not help that I have watched him die—this wonderful man—again and again.

When he promised to protect me with his life, he meant it.

He meant everything.

I am a different person from the one I was yesterday. The visions have hardened me. Broken me. Experiencing alternative realities, without knowing the science behind them, and fearing that a single misstep could fracture existence, has left me deeply unsettled. I never want to do it again.

I smooth my fitted, mid-length blue dress, a shade that flatters my eyes, emphasises my pallor and somehow makes my blonde hair glossier. Six-inch heels would have crippled me when I was human but vampiric balance keeps me upright, and though I loathe every step, having extra pointy things that can be used as weapons is comforting.

Beryl is strapped to my thigh beneath the fabric, silent and unnervingly cold. I must trust she will wake when it matters.

"Going to tell us we can't enter or that we have to cartwheel through the door?" James sneers.

My visions insisted James accompany us, otherwise, Valdarr would have left him behind. I give him a tight smile. "No cartwheels, James. We are all good."

During the drive, I revealed our route in fragments. The detours infuriated everyone but Valdarr, who simply watched me, storm-grey eyes understanding. He knew what I was doing. He would not let anyone override me. I threaded us through side roads, turning a half-hour journey into more than an hour. James—mercifully—in another car.

Security waves us through and we step inside.

I have walked this moment countless times, yet never enough to banish dread. My stomach flips. It's like rewatching a familiar film—but different. The visions were scent-free; being here is overwhelming. My senses flare, fangs sliding down of their own accord.

At least my vampiric nature keeps the sweat at bay.

The Hall of Silence exudes oppressive grandeur—an eighteenth-century court dipped in chrome, polished to a mirror shine and set inside a curved skyscraper.

Cold, clinical light pours from invisible sources far above, catching on steel fittings and glass balustrades. Everything gleams. The open-plan space feels deliberately cavernous, designed to make you small, and it succeeds.

It makes you think you have stepped into the belly of something ancient, ruthless, wholly indifferent to your survival.

Tiered rows of bone-white seats sweep around the central floor, where I will stand—an insect in a very clean, very expensive trap.

The higher a clan ranks in the hierarchy, the higher the members are seated. Clan Nocturna occupies the middle rows; I spot them at once, and they are glaring. The old adage "if looks could kill" springs to mind.

I know the other clans too—their rivalries and who they would kill if given the chance. I watched them closely in my visions and then carried out extensive research. They mingle in small groups, gather in force. Others stand alone —some stare, some smirk, and others look keen to behead me where I stand. All of them relish what they see as Valdarr's epic mistake.

By contrast, Valdarr's clan has remained impartial for more than a thousand years, helping rather than hindering. He has kept his head down, allowing the newer clans to squabble.

I recognise faces, reactions, intentions. The elegant lady across the hall plans to strike Simone. The scowling man near her, furious even among his own clan, will unexpectedly shield me.

Foreknowledge matters now, but I am glad I don't live with it daily. I will not make a habit of using this power. Last night I pursued the threads of the main players and nothing more. The future is a spider's web of possibilities.

One careless tug and the whole thing tears.

I must handle these next few moments very, very carefully.

Many thoughts spin through my head: be humble yet confident—do not look coached. I am no actor—my heart lives on my sleeve—but I must pretend every word is new, must perform to save our lives.

Valdarr angles his body protectively before mine. He is ready—willing—to throw himself into danger, and I dearly hope I do not ruin everything. I must keep him safe. I do not want to watch him die again.

Our clan spreads out behind us, outwardly relaxed. Simone mutters at James, who snaps back. Ralph stands aside, all warrior. Tony is quiet, watchful. Harrison, the head of our security, draws sneers from other vampires. They have no idea. If things go wrong, they will never see him coming.

Valdarr has surrounded himself with capable people.

My eyes drift around the hall. In the Hall of Silence, vampires must represent themselves, and it rarely ends well for the accused. Sometimes, when a vision went wrong and I didn't have the heart to watch the outcome, I wandered—eavesdropped, explored, learnt this building. I probably know it better than most here—better than the Council, the guards, perhaps even the Grand Master himself.

He enters exactly on time.

Everything stills.

Chapter Thirty-Two

Had I not seen him countless times before, I might have dropped to my knees. In earlier visions, I have been paralysed by terror.

It is not that he cannot hurt me—he can—but this is the Council's arena, and even monsters have rules, rules he has broken whether he intended to or not.

I meet his gaze. The burgundy ring around his dark grey eyes has widened, the irises shading towards red, as though whatever he is has started forcing its way to the surface. He licks his crimson lips, tongue sharp, almost reptilian.

I can smell iron, ash, and rot drifting from his skin; the stench turns my stomach.

It takes everything not to sneer or scream. No one should have to lock eyes with their murderer. Rule number one: do not antagonise. Rule number two: do not show fear.

I bow my head instead and as though rehearsed, Valdarr mirrors me.

"Father."

The Grand Master's mouth curls. "My son," he replies, thick with disdain. "What abomination do we have here?"

Me, the woman you drained and killed, who lacked the decency to remain dead. Surprised we survived your many assassination attempts? I keep my mouth shut and my expression vague.

Standing together, they share an unmistakable family resemblance, yet I can also see how character etches itself onto a face. How sustained evil warps even a vampire's features.

Before Valdarr's father can spew more vitriol, the rest of the Council arrives: twelve clan-less elders—male and female—draped in royal-blue capes trimmed with fine gold thread bearing the Crest of the Vampirical Council.

The Grand Master strides away, his regal black robe sweeping the floor, and settles on a polished stone throne at the very centre of the council's raised white marble platform. Scowling, eyes fixed on me, he waits as the court officiant steps forward with all the pomp you would expect from a man wielding a staff taller than himself.

The officiant moves to the centre of the chamber, red robes rustling, and bows—first to the Grand Master, then to the assembled Council, who have now taken their seats. Raising the ceremonial staff high, he slams it down.

The boom ricochets off marble and glass; magic whips across the hall, prickling my skin and lifting every tiny hair.

So this is what always snaps vampires to attention. It is not pleasant.

A small grunt escapes me. Valdarr's little finger brushes mine with a whisper-light reassurance. He is already watching me, trust and certainty blazing in his eyes. Humbled, I swallow, lift my chin and manage a confident smile.

"Order!" the officiant bellows. "The Court is in session."

And the trial begins.

A ward seals the gallery in silence as the charges are read.

"I, the Herald of Silence, speak as the voice of the Council. Winifred Crowsdale of Clan Blóðvakt, you stand before this Hall charged with the following articles:

Unlicensed turning and failure to register, in breach of Accord Code 675.3 and the related registration provisions;

Unlawful feeding and assault upon a claimed human of Clan Nocturna, contrary to Accord Code 561.0;

Trespass into a sovereign clan's warded territory without leave, in violation of Accord Code 421.9, as recognised under Accord Code 302.1;

Final death of Accord-recognised persons, absent protection under Accord Code 765.0.

How do you plead?"

Valdarr opens his mouth, but I step forward.

"I thank the Vampirical Council and the Court," I say, my words riding the ambient magic. I bow once more. I recall the vision in which I pleaded not guilty to every charge—a tactic that ended matters swiftly.

They cut my throat.

"On Count One, the unlicensed turning, I plead guilty—on paper—but I will show extenuating circumstances."

The ward blocks all sound, yet I watch the vampires in the gallery shift in their seats; some even lean forward, eyes gleaming with glee. They think I have just signed my own death warrant.

"On Count Two, the alleged unlawful feeding, I plead not guilty. The donor wasn't a registered thrall at the time, and I never fed."

Crystal was only a human blood donor, and although that makes no difference to me—since taking blood unwillingly is evil—to the Court, it means everything.

"On Count Three, trespass, I plead guilty, with mitigation: I crossed to save a human life. On Count Four, so-called murder, I claim immunity under Accord Code 765.375: Right of Self-Defence. Every act of violence was in response to an attempt on my life."

The Herald's eyes gleam with interest at my responses.

Vision me must have died a score of times before stumbling upon his office and the cache of Accord law books and articles I needed—conveniently open on his desk with notes for today's trial. In this court, every defendant is set up to fail. Yet, no one can claim the Herald does not do extensive case preparation.

I have never been so grateful that the memories from my visions come with near-perfect recall.

"The Court records your pleas as tendered: guilt with mitigation reserved, trespass admitted, assault denied, and self-defence invoked under Accord Code 765.375. So entered. The Council will confer under seal. Raise the Veil."

The staff strikes, and a sheet of noise-cancelling

warding rises from the floor, encircling him and the Council. He steps back into their midst, and they begin to confer.

The Grand Master argues with the Vampirical Council. The vampires are told the Council is impartial; they are not. Each has an agenda.

I have stood on the other side of that ward, listening to their deliberations, gaining valuable information, and today I have planned my words, chosen my targets—the ones who might listen. I practised my plea, honing the phrases that carry weight: clear, concise, honest speech. Begging never works on them, but precision often does.

Even so, it may not be enough. I may have misjudged them—misread the moments. Hope is a dangerous thing.

In the visions it was easier, events unfolding out of sync with reality. Now there are no second chances, no redos, no margin for error. I am here now. And I pray I have judged correctly.

I can see into the future—but I cannot go back.

After a somewhat silent but lively debate, the ward drops and the Herald moves to the lectern. "The trial shall proceed." He turns a page with ceremonial precision. "You claim justification for your turning?"

"Yes."

"*Let the Silence record*: the Council will dispose of the ancillary counts first. On the allegation arising from the so-called assassination incident, the Council has reviewed the evidentiary bundle submitted by Clan Nocturna, together with the defence materials. Civic CCTV confirm that the accused extracted and conveyed a human donor who, at the material time, was not a registered thrall within the meaning of Accord Code 302.1; no compact had been signed or sealed."

He glares at the Nocturna delegation. "Clan Nocturna's submission is therefore defective in law and in fact. The count is dismissed with prejudice; judgment is entered in Winifred Crowsdale's favour."

A ripple moves through the room.

"On Charge Three: Trespass," the Herald continues, "*let the Silence record:* the Council finds the accused newly turned and non-indoctrinated, a mitigating factor recognised under Accord Code 402.3, of Novitiate Leniency. The evidence shows her incursion into Clan Nocturna's demesne was in aid of a human life and not in interference with clan prerogatives, thus falling within the humanitarian carve-out of Accord Code 211.9c, Territorial Integrity and Wayleave—Good-Faith Rescue.

"Ordinarily, a compensatory levy would issue; however, Clan Nocturna acted in bad faith, instigating unlawful force and subsequently escalating to a daylight assault upon Clan Blóðvakt, in breach of Accord Codes 118.2 and 703.4.

"Accordingly, no further action shall be taken against Winifred Crowsdale. Clan Nocturna, be formally censured: cease and desist. A second violation will trigger sanctions under Accord Code 910.1."

The Herald waits for the gallery of vampires to settle, then turns back to me. "On Charge One: Unauthorised Turning—in contravention of Accord Codes 101.1 and 203.7. You have entered a plea of guilty with mitigation. *Let the Silence record it so.* The Council will now hear your justification. Speak it plain, and let the record hold you."

Now for the hard part.

"I was assaulted and killed. I am an unwilling product of the turning. The vampire who fed on me did not intend to sire me, he believed I was dead and discarded. I rose alone—unregistered, untrained, and without guidance."

"Assertion noted," the Herald's tone edged with scepticism. "The Court does not sit on sentiment nor accept naked allegation. Accord Code 214.2 bars hearsay without substrate. What proof do you tender?"

"Test my blood and memory. They will name my sire and show the turning lacked intent. I exist only by mistake."

The Herald frowns. "Blood will name your sire; it cannot divine their intent. Tread carefully, Winifred Crowsdale, if this petition proves frivolous, the Council will consider sanctions under Accord Code 12.2, Contempt of Tribunal. Proceed, if you still wish."

I pause, letting the moment stretch.

Valdarr's father smirks.

I draw a deep—though unnecessary—breath and steady myself.

"The vampire who broke our laws, who fed from an unwilling human, killed her, and turned her by accident..."

I raise one hand and point at the throne.

"...is our revered Grand Master."

Chaos erupts in the gallery as vampires leap to their feet, shouting.

Down here, silence.

The Grand Master does not protest at first; for a second, his eyes flash red. He inclines his head a millimetre towards the Herald. When he speaks, the temperature in the hall seems to drop.

"Strike that from the record. A rogue mistake dares to spit slander at this court. Have we sunk so low that any unregistered aberration may level a charge at the Crown without evidence? Herald, you will silence her, or I will. Sanction her for contempt. Tear her tongue out if you must. I do not answer to gutter-born lies."

His gaze spears Valdarr. "And you, you bring this thing into my hall to bark at your betters? You disgrace your blood."

"You will stand down, Grand Master. The Council—not you—decides what is stricken," the Herald replies.

"Then decide quickly, before I decide for you."

The Herald ignores the Grand Master's threat and narrows his eyes at me. "That is a grave accusation, Winifred Crowsdale."

"I stand by it, and I invoke Accord Code 101.4, the Right of Blood Provenance, and Accord Code 212.3, Ethereal Memory Capture and Admissibility. Let blood and memory speak."

A hairline crack appears in the marble arm of the Grand Master's throne.

"So entered. By authority of this Court under Codes 101.4 and 212.3, the Ministry of Magic will perform bloodline verification and an Ethereal Memory Capture—"

"When her blood speaks and fails, will you cut her head off here or drag her through the streets and make it... poetic?" the Grand Master snarls, interrupting.

"The Council withholds judgment until both attestations are complete and places Clan Blóðvakt under Court protection pending sentence," the Herald continues.

We have won, for now. I betray no relief.

There's no chance the bloodline verification will succeed. House turned me—at best, she borrowed a little magic from the nearest vampire.

The Grand Master knows he didn't sire me, so he may hesitate to kill us while he seeks vindication before the Court. No one enjoys being accused of a crime they didn't commit. I can practically see steam rising from the heat of his temper.

The Grand Master's fingers twitch—a signal too subtle for most. But I have seen this before—he is about to run and he needs a distraction.

Gripping Valdarr's wrist, I signal the clan with my other hand, held low behind my back.

Five—my splayed fingers mark the countdown.

Four—I drop one finger and squeeze Valdarr's wrist.

Three—another finger, another squeeze.

Two.

One.

I clench my fist.

The wards collapse. All hell breaks loose.

Chapter Thirty-Three

Violence ripples from the back of the gallery, where agents, acting on the Grand Master's orders, slaughter a smaller, insignificant clan. Screams rise; fangs flash. The hall descends into chaos. The scent of spilt blood thickens the air, mingling with snarls and the clash of blades. Vampires, driven by bloodlust, seize the moment to settle old grudges. Those who try to hold back are dragged into the fray when they are attacked.

I slam into Valdarr's chest, knocking him clear of a throwing knife that whistles past my head.

"Simone—left, the lady in the red dress!"

Her head whips round. The woman charges, fangs bared. Simone flips her skirt aside and twin blades gleam in her hands. She twirls them, grinning. "You always were a sloppy fighter," she spits as they clash.

Our companions form a defensive ring around Valdarr and me.

"How does she know all this? How does she know the accords better than I do?" James snarls. "My liege, she did a countdown! Winifred isn't who she pretends to be. Last night she was shaking just talking to the clan, and now she faces the Vampirical Council without flinching?"

"I told you she was a worthy mate," Valdarr replies, grinning. "Fred, you are incredible."

"A mate who, not even twenty-four hours after your declaration, has tipped our clan into outright war. She publicly accused your father."

Tony intercepts a blood-soaked vampire mid-rampage; they grapple violently before vanishing from sight as a second attacker charges.

Harrison steps forward. The foolish vampire laughs and tries to bat him aside, but Harrison is armed to the teeth. The creature lunges—it's a fatal mistake. In one fluid motion Harrison slices the tendons at the man's elbows. His arms drop uselessly, blood pouring freely. He stares in stunned silence, unable to raise a hand.

Then Harrison reverses the blade and strikes him in the temple, knocking him unconscious—a blow that would kill a human. He grins as he drags the body clear so no one trips over it.

Movement in the gallery catches my eye.

"Clan Nocturna incoming," I warn.

James emits a squeak, rummages frantically through his pockets, and clutches his tablet to his chest as though it were a shield.

The vampire, Ian, whom I stunned with a spell—and

his furious brute of a friend—appear at the balcony rail. They ignore the stairs, leaping instead.

One rolls smoothly; the other lands fist-first, rising with a growl.

"You're dead, baby rogue."

Been there. Done that.

Valdarr shifts me behind him. "I've been waiting for this," he says softly. "You came at us with humans in daylight, you broke every rule, upset and attacked my fated mate. Then you squealed to the Council."

I did not realise until that moment how much of his incredible power he normally keeps contained. Everything that makes him a vampire—everything ancient and terrifying—has been held in check.

But now it radiates from him.

He is more than a thousand years old, ancient in every sense. The air crackles, and I feel it, the heat, the power—the sheer weight of him in the room. It rolls off him like a storm about to break. His eyes glow violet.

The Nocturna brute's eyes widen at the weight of Valdarr's power. A sword slides from its sheath so fast it seems like magic. He swings—futilely. Valdarr blurs, and the blade whistles over his head. A single pivot, a single blow to the face, and the brute sails across the room, slamming into the gallery steps. Stone cracks into shards and dust, and the sword clatters across the floor.

The second attacker—Crystal's vampire, Ian—barrels towards me, claws extended, fangs bared.

James tenses beside me, but Ralph materialises behind Ian, silent as a ghost. He twists, bones crack, and the body drops.

I flinch.

"It's all right," Ralph says. "He won't die, just sleep for a few days."

Harrison, now wielding the brute's sword, plunges into the fight, felling two more warriors with a single sweeping strike that sends them crashing through a row of chairs.

Away from the chaos, I spot the Grand Master slipping through a concealed door behind the dais.

Valdarr sees him too.

"He's leaving," he growls, stepping forward. "Ralph, James—keep Fred safe. I need a quiet word with my father."

Harrison appears beside him, a blood-slick sword in hand.

The others nod their agreement.

I am still holding Valdarr's wrist, but my grip slips, and fear spikes. If he disappears through that door, the Council will kill him, and I will never see him alive again.

"Valdarr," I whisper, my voice cracking. I pull him closer. "No. You—"

Those violet-grey eyes—moments ago ablaze with fury —soften. He brushes a kiss across my forehead. "The clan will keep you safe. I won't let you down."

"No—listen, you can't—"

"I can." His thumb strokes my cheek while the ache of all those visions echoes inside me. "I'll see you soon, sunshine." Before I can utter another word, he turns and strides away, cutting a path through the melee.

"Valdarr, no!" I cry. I do the only thing guaranteed to stop a vampire mid-hunt. Using vampire speed, I launch myself at him. He has a choice: catch me or let me fall. Of course, my mate scoops me up, holding me tight against his chest.

"Fred, what is it? What's wrong?" He sounds confused.

"He is getting away."

"You can't go."

Summoning all my courage and fear, all the emotions I have kept inside, I slam my lips to his.

His body tenses around me; his warm lips remain unyielding.

I kiss him again, more deliberately, drawing his lower lip, lip-ring and all, into my mouth and nibbling lightly. My tongue flicks forward to taste him.

He growls, threads his hands through my hair, and kisses me back.

Amid the battle, with vampires clashing around us and blood spattering the floor, this is the only way I know to save him. To give him something else to stay for.

Me.

My senses ignite. Valdarr cups my jaw, tilts my head, and deepens the kiss. Fire races through me; my fingers knot in his coat. He spins us aside, and a green spell slashes the space we had occupied.

Tony steps in, fells the caster, and vanishes again. The world could burn to ash while Valdarr and I remain locked together.

Nothing beyond this man matters. It doesn't feel like a first kiss; it feels as though our souls have practised this for years. It's as if time stands still. We exist in a bubble of intimacy that excludes the outside world. His mouth moulds to mine with aching perfection, soft yet unyielding, warm and demanding. All-consuming. My whole body tingles.

This...

This I could never have prepared for.

We break apart, gasping. His lips are swollen; his eyes, stunned.

Well, Fred, that was one way to claim his attention.

"I know you want to speak to him." 'Speak' is the polite way of saying Valdarr wants to rip his father's heart out with his bare hands. I've seen how that would end: there is no mercy for anyone who deliberately attacks the Grand Master.

I lower my voice. "But you can't go after him, not yet. Yes, he threatened me in public, and you can't let that stand, but now isn't the time. Soon. Trust me."

"Very well," he answers gruffly.

The Vampirical Council's guards surge in, and I slide down Valdarr's rock-hard body just as a spell crackles overhead. Silence drops like a curtain as every vampire freezes, magic pinning us to the marble floor.

Harrison growls, furious at being immobilised.

I am exactly where I want to be, safe in Valdarr's arms. I rest my head against his chest, breathing in his distracting musk, metal and power scent. For one brief moment, all is well. We have survived the trial and the fight.

I. Kissed. Him.

Grinning like an idiot, I make sure no one notices. Worth every ounce of fear and stress: I saved the prince with a kiss—this time, fairy-tale nonsense of my own making.

The Herald, robes askew, sweeps the hall with a withering glare.

"You are a disgrace. Have you lost your minds and all common sense? You have made a mockery of this court. We will review the security footage, investigate how the wards failed and who spilt the first blood. All clans should expect repercussions. We may even close the public gallery for good—animals do not deserve public trials."

A ripple of hushed murmurs spreads through the chamber.

"Winifred Crowsdale, before this disgraceful interruption, the Court granted your petition. Under Accord Codes 101.4 and 212.3, the Council orders a full ethereal-memory and provenance assay. The Ministry of Magic will conduct the testing under Council ward and seal. The Court will reconvene three nights hence at first bell.

"Until that time you remain under interdiction: you will not quit the protection of Clan Blóðvakt, you will not conceal, alter, or destroy any evidence, and you will submit to summons on pain of contempt. So entered. Let the blood speak; judgement will wait until it does."

He makes no mention of the absent Grand Master.

A commotion erupts to one side as guards haul the Nocturna delegation forward.

"Clan Nocturna," the Herald intones, "by breaching Accord Code 301.2, Sanctity of Council Proceedings, 512.6, Armed Hostility Under Ward, and 12.1, Protection of a Petitioning Clan, you have placed yourselves outside the law. You exploited this hearing, ignored my explicit warning, and attacked Clan Blóðvakt while it stood beneath the Court's aegis. We are not human; our law is not a suggestion. Judgment is final.

"Under Accord Code 903.11, Forfeiture and Dissolution, your name is struck from the roll. Your titles, assets, and territories are seized by the Council treasury to remediate the damage to this Hall and compensate the injured. The penalty is death."

He does not need a dramatic gesture to summon the vampire I have seen many times before.

One might expect an executioner to dress in black leather. Instead, he wears a tailored suit. Calm and precise, he glides across the chamber like a shadow—face expressionless, eyes lifeless. A sword rests loosely in his grip.

I have watched my own execution in visions delivered by that very blade.

The clan struggles, yet the many guards keep everyone contained. I do not look away when a sword claims them. One by one, beginning with their still-unconscious leader, their heads come off. Blood sluices across the marble, seeping into the grout.

Eight lives, wasted.

I no longer flinch at the sight of blood, no longer feel sickened by the violence. Perhaps it is my vampire nature, or perhaps I have seen too much, too quickly, to react.

Crystal flashes through my mind, and the tired waitress at One Bite Won't Hurt. "What about their humans?" I rasp.

"They fall to the Council under the accord," Valdarr says quietly. "They will be protected."

The upper-tier clans depart first, and the spell anchoring us releases. Our feet peel free of the stone.

Outside, Harrison produces a canvas bag.

"All phones and electronics—now. We're compromised. War status."

I drop my mobile in. Ralph, Tony, Valdarr follow.

Simone shrugs and tosses hers. James clutches his tablet in horror.

"But my schedules—our entire life—"

"Tablet. In." Harrison's growl brooks no argument.

James appeals to Valdarr.

"Do as Harrison asks."

With a pained hiss, James drops the tablet and his phone into the bag. Harrison grins and throws in a swirling purple spell, incinerating the contents into a bubbling, molten lump.

A matte black minibus pulls up at the kerb, pulsing with layered wards.

"Oh, no," Tony mutters. "The war machine. Embarrassing. Quick—inside before anyone sees."

"It's magic-proof, bullet-proof, and seats all of us," Harrison says proudly.

I wish we had the 'war machine' for our journey here.

"It weighs a ton and drinks petrol," Tony grumbles.

"Feels like a school trip," Simone says with a grin. A cut on her cheek is already healing, and the skirt of her suit is torn at the seam.

"Get in," Harrison snaps.

Valdarr fastens my seat belt. "We are going to a new safe house. Baylor is waiting."

I watch as the lights and glow of the city slowly turn to dark roads and dilapidated buildings. The house sits at the end of a row of other homes in disrepair. It's unremarkable, rundown—peeling paint, grass in the leaking gutters, a patch of moss creeping up the far wall. It looks like it hasn't been lived in for thirty years.

Inside, the hallway smells of damp. Harrison slides a

crooked wedding photo aside, keys a code, and an inner door hisses open.

Beyond lies a sleek, modern hideout.

Baylor hurtles around the corner, howling with joy. He slams into my legs, then bounces between Valdarr and me.

"Hey, buddy." I scratch his ears. He pants happily; I kiss his nose.

"So this is Baylor. What a beautiful dog," Ralph says, dropping to his knees. "I love dogs."

My Husky, delighted to meet someone with great shovel-like hands, flops onto the floor. All four legs splay out as he presents his belly for tickles, and Ralph laughs with delight.

"Drinks?" Valdarr offers.

"I'll pour." I brush his arm, head to the kitchen, wash my hands, and prepare the blood. My hands tremble slightly at the thought of what is about to happen next.

Glasses distributed, Simone—cool as ever—leans against the wall and sips her drink. "So, next steps?"

"Meetings with the Ministry of Magic and the shifters," Valdarr replies. "Sooner than ideal, but Father is up to something. No one in the clan is harmed, so today counts as a win." He squeezes my hand.

"About that," James says, taking a swig of blood. His eyes narrow. "How did you know everything today? Who is your contact?"

A thud. We turn: Simone has crumpled, her glass shattering, blood pooling.

"Simone—" Tony lunges.

"She's fine," I say. "Sleeping spell."

James splutters. "You—my liege, she's knocking out clan members!"

"Yesterday, you wondered who leaked our location to Clan Nocturna, who arranged for the wards to fail, who allowed the human assassins inside, and who aided your father."

I meet Valdarr's gaze. "It was Simone."

Chapter Thirty-Four

Valdarr believes me without question; I can see it in his eyes. He understands I would never make an accusation without proof.

"She's been right all night," Ralph says quietly, flicking a glance towards me.

"Not about this. This isn't right. I'll carry Simone to her room. I can't believe you had the gall to spell her. She's going to be furious when she wakes up. Do you have an antidote?" Tony demands.

"She will wake soon enough," I murmur, "but you had better tie her to a chair before she does."

"I've known this woman for fifty years," James protests. "The rest of you have known her for centuries. Now you believe a stranger over Simone?"

"I certainly wouldn't have knocked her out if I'd had any other choice."

Harrison stares at his glass, slides it onto a side table, and watches me as though he expects everyone to drop. His fists clench, and he looks ready to snap my neck at the slightest excuse.

The others look utterly bewildered. James seems frightened, shaking his head as he stares at Simone, disbelief etched across his features.

After everything, they still do not trust me, and I understand. They have no idea what I can do, and for my own safety I'm in no hurry to enlighten them.

"Give us a moment." Valdarr draws me aside, away from the others, into another room. "This office is soundproof. How much more do you know?"

"A few hours ahead, then nothing," I whisper. "And I wish I didn't know even that."

"Can you tell me anything about what's coming?"

"No." I shake my head. "One detail could shift everything. The future feels delicate—dangerous—and I don't yet understand the rules. Instinct says one wrong word might shatter it." My lower lip trembles. "I'm frightened. This power scares me, Valdarr."

He pulls me to his chest and folds his arms around me. Just what I need. After a minute, I reluctantly step back, and his intense gaze darkens. "How vivid are your visions?"

"They feel real. I'm there, watching, a ghost. I can't interact, but I can move."

The words pour out. This time nothing blocks them, no overwhelming dread like everything will fall apart if I speak. Even my power knows I'm safe with him.

"It's strange. I don't know *how* to explain it, but when I'm in a vision, thirty seconds here can be hours for me. Tonight I knew what would happen. I knew what to say so we could walk out alive."

"You did back-to-back visions for hours," he says, horrified.

I close my eyes, letting myself feel the full despair of my gift. It's a curse. "I saw you die. I saw us die again and again. I don't know how it works. Perhaps every change splits the timeline, and those versions of us... end. I'm no theoretician, but I know this is dangerous."

My voice wavers. "Maybe we have only delayed the inevitable, but we are still here, and this is the last piece of the path I know."

"I'm sorry you faced that alone," he says softly.

I shake off my melancholy. "I wasn't entirely alone, you were there, even if you couldn't see me." I manage a small smile. "Across all those visions I saw you—saw the man you are. You call me 'sunshine,' but you are the one who's blinding. I was terrified and confused about being your mate, yet now I understand. I see you."

I open my eyes and meet his gaze. "Us—this—will take adjustment." I rest a hand on his chest. "I watched you protect me. I have watched you die for me so many times. And I realised... you are not merely a good man. You, Valdarr Blóðvakt, Raven of the North, are extraordinary. I'm scared, but I would be honoured to share this life with you, if you will have me."

"Is this your romantic declaration?" he asks, wiping my cheeks before kissing me. "I can tell you practised. Why are you crying? That was a ten out of ten."

"Because I'm overwhelmed."

He gently grips my upper arms, solemn. "I'm all in, Fred. And you never have to use your power again. We will find another way, together."

"I have this magic for a reason. Part of me wants to run, wrap you in bubble wrap and keep you safe forever, but we can't, can we?" I glance at the door—the clan waits beyond it, Simone still unconscious. "No. We can't."

He tries to lighten the mood. "I haven't got nice boobs, but I do have great abs."

He lifts his shirt. I laugh despite myself. "Yes, your abs are beautiful."

He smiles. "If we are together, things will work out. Let's sort this mess out first." He starts for the door.

Softer, I add, "For what it's worth, I hope you understand why I couldn't tell you, and I'm sorry about Simone. If we don't restrain her—" I stop and swallow hard. I *can't* finish the thought.

"Say no more," he murmurs.

"I know she's family. I know you love her."

"I do. We all do. This will be hard. Looking back, Simone was an obvious target. My father always uses whoever stands closest to me. It's his modus operandi." He kisses my cheek. No speech is needed; as soon as I said her name, his posture—shoulders bowed, eyes bleak—speaks for him. He is devastated.

I had known Simone only briefly, yet I liked her; I had hoped we might become friends. I have precious few friends.

Friends... my insides leap. I hope House is all right. Later, I shall reach out and see whether I can sense even a trace of her. She is not exactly human, yet I must try, though doing so will send me sliding once more down the slippery slope of using my magic.

I'm never going to win, am I? Not now that I've opened Pandora's box. The gift is too tempting and I'm not strong enough to resist.

"Get Simone up and secure her to a chair," Valdarr orders when we get back into the room. Someone has tucked a pillow under her head. "Bind her."

They hesitate—they don't want to do it. But he is their leader, and in the end, they obey.

In a few minutes Simone will wake, and they will see for themselves.

"Check her pockets. You will find her phone."

The unspoken question hangs in the air: *How do you know?*

Harrison searches her suit coat and produces a compact, password-free phone.

Even though they discovered the hidden phone, they still do not quite believe me. I have already decided I do not have to justify myself or explain anything. As long as my vampire believes me, I could not care less what anyone else thinks.

I am done trying to prove myself.

"You won't find much on it," I say, "but she's expecting a call. She planned to reveal our location."

James turns to Valdarr. "My liege, please explain." He glares at me; his confusion has evaporated and switched back to hate.

Valdarr just shakes his head.

Poor guy keeps asking for answers, and I feel kind of

bad. At first, I suspected James. I watched him, and a part of me wanted him to be the bad guy. But he is loyal.

When Simone wakes, we all stand before her. She blinks groggily, then strains against the ropes.

"What's happening?" she slurs. "Harrison—"

"Is it true?" Harrison asks, voice cold. "Did you betray us?"

The shock on her face looks genuine. "Why would I betray you? You're my clan—my family! What has she told you? She's lying! She's used magic to trick you. My liege, there's no mate bond. She's a witch; that's how she turned. She'll kill us all and take our clan."

Valdarr growls—a low, warning sound—but the others still glance at me as though I'm the villain.

"He left you," I say, studying my nails. "While you were fighting that woman and her clan, he slipped out the back like a coward."

"He didn't do it on purpose," she snaps, baring her fangs. "He left because his life is more important."

Silence falls. Everyone stares at her.

She tilts her head back and sighs. "Let me go. Knocking me out and tying me up is childish. If anything happens to me, he'll kill you. Well, he's going to anyway, but he'll make you suffer."

She tugs at the restraints. "Let me go, and I'll give you a five-minute head start before I call in the cavalry. Face it, you're on the losing side."

Harrison steps forward, voice quiet and hard. "Why, Simone? Why did you do this?"

Her eyes widen; a slow smile spreads across her face. "I love him."

"Our liege?" James frowns.

"No, dickhead, Eirikr," she spits. She rolls her eyes and sneers at Valdarr. "I have loved your father all my life. We could have been together if not for you."

"So you conspired against your own clan?" Harrison presses.

"You were never my clan. I have always belonged to him. I watched you only to protect him. Every scheme, every plan, I told him everything. You wondered how he was always a step ahead? It was because I gave him the advantage. You're a fool, Valdarr. He'll kill her, destroy the Council, and crown himself king."

"But he's already Grand Master," Ralph says softly. "He is already our king."

"A monarch in name only. A figurehead. You saw it today," she snaps. "They discarded him, treated him as nothing. He's destined to rule the world, not just this poxy little country."

She turns her loathing on me.

"And you—James was right, you couldn't even remain a *meal*. You had to turn, instead of dying. You're a cockroach. I'm surprised you're not dead already with the way that you fight."

"Simone," Valdarr warns.

"I did it for love," she hisses. "Centuries of planning, and *you*, a mere human abomination, ruined everything. I hope he kills you slowly and mounts that mutt of yours on the wall."

Ralph pales; the others stand silent, shattered.

"We love you," Tony whispers.

She shrugs. "I never even liked you. Any of you. Pathetic. Weak."

Then it happens.

The phone rings.

"They will accept a text," I tell Harrison.

"They won't," she snaps. "They'll speak only to me—"

"Text them she can't talk," I say calmly. "The code word is *Winter Green*."

Her eyes widen. "How do you know that?" she shrieks.

Harrison starts fiddling with the phone. "Use the rope and tape in the drawer, bottom left; don't waste a spell on her," he says.

Simone kicks, screams and thrashes. The chair rocks from side to side, threatening to tip. Ralph steps behind her, steadying the frame, while Tony appears with a roll of tape. Hands shaking, he tears off a strip and presses it firmly across her mouth. Simone's protest becomes a muffled, furious howl.

"It was better when she was unconscious," James mutters.

I nod in agreement.

Harrison sends the message.

Within minutes we have her lashed more securely to the chair. A full search yields several concealed weapons, which Harrison pockets before we leave. The war machine is abandoned for a fresh convoy of blacked-out vehicles. Daylight is coming, and we must move.

The new safe house occupies a discreet, modern block of luxury apartments in the Human Sector. Geometric lines and clean angles define the structure, its facade sheathed in sleek grey cladding broken only by narrow, glass-edged balconies.

Once inside, we switch to the live feed from the cameras left behind. The assassins arrive moments later, clad once more in black-and-grey tactical gear. They breach with chilling efficiency.

Harrison narrates the assault in a low, clinical voice. I feel anything but calm. Valdarr stands behind me; I lean against his abs while Baylor presses against my legs. My fingers curl into his soft fur.

The attackers enter the building.

Had we still been there, we would be dead.

I count the seconds. Wait. The building explodes.

The interior feed whites out. An external camera, hidden in the trees, shows fire tearing through the structure. Smoke billows. Wreckage burns.

No survivors. Simone is gone.

In the time I have known Valdarr, I have seen his kindness, his control, his patience—but also his ruthlessness. Other clans do not challenge him because they remember what happens when they do. He never starts a war; he merely ends it. Completely. No second chances.

That is how he stands unopposed as heir, and why only the young or the foolish imagine he has gone soft.

By tomorrow night, every clan will have heard the gossip: another assassination attempt has failed.

Chapter Thirty-Five

I KNOW the clan is hurting, and because Valdarr refuses to tell them anything about me—about what I can do—they treat me like some sort of super spy and give me the cold shoulder.

I understand; it's fine.

If I hadn't knocked Simone out, it would have been much worse. She *is*—*was*—incredibly strong and talented.

Harrison has taken it hard. He has locked himself in the apartment's study, analysing every scrap of data and trying to work out how she managed to outmanoeuvre him.

Valdarr is a tangle of emotions: delighted that I am willing to try a relationship, yet wounded that someone he trusted so completely has proved a traitor.

Daylight arrives quickly, and the vampires retreat to

their rooms. The penthouse is open-plan, with kitchen, dining, and living areas, each opening onto a slim glass balcony. Fortunately, the apartment is large enough for everyone to have space. Valdarr invites me to his room, but I decline; I'm not ready to watch him die for the day.

I shower, change, and after toast and tea, curl up on the brown leather sofa to try to reach House. I know I ought to have someone beside me in case anything goes wrong, yet I also need to manage this on my own. I'm sure I will be all right. I tap the faint threads of my magic, searching for any trace of her, but all I gain is a splitting headache and a nosebleed.

Perhaps daytime and being human dulls the link; perhaps she is too *other* to be found. Perhaps I am simply tapped out. It is maddening.

Around midday Valdarr reappears.

I have not seen his hair loose since we first met; it falls in glossy waves around his shoulders. He is wearing grey tracksuit bottoms that sit low on his hips and a plain white T-shirt that clings to every muscle. Coherent thought deserts me. It is such a simple outfit, yet he wears it like sin. He gives me a lazy smile, then strolls to the kitchen and begins pulling things from the fridge.

"You have not eaten lunch yet, have you?" he asks.

"No, I have not," I admit.

"Great," he says, sounding genuinely pleased.

He starts assembling a salad—a huge one. I watch as he whisks together a dressing from vinegar, oil, mustard and some lemon juice.

He slides a glass of orange juice across the table just as

I'm rubbing my temples, trying to ward off the growing headache.

"Hydration," he says, placing a glass of water beside it.

I don't have the heart to tell him I was trying to search for House—that I have probably pushed my power too far and need a break.

Then the salad appears in front of me, and he sits opposite, watching with a soft smile, as though he genuinely enjoys taking care of me.

We sit at the dining table and talk nonsense. I tell him about my podcast obsession and how, two years ago, I fell deep into a rabbit hole of flight-simulation crash analysis. An internet pundit dissects every cockpit procedure; I now know all the jargon.

Valdarr grins, amused.

I try to eat delicately, but when I cut into a cherry tomato, it bursts beneath my knife, splattering seeds across his white T-shirt. Mortified, I leap for a cloth. "Oh no! I'm so sorry."

"It's fine," he says, smiling. "I like abstract art."

I slip my fingers under the fabric to dab the stain. "I didn't mean to get you."

"It's all right," he murmurs, gripping my thighs and pulling me close before kissing me. The kiss is soft, slow, lingering. Somehow I end up perched on his lap, my fingers tangled in his silk-smooth hair.

Eventually I rest my head on his shoulder. We need this, laughter and tenderness, if only for a moment, to feel alive.

"Lander is coming tonight," he murmurs.

I groan.

"The Vampirical Council appointed him and his team to handle your tests. We need someone we trust; a stranger might be working for my father."

Ministry of Magic tests. A blood test must be simple, but I have no idea what the memory one involves. Everything is cloaked in secrecy. House's magic is bound to interfere with everything. Lander will be overjoyed about getting evidence of that.

I don't even know how she managed to turn me into a vampire, and she isn't here for me to ask. I've gambled with a losing hand to buy us time we never had, and I've no idea how it will play out.

Perhaps the Grand Master will get his wish, and I will lose my head.

"He's doing multiple samples, yes? Back-ups, in case something vanishes?"

He nods. "Exactly."

"And we are meeting the shifters?"

"Yes. They will help track my father."

"Perhaps, once it's dark, I could try to find him," I suggest, tapping my temple. "It would be easier."

"No," he says, hugging me. "You said yourself you don't know what those visions do to you. We will hunt him the old-fashioned way. The shifters owe me a favour; they'll come through."

I lean into him and nod. "All right."

Baylor nudges me and grumbles. He does his I-need-a-wee shuffle; he wants to go for a walk. We are in a apartment, so I can't simply let him out into a garden.

Down below, there's a small park.

"I haven't got my ring," Valdarr says, glancing from me to the grumbling dog. "It can't be worn constantly—it needs to recharge."

"Oh, I wonder if that's the same as Beryl?"

"Perhaps. I have books on the subject, but you could ask Lander tonight. He's very knowledgeable."

"I'd rather not."

"Our security will take you across the road. Please don't be long, straight there and back." He gives me a sheepish smile. "I worry."

"Okay."

I grin, clip on Baylor's lead and head out.

The guards nod in silent acknowledgement: one walks beside us while the others fan out in plain clothes that draw no attention. We are, after all, in the Human Sector. An odd place for a vampire safe-house.

The park is quiet. A winding path curves through clusters of trees and neatly kept grass, flanked by evenly spaced wooden benches. At the far end, a children's play area—with a bright red slide—adds a splash of colour against the surrounding greenery.

I stand awkwardly, pockets full of 'poo bags,' while Baylor does his business. He sniffs everything.

A Jack Russell spots him and erupts, barking and snarling as if defending sacred ground. "Pickle, stop it," the embarrassed owner pleads, tugging the lead while the dog shakes it like prey.

Once Baylor has finished, we cross back towards the apartment building's glass doors.

"Oh, look who it is." Theresa—hands full of bright-red sale bags—marches towards us.

When did Theresa ever shop at a discount, and what are the odds of running into her here? Fate really does enjoy playing games with me.

"Still wanted, are you?" she sneers.

I look skyward for patience. The nearest guard shifts, tense.

"Excuse me," I say, clearly.

"Still wanted?" she repeats, louder. Juggling her bags, she pulls out her phone. "I'm ringing the police. I told everyone you were trouble, and then you turned up at the wedding with that cosmetically altered face. You do realise that shoddy magic won't win Jay back, don't you? Do you know how many awkward questions I had to field? I had to explain why a thief was at *our* wedding, and then you pop up on the news in a kill-on-sight segment."

I fold my arms. Baylor merely tilts his head. The guards drift closer; one subtly adjusts his coat.

After facing down the Vampirical Council, confronting a human woman in her late sixties feels like nothing. Experience does change perspective and it's freeing. I no longer care what she thinks. Of course, I don't want her calling the police, but my security would stop her long before that.

I don't care what she says or what she thinks. It's liberating.

Her face reddens, and I catch the familiar, nasty gleam in her eye. She assumes she has won. I feel sad for her. Theresa is flawed, and she doesn't see it. Her life revolves around a spoiled son who will never appreciate her.

In her head, she is the self-sacrificing mother defending her family from a wicked woman. To everyone else, she is the villain. The truth? She is neither—just a woman with no real power. She steals power by hurting others. Ultimately she only hurts herself.

"I spent hours trying to give a statement. They said you were a vampire—*a vampire*." She gives a squeaky huff and glares at the overcast sky. "I'll get them here and prove you are as human as I am."

"Yes, I'm still wanted," I reply. "The Vampirical Council is furious with me."

"Pardon?" She lowers her mobile and rapidly blinks at me.

"Oh, yes. I'm terribly violent. This is my gang." I gesture to the guards she has only just noticed.

She turns in a slow circle, her confidence crumbling.

"It's hard," I continue, "deciding whether to murder people who annoy me or let them live. Still, you never know, Theresa. Someone starts shouting accusations or more lies... Jeff here"—I point to the nearest guard, who is definitely not called Jeff—"might shoot you."

He eases his coat open, revealing a holstered gun.

Theresa pales, takes a step back, her heel catches on a pavement slab, and she wobbles.

"What you need to learn," I say sweetly, "is when to keep that big mouth shut." I don't give her time to retort. "And for the record, I wouldn't take Jay back if you paid me. Bog off, Theresa. Go and ruin someone else's life."

"You... you—"

"Yeah, yeah. You have a new daughter-in-law to torture. Why are you bothering me? Next time we see each other, let's pretend we are strangers."

We walk away and circle the block before returning; no sense letting her see the safe house.

Fake Jeff chuckles. "You certainly told her."

"Ex's mother," I sigh. "Give me five minutes, and the guilt will set in. Ten years of that woman." I shake my head. We reach the apartment building without further trouble. "Thanks for backing me up."

Chapter Thirty-Six

Night falls, and security announces our guests.

The Ministry of Magic is here.

Lander Kane enters with a redheaded woman who is effortlessly pretty. Both are dressed in everyday clothes. She glances around, cautious rather than afraid—fair enough, she has just walked into a flat full of vampires.

I hush Baylor when he growls at Lander.

"This is my sister, Dayna," Lander says.

I wave. "Hi, Dayna."

"Hello, Winifred," Dayna says, stepping forward, her handshake firm. "I'm here to perform the Council-ordered tests. We will need some privacy."

"I've got security matters," Harrison mutters, slipping out. One by one, the others scatter. Ralph takes an unhappy Baylor.

James remains, tablet on his knee.

"James," Valdarr warns.

"What? Do I have to leave?"

"I'd prefer it if everyone but Winifred left," Dayna says, giving him a teacherly stare.

James huffs but skulks into the hallway.

"You will need to lie down on the floor," Dayna tells me. "A bed won't do, it is not stable enough, and we will need to use a circle. All right?"

Valdarr nods. "You could use the embedded circle in the living room."

"You have a circle? Perfect."

We roll back the heavy rug, revealing an eight-foot circle etched into the floorboards. Dayna kneels and spends forty-five minutes chalking runes, while Lander, wielding a council-sanctioned camera, records every step.

Finished, she sits back, sighing, "Hell on the knees."

"Would you like a drink?" I offer.

"Oh, I'd love a cup of tea with just a splash of milk."

"Would you like one as well, Lander?" I grit out.

"No, thank you; I prefer my tea without spit."

I scowl and head to the kitchen. "Spit? More like poison," I mutter. Lander puts the camera down and follows. My spine stiffens as I switch on the kettle—I don't like him at my back. Valdarr is only a whisper away, across the room, and I know I'm perfectly safe.

"How are things? Any contact with the house?" he asks.

"No. I don't know where she is." I turn, lean against the worktop and fold my arms.

"Look, Winifred, we got off on the wrong foot. It was never my intention to upset you."

"No, you just wanted to hurt my friend."

"I don't want to harm the house, but you must understand how dangerous she is."

"So you keep saying."

"That house killed people."

Yes, to protect me. "You have no evidence of that." He needs to understand, he thinks the house is merely magic, but she is so much more. "Look, Lander, after I turned into a vampire, something in my magic let House and me communicate; I could speak to her."

"What?" His macho mage mask slips, and he looks dumbfounded.

"I can talk to her, proper conversations. She's a person, even if she is trapped in bricks and mortar. She has thoughts and feelings—she isn't just a thing."

He rubs his forehead. "She shouldn't *have* a personality. You shouldn't be able to speak with her. And when you say 'talk'—do you mean aloud?"

"Exactly like I'm talking to you, but she answers in my mind."

"That's not possible." He turns away, shaking his head, and begins pacing the kitchen. "You talk to her and she responds? I thought you were personifying the magic, giving it human traits. People do that all the time."

"I don't. I'm telling you the truth. After I turned and could hear her, she became my friend. My family." My voice wavers as I pour hot water over the teabag; the teaspoon clacks against the cup. I'm not opposed to begging. "Lander, if you ever have the chance, please help her. Don't hinder her and for all that is good in the world, do not hurt her. She is more than a wizard's house.

If you insist on hunting her, at least give her a chance—be kind."

"I can't promise that."

"No, you can't." I wipe my eyes with the back of my hand. I shouldn't let him upset me; people like him never change. I silently finish making the drink. "And that is why you are a horrible person." Shouldering past him with Dayna's milk-splashed tea, I leave the kitchen.

Valdarr looks up as I stomp into the living room. I shake my head. "I hate him," I mutter, low enough for only my vampire to hear.

I hand Dayna her tea with a tight smile.

Dayna chats with Valdarr while she sips her drink, and Lander stares at me like a puzzle he'd solve with a scalpel. I shift so Valdarr stands between us.

"Right," Dayna says, placing her empty cup on the side. "This won't be pleasant. Would you like an explanation, or shall I just proceed?"

I've had days of knowing exactly what's coming. This is going to be unpleasant, so I'd rather wing it. "I'm fine not knowing."

"Lie down inside the circle, then. I'm just going to wash my hands," Dayna says, nipping into the kitchen.

Lander gives Valdarr a wary look. "I know you want to be here for your mate, but for Dayna's safety it's best you leave. I realise it goes against all your instincts, yet I must protect my sister. I don't need an angry vampire trying to rip her throat out."

I frown. "He would never—"

"I would," Valdarr interjects. "If someone hurt you, I would."

Images from the court hearing—and every vision in which things went catastrophically wrong flash through my mind: Valdarr stepping in front of me, shielding me—

I nod.

"I'll wait outside," he concedes, and slips into the hallway.

Once I settle on the floor, Dayna's magic threads through the wood, lighting the circle rune by rune. I feel the ward activate as each segment flares to life, like a switch being thrown. Then she unwraps a surgical packet containing an alarmingly long, rune-etched needle.

"Where's that going?" I ask, voice tight.

"Your tear duct. If we went through the cornea, you'd lose vision."

Tear duct! "Oh, great, how reassuring: a huge needle in my eye. Why is everything connected with vampires so bloody awful?"

Let's hope all this will be worth it. If it's not—if there's nothing there but House's magic—I don't know what we will do. Run, I guess.

"I wish there were a simple spell. You were turned without consent, so it's complicated."

"She was murdered," Lander mutters. "The wizard's house magic did the turning."

Dayna levels him with the same teacherly stare she gave James. "Winifred was turned without her consent." Then her expression softens as she turns to me. "To prove your memories of your murder, we need undeniable, soul-bound, court-acceptable evidence. The signature sits in the lacrimal nerve cluster—both magical and biological."

"Will it hurt?"

"Yes, it will hurt." At least she doesn't lie. "Your body will fight it. But the needle draws more than fluid. It pulls memory and lineage. *Ethereal Memory* is the residue of formative, high-magic moments—trauma, turning, oath-taking—imprinted into a vampire's aura and recoverable under warded conditions. If he turned you, his essence is there. If he murdered you, the memory will be there. If not..." She shrugs. "We will know."

Lander places two fingers on my temple. "Do not move, Winifred."

It takes everything I have not to aggressively flash my fangs.

Dayna states who is present, along with my full name, clan, and the time and date for the camera. Then she continues, "This Ethereal Memory Assay is conducted under the authority of the Ministry of Magic, pursuant to Accord Codes 101.4 and 311.2. For the record: the subject is unrestrained; no coercive magic is in effect, and all counter-compulsion wards have been checked and hold.

"Winifred Crowsdale, do you affirm that you understand the nature and risks of an Ethereal Memory Assay as defined in Protocol EM-7, and do you consent to proceed?"

"I do."

"Beginning assay... now."

They don't have to restrain me physically. Dread does that job.

The needle glints. I try not to focus on it as it approaches, and I hold my breath. Pressure at the inner corner of my eye, then pain, sharp and lancing. My eye floods with tears, the ceiling blurring grey and white.

"Steady," Dayna murmurs. "Do not resist; resistance corrupts the magic."

The pain shifts, deepening, a spectral tug as though something ancient is being siphoned through a straw. Heat pulses, then a flash—fangs, red eyes, the Grand Master's face, then darkness. The needle withdraws; vision doubles, steadies.

"There it is," Dayna says softly, holding a vial up to the camera. The fluid inside is white, threaded with dark burgundy. "The Grand Master's signature."

"Match confirmed," Lander says, voice flat.

The relief I feel makes me want to sink into the floor.

But we are not done yet.

"Winifred Crowsdale, do you acknowledge you understand the nature and evidentiary use of a Hematic Lineage Assay as defined in Protocol HL-3, and do you consent to proceed?"

"I do."

"Commencing draw... now." She informs the camera.

Dayna unwraps another sterile packet: a rune-etched blood-collection needle, sturdy enough to pierce vampire skin. She professionally draws three glass tubes of blood from the vein in my elbow.

I don't know what they will find in my blood—human, vampire, or some mixture of the two. House's magic? I'm reaching. They are searching for lineage, yet I was turned by magic. This is not going to work.

She sets out a silver-rimmed obsidian bowl and murmurs a spell. Blue light shimmers across the surface, and when she tips in three drops of blood, it smokes, blooming into runic geometry.

Dayna studies the forming glyphs. "Marker pattern... ancient. Primary vector: Elder Signature Three. Cross-checking—"

Above the bowl, a ghost-sigil sharpens into focus and locks in place with an audible click of magic—then it shatters. Bowl and sigil explode together; I throw up an arm to shield my face from flying obsidian shards.

"Match inconclusive," Lander says, wearing a thin, satisfied smile.

I don't know what the council will do with an inconclusive blood test. Anything that makes Lander smile is bad.

"The Ethereal Memory Assay and Hematic Lineage Assay is complete," Dayna announces, her voice clear. "Chain-of-Custody Seal CS-8842 remains intact. All recordings will be duplicated to Ministry Vault Theta under Accord Code 902.1. Preliminary finding: the Grand Master's signature within the Ethereal Memory. Hematic Lineage inconclusive. 'Sealed Pending Council Review.' This record is closed."

Dayna seals the samples in a lock-box, signs and wards it, then signals for Lander to switch off the camera.

"Has that ever happened before?" I ask her, brushing black shards from my sleeves and torso.

"No. Either your lineage sigil isn't in the Vampirical Council's records, or your blood was so magically potent it overwhelmed the test."

"This is what happens when a wizard's house meddles with illegal magic," Lander mutters as he packs up.

"Lander, drop it," Dayna scolds.

"I'm not denying that the Grand Master murdered her; clearly, he did, according to the eye juice results. But he didn't turn her. Her precious house did, and the Vampirical Council, along with the Ministry of Magic, won't let that stand. They'll kill you to keep the secret. Face it: you're screwed." He grabs an armful of gear, steps out of the circle, and leaves the room.

Dayna gathers her things. "You will have to excuse my brother, he takes his work very seriously. He's seen the worst of people and magic, and now he spots corruption even where none exists." She smiles sadly. "That's everything. I'm sorry it was uncomfortable. You might be dizzy for up to an hour. The Ethereal Memory is magically draining."

"Thank you for coming."

"You are welcome." She squeezes my forearm. "I can't imagine how hard this has been. I thought about what I'd want if I were turned into a vampire, and the answer is simple: information. All derivatives can be incredibly tight-lipped about everything, and it must be terrifying. I've brought a few magic books that might be of interest." She produces a small stack.

"Thank you, that is very kind of you. I have been wanting to find out more."

"This one deals with soul-infused objects," Dayna says, tapping the hefty red-leather volume. "They are more than a century old, so handle them with care." She steps out of the circle and places the six antiquarian tomes on magic carefully on the coffee table. "You will need to stay inside until the magic drains; it won't take long—just another couple of minutes. Good luck, Winifred."

"Thank you."

She leaves me to my thoughts, following her brother.

Valdarr returns, watching me intently.

"I'm all right," I whisper. "The blood test came back negative."

"I heard what Lander said. I thought it would. Whatever magic House used to alter your DNA, it wasn't my father's. I'm sorry, Fred."

"I'm sorry I let you down," I murmur.

"Never. Not in a million years."

As soon as the circle's magic fades, Valdarr steps in and scoops me up so I'm not standing on the shards in my socks.

He carries me to the sofa and settles me gently.

I have never experienced that. A man lifting me as easily as he does, rearranging me so deftly. My mouth parts as I stare at him in shock. He gently rubs his thumb across my bottom lip.

"The Council are going to eat us alive."

"Not necessarily. You are only one person. Everything will be fine—I have a few tricks up my sleeve. We will sort it out, together."

Chapter Thirty-Seven

Valdarr wants us to move again, saying the safe house has been compromised after Dayna and Lander's visit, and the run-in with Jay's mother. There's no telling who might talk. It simply isn't worth the risk.

He rearranges the meeting with the shifters for tonight. It's easier for him to go alone while the rest of the clan packs up and secures the new location. Besides, he doesn't really need my help, and I'm still a little shaken from the revelation about House, Dayna's magic and the failed blood test.

And honestly, I'm peopled out. I don't want to meet the shifters or stay on guard; I just want to curl up and let the world pass me by.

When everyone is ready to move, we load the van. Baylor, half-asleep, leans against my leg as we drive.

The next safe house is the townhouse I escaped after the border station, the one with the lion-headed brass knocker and the spiky window boxes.

The house now has even more upgraded security. Each of us must give a drop of blood to the warded threshold, just to get inside.

What is it about vampires and blood?

Baylor and I settle in Valdarr's modern office. The rest of the townhouse features silk wallpaper, expensive furniture, and honey-gold parquet flooring—none of which is designed for paws, and he keeps skidding about. The office is simpler by comparison, and it boasts a thick grey carpet.

I try again to find House, using my usual phone-scrolling trick. I know I must eventually practise without the phone, yet the mindless music and endless reels help me drop in.

The vision almost takes me, then lightning strikes behind my eyes. A blinding headache flattens me. Perhaps the magic doesn't recognise her—she isn't human. I switch focus to Ralph, who's in the next room, and my nose starts to bleed.

Head tipped back, tissue pressed to my face while vampire healing does its work, I reach an unwelcome conclusion: I can manage only so many visions before the well runs dry. I'm tapped out.

Or perhaps I can only have a vision when the person is in immediate danger. I don't know, I'm winging it at this point.

The power might recharge in a few days, or it might not return at all. With my skull throbbing as though it might split open and ooze all over the floor, I'm in no mood to test the limit.

The Vampirical Council hearing looms. If I cannot navigate it with foresight, we will be in a pickle.

When the bleeding stops, I bin the tissue, sigh, and decide to read.

One of the books, the red one, tingles in my hands; I seize it at once. Relief washes over me when I find in the index that there is a chapter on recharging magical objects.

I leaf through, searching for mention of sentient artefacts, and find exactly what I need: *when such an object expends all its magic, it enters a restorative slumber, sometimes for years.* This proves our theory that Beryl must have exhausted herself.

Perhaps House's magic once replenished her; deprived of that, she has slept.

The book explains that a simple rune-circle can deliver a modest magical boost, enough to wake a slumbering object, though it will be sluggish at first.

It's better than nothing.

I want to try to revive Beryl. I double-check the runes; the text states plainly that the caster need not be magical. I can't manage the proper ritual chants, but the book insists that, so long as the runes are correct, the circle should still work.

Ralph is pottering about, so I show him the diagrams. I don't mention it's for Beryl—only that I have a magical object that needs re-charging. He helps me locate a circle and redraw new symbols.

James wanders in, surveys our handiwork, and tuts. He vanishes, then returns in a shell suit straight from the late

'80s. I bite my tongue. He flicks his boy-band fringe, snatches the chalk from Ralph, and sighs in theatrical despair before grudgingly re-drawing a fresh rune circle, every line drawn with perfect symmetry.

"Why are you helping us?" I ask.

"Because you're making a mess," he says. "If you're going to do something, do it properly or don't bother."

When we finish, we stand around the circle, admiring it.

"Well, then," James says. "Where's this magical object?"

"Er... in my bag." I have Beryl tucked safely away.

"Aren't you going to fetch it?"

"No."

"God, you're so cagey. Everything you do is cagey."

"Unfortunately, James, that's just me, and you haven't exactly earned my trust."

"I haven't done anything untrustworthy," he huffs.

"Mm-hmm."

Ralph grins.

I place the bag gently in the centre. Beryl rests hidden inside. A faint buzz creeps up my arms at once. I step back. The circle begins to draw magic in.

"Feel that?" I ask, waving a hand through the shimmering air.

"No," Ralph answers.

James merely arches an eyebrow. "Must be one of your weird things." He departs to wash his hands.

"Thanks for your help, James," I call after him. "Thanks, Ralph."

"I did have an ulterior motive: can I take Baylor for a walk?"

At the word *walk*, Baylor opens one eye and his tail thumps.

"What do you think, Baylor?"

He springs up, stretches, then performs a dizzying wall-of-death circuit around the room—white and grey fur drifting in his wake. We laugh, and I hand Ralph the lead.

Once they have left, I place Beryl directly on the floor inside the circle in case the bag was muting the magic. I cover her with a handy scarf from my bag. I tidy the chalk and sit nearby with a book, though my knee bounces.

I'm worried about Valdarr. I know he can look after himself. *He didn't fare too well with the Council, did he?* whispers my nasty inner voice.

"Shut up, Doris," I mutter. "He will be fine."

James re-enters, tablet under his arm. He selects a volume from a shelf and begins leafing through the text. After half an hour, he makes a low sound.

"What?"

He marks a page and puts the book down, eyes gleaming. "I know what you are."

"Pardon?"

"That detour with the car," he says. "Pushing my liege clear of that knife. The way you kissed him, like you expected him to die. It all fits."

"James, perhaps you shouldn't—"

"Oh, I should. It's been driving me mad." He leans closer, voice a whisper. "I know what you are."

I fold my arms. "Go on, then. Enlighten me."

He points, certain. "You're an oracle."

I point at myself. "Me? An oracle? Is that even real?"

"Yes, I believe so." James taps at his tablet with practised fingers. "Here, look—though I want that back." He hands it to me as though it were priceless.

I feel oddly privileged to be trusted with it. I scan the screen.

Oracle: a person or thing believed to offer wise or prophetic insights, often inspired by deities.

"Deities? That doesn't sound right."

"Nor does *wise*," he mutters, snatching the tablet to scroll further before handing it back. "What about precognition? You can see future events, can't you?"

"Yes."

He grins. I realise I've answered all his questions by saying one word. I groan and wipe my hand across my face. I'm no good at this cloak-and-dagger shit.

"Do we have any books on this?"

"Possibly," James murmurs, his eyes almost glazing over as if already mentally cataloguing.

"How did you come to that conclusion? An oracle?"

"It's the only thing that fits." He puffs out his chest, pleased with himself.

"James, you are like Sherlock Holmes."

He beams. "Who knew?"

"You worked it out because I knew about Simone and everything else?"

He nods. "It all clicked. I'm right, aren't I?"

I sigh. "Yes, but it's a secret."

"Understood. If my liege doesn't want it known, I won't breathe a word. But I can help." He leans forward, eyes bright. "So, what's it like?"

"Horrible," I admit.

"Oh." He looks disappointed.

"If it were, say, predicting lottery numbers, it might be fun. But it's not. I relived our Council visit—and everything after—so many times. I watched people die, over and over."

"So, how does it work? If you relived the Hall of Silence, that means the power takes direction, and it's not just random. How does that happen? Do you think of a person?"

I pause to check in with myself—to listen to my gut—and realise that sharing this with him doesn't bother me. Nothing inside me screams *Don't*. My throat isn't tight; there is no hint of danger or wrongness. Everything feels... easy. Whatever power lives in me trusts James.

Had you told me a few days ago that I'd feel this way, I would have said you were mad. But I shadowed him in that vision for a long time—watching, waiting for him to slip—and he never did.

James may not like me much, but it isn't out of cruelty —there's no malice in him. He will always put the clan first, and because he's so blunt, so black-and-white, I know there's no hidden agenda. He simply calls things as he sees them.

"Yes. I focus on someone, and it drags me into a future event—usually something dangerous."

"Who have you followed?"

"Other than Valdarr? Simone. And you."

"Me?" His eyebrows shoot up. "Really?"

"Yes."

"How far did you see?"

"Up to our arrival at the last safe house."

He falls quiet, then asks, "How are you feeling? Overwhelmed? Frightened?"

"It's a lot," I confess.

"I bet. But if you're doing what's best for the clan, for my liege, I'm with you. I'll help however I can."

"Thanks, James."

"But if you hurt him, if you break his heart, I'll use that stake you like to wave about and stab you in yours."

He stares at me, unblinking.

"Bugger," I mutter. I'd thought he was nice; clearly, I was wrong. "I won't break his heart," I say. "He's far more likely to break mine. Have you seen him? The man's a walking, talking vampire god. And then there's me—"

"The oracle," he interrupts.

"No. I'm not an oracle."

He arches a brow. "If it looks like an oracle, walks like an oracle, talks like an oracle..."

"It's just a psychic gift—premonitions. I'm closer to a seer, if we need a label."

"Yet you can trace people, find them. That's a bit more than an average psychic gift, isn't it?"

I don't answer.

"I like the title, clan oracle," he grumbles, burying himself in his book.

Chapter Thirty-Eight

It's a few hours before dawn, but Valdarr still hasn't returned. I keep glancing at the clock, worry gnawing at me —he's cutting it close.

The mobile Harrison gave me rings: it's him.

I take a steadying breath. "Hi. Are you all right? I was worried about you."

"I'm fine. I'm sorry, I should have called earlier. I'm too far away to get back before sunrise. I went hunting with the shifters. We almost caught up with my father, but it ended in a fight with his people."

"As long as you and the shifters are safe, that's what matters. Everything here is fine, everyone is looking after me."

"Are they?" he asks, with a hint of amusement in his voice. "How's your friend, Beryl?"

"Still in her restorative sleep. James drew a new circle using runes from a book Dayna gave me. I think the magic is working, as she's no longer cold to the touch."

"That's great news. I'm glad he is helping you."

I cringe. "I messed up. He knows about the visions. He is sneaky, and I'm a terrible liar. He thinks I'm an oracle."

A long pause follows. I hope he isn't angry.

"Interesting," he says at last. "If James suspects you are an oracle, we should research it. We need to discuss registering all your gifts with the Vampirical Council; it would add another layer of protection. The Council is not in the habit of discarding powerful talents—no, it hoards them."

"So we need to tell them about the day-walking?"

"Yes, we will push the day-walking angle, not the human-by-day-and-your-heart's-beating issue. Only the oldest vampires would know the difference, and we will make sure you are nowhere near the elders while you are human."

"But what if... because House isn't here, I stop being human during the day?"

"I believe your friend House is too powerful; none of the changes made to you will wear off. What happens, happens. We can't change it, Fred; all we can do is react. We will be careful, and I will ask Harrison to arrange extra security for you."

"Why extra security?"

"Because, sunshine, it makes you very valuable. Everyone will want the shiny new gifted vampire." His voice softens. "But that shiny new vampire is my mate, and as long as she wants me, she is not going anywhere."

I laugh; he makes me feel warm inside. "It's nice to feel wanted."

"I will always want you. I had better go."

"Please be careful."

"You, too. I will see you after sunset."

Baylor and I retreat to the bedroom I once fled and curl up with a book on the Council's rules, reading about their stance on gifted vampires. Valdarr is right, it may prove our saving grace.

I spend the day reading, walking Baylor, and brushing his coat with a cushioned hairbrush I found, as he stretches blissfully beneath each stroke. When he trots to Ralph's door and howls, I hush him. No one wants to wake a day-dead vampire with a slobbering Husky.

I force myself to eat—cereal for breakfast, a sandwich for lunch—and then count the hours until Valdarr returns.

Darkness falls. I keep waiting.

One hour passes, then two.

Harrison appears in the doorway while I sit curled on Valdarr's office sofa. He looks worried. I know then that something has gone horribly wrong.

"Valdarr slipped his security," he says quietly. "He abandoned both his phone and his tracker in the vehicle."

I stare at him. "He did that on purpose?"

"He wasn't taken. He wasn't coerced with magic—he's too strong. I believe it was deliberate. We've had no word."

"Has he done this before?"

"No. But it could mean the Grand Master has been in contact, and he wants a private meeting. It's a game to him; he enjoys seeing how far he can push Valdarr."

James bursts in, followed by Tony and Ralph. He

marches to the sofa, grabs my forearms, and gives me a little shake. "You have to do something," he says. "This isn't like him. We need to know what's happening."

Baylor lets out a grumbly growl. Harrison shoves James back with a snarl. "Do not mishandle the youngest."

"I—sorry," James stammers. "It's just—"

"I'm frightened too," I say. "When did he go missing?"

"Five, ten minutes ago—if that," Harrison replies.

Huh. I'm surprised he came straight to me.

I know I shouldn't be using my power—if I can, I should be saving it for the council meeting tomorrow.

But James's anxiety is catching. I try not to let other people's emotions affect me, but it isn't easy. He's incredibly smart and knows Valdarr and the Grand Master better than I do.

Half-knowing this is a huge mistake—and that my vampire doesn't need my help—I grab my phone and open my favourite app.

"Okay. Okay. Let's fix this."

"What are you doing?" Harrison asks.

"Shush," James murmurs, nudging him aside.

"Are we going after him? Do we know where he went?" Tony demands. "I'm sure the shifters would help us search."

James raises a hand for silence. "Fred will find him—won't you, Fred?"

"I will. But I need some space and I need to concentrate. Can you speak over there?" I point to the other side of the room. "Please, tell them everything about your oracle theory."

"Right. Okay." James hustles them out of the way.

Fear claws and writhes inside me. *What if this doesn't work?* I push the thought aside. *Come on, Fred. Be brave. You can do this.* I sit cross-legged on the sofa, close my eyes, and reach for the power. The phone lies forgotten in my lap.

I think of him.

And I fall into the vision.

Chapter Thirty-Nine

Valdarr stands on a kerb in an unfamiliar street, perfectly composed. He wears a different suit, his hair plaited intricately over one shoulder, tattoos gleaming under the streetlights. He looks as if he is going to an important meeting.

A car pulls up. He remains loose-limbed.

"If you are here," he says softly, "do not worry. I have a meeting with my father. I know what I'm doing."

He's talking to me. Relief floods me. I did the right thing, and I didn't overstep by using a vision to find him. He *knew* I would look for him. I go with my gut, reach out and brush his hand; his fingers twitch, and Valdarr smiles.

He felt me. Wow. That shouldn't be possible. But I have no idea what is possible between fated mates.

Four men step from the car. Three vampires and a

mage. "Master Blóðvakt," the spokesperson says, bowing. "We are here at the Grand Master's request. To collect you for a meeting."

"We need to scan you, sir. Is that all right?"

"Of course," Valdarr replies, his voice calm. He lifts his arms and spreads his legs as a nervous mage runs his wand over him.

Though shaking, the mage is admirably thorough. "He's clear," he mutters, stepping back. He pockets the wand and stares at the floor.

"If you wouldn't mind..." the spokesperson says. His hands also tremble as he raises a black hood. "You can't know where you're going. It's for security reasons."

Valdarr elegantly bends so the hood can be slipped over his head, then slides into the car and fastens his seat belt.

The men exchange uneasy glances: his serenity disconcerts them, as they are accustomed to fear. He radiates the message *You are nothing to me.*

The car pulls away.

I fold the vision, using the magic to trace where the car will end up because that's where the Grand Master and danger is.

I arrive outside an apartment block—fourteen storeys—on the edge of the Vampire Sector. If I have to come here in the flesh, I mentally note the street name and building number.

Now I must choose: do I snap back and tell the others or stay and watch this through? My power is limited; if I leave, I might not return. And what seems like hours here will be minutes in the waking world. Valdarr may not even have been taken yet.

I have time, so I decide to stay and study the building, counting guards, mapping exits. I trust my magic will let me know the moment Valdarr arrives—there will be a faint ping, almost subliminal.

The Grand Master owns the entire place, and security is tight.

On the ground floor I start with the security office, a control centre behind a reinforced door. I note the camera angles and their coverage, anything useful. I skim the paperwork left out, but find nothing helpful.

Next I move through the armoury and the break room. It apears some staff even live on-site, packed into bunks like an army barracks. For all the Grand Master's wealth, he treats his people poorly.

Each floor serves a different function. One is devoted entirely to PR and marketing. For a murderer of his calibre, he is meticulous, and that thoroughness has kept him in power for so long.

Floor by floor, I work my way up. Just before the top storey—an hour and fifteen minutes later, far longer than necessary—my magic pings to let me know the car is pulling in. They must have driven in circles to confuse him. Without having to think too much about it, I'm back at street level. No matter, he knows I'm watching.

They lead him inside. A lift whisks them straight to the top floor.

The doors open onto a suite of velvet, gold and ostentatious luxury. Heavy drapes. Polished stone.

They remove the hood. Valdarr neither blinks nor flinches. He simply surveys the room.

They make him wait. It's a power play. The kind men

use when they fear they have already lost. Guards stand at parade rest. Silence lengthens until it creaks. Then a guy appears and flicks two fingers. Valdarr strolls forward as if he has all the time in the world, obliging his father to wait those extra, deliberate seconds.

He enters the inner office. Closes the distance. Each step is measured, deliberate, until they are close enough.

"Son." The smile is all fang.

"You wanted to speak to me?"

"Still playing at rebellion? How quaint."

Valdarr's eyes are half-lidded, as if bored. "You fed without consent. You killed her. Dumped her like rubbish. When she rose, you sent knives and assassins—humans, even—to fix your mistake."

"A mistake?" The Grand Master's eyes glitter, cold, delighted. "Do you know how many mistakes I have buried, boy? Empires. Wars. Lovers. You think I remember every throat I drain? If she lived, some other power meddled, not my hand."

"You know who she is to me."

"I know what you *want* her to be."

"Winifred Crowsdale is my fated mate." He drifts closer.

"And the instant you called her mate, you made yourself weak enough to break. Do you remember what I taught you about weaknesses?"

"I remember you taught me to hide mine." Valdarr's mouth flattens. "I'm done hiding."

A low chuckle. "You think that Court will save you? You tossed a torch into tinder. The Twelve won't kneel to a boy who drags his pet *human* into their chamber and names her miracle."

"She's not just a miracle," Valdarr says softly. "She's proof."

The Grand Master's smile holds; his eyes harden. "Proof of what, exactly?"

"That you're not a god," Valdarr replies. "That you can make mistakes. That the Accord still binds you, whether you believe it or not."

"Then I will break the Accord," the Grand Master murmurs, voice like silk. "I wrote half of it. I can unwrite it."

"You won't get the time." Valdarr lets anger show. "I will drag you into Court by your throat. Call a formal challenge. Let the world watch you lose."

"Lose?" He laughs. "To *you*?"

"Yes."

Something flickers—admiration curdling into hate. "You have grown teeth, little raven."

"I had them the day you made me watch you burn cities," Valdarr says. "I just chose not to use them on my own blood."

"And now?"

"Now, I choose differently. I choose *her*."

Crimson magic curls over the Grand Master's fingers, an ancient kill-spell purring to life—a warning not to come closer. I fight the urge to throw myself in front of Valdarr to shield him from the deadly power.

"You are not ready."

"Try me."

The Grand Master studies him, pride souring to

contempt. "Careful, my son. Thrones cut deeper than swords."

"I will bleed," Valdarr says. "But I won't feed on the innocent to stay seated."

The Grand Master leans back, almost idly. "Innocent? I've been killing innocents for centuries. There was a human couple, very much in love."

The whole conversation feels like the performance of a man who delights in horrifying his son.

"The woman had dark curls and big blue eyes." His tongue wets a lip. "I drained them both outside Nocturna's ghastly bistro and left their bodies at my favourite disposal site."

I gasp—*Amy and Max.*

The vision stutters; I clutch the thread and force it still.

The Grand Master casually admits to murdering my friends, yet he is not finished; a still more horrific point must lurk in this macabre tale. I think I know what's coming.

"Then a middle-aged human began to poke around," he goes on, amused. "My people followed her to *your* safe house. You, ever the gentleman, gave her a jumper. A delivery driver. Unusual. So I kept watching. When you moved, I ordered a takeaway to your address. She arrived and was so disappointed it wasn't you at the door." He taps a claw against the desk. "I drained her and binned the corpse."

His smile strips the room of warmth.

I shiver.

"But then came the surprise. The waitress who'd reported her nosing—the one who set that couple up—told my people the little problem was still alive. Not only alive. *Turned*."

I don't even know the waitress's name—the one who handed fellow humans to monsters without a qualm. Amy and Max. Me. I try to recall our conversation in that themed bistro so long ago, but I cannot.

I thought she was frightened.

The moment I left, she was dobbing me in to the vampires, and I had no idea. Then I drove Crystal home and made sure she was safe. The bloody waitress answered the door.

"I don't make mistakes. I don't turn. Yet this creature *rose*. It didn't take much to nudge Nocturna into a rage after the thrall incident. We sent assassins; she survived. The little bitch. Then my *agent* informs me she is human by day, vampire by night, and that you are protecting her." He thumps his chest. "I won't have that abomination tied to me."

Simone. He does not say her name. He doesn't need to. My stomach drops.

"Another trap—humans, mages, then the Council," he purrs. "She wriggled through those, too. Made me look incompetent. Stood there in the Hall of Silence and *pointed at me*. Cost me Nocturna, a human spy and an agent I'd placed for centuries."

Valdarr tilts his head. Gentle. Murderous. "Yes, Father, tell me about that agent. Tell me about Simone."

"Beautiful toy. Loyal. No compulsion needed—love makes fools of women." A small, pleased exhale. "Didn't expect you to throw her away."

Valdarr doesn't bite.

"See that your mate keeps her mouth shut," the Grand Master continues, as if swapping one topic for another costs him nothing. "Publicly, she's a day-walker. You will keep the rest quiet. She is my gift to you—*if* you accept your responsibilities and take what is yours.

"I'm old," he says, satisfied with Valdarr's silence. "This avoidance of your birthright is over. You will take the throne, dismantle that pathetic Council, and I will retire somewhere far away."

Valdarr's expression doesn't change. "You will stop sending assassins? Leave my clan and my mate untouched if I accept your title?

"Yes."

"Anything else?"

"Unity with the shifters and the magic-users is our downfall. End it. Do this, and I will let you enjoy your eternal love story."

"I will need to speak to her first."

The Grand Master barks a laugh. "You will *ask permission* to seize a throne? Her opinion matters?"

"Yes," Valdarr says simply. "I put her first."

"What a fool. I thought I raised you better."

"I raised myself."

"And that is your first mistake." His voice goes soft. "I have always been in the background. You would do well to remember that. Every word from the agent's mouth was mine."

Silence settles.

"Fine." He flicks two fingers, magnanimous and cruel. "Be modern. Ask your little mate. While you play at ruling this country, I will take the world—one bloody corner at a time."

"I thought you were tired," Valdarr says. "Ready to step down."

"Oh, I am." The smile widens. "And I am bored."

"Anything else you'd like to discuss?" Valdarr asks, voice level.

"No. You may go. Enlightening, as this conversation has been, I have things to do."

Valdarr stands. Bows his head without lowering his eyes. The smallest, unreadable smile tilts his mouth.

Guards step in; he accepts the hood without complaint, a prince allowing ritual to pretend to be power, and lets them steer him back to the lift.

I remain until Valdarr has safely left the building. I follow them to a drop-off point, and only then do I release the vision.

Chapter Forty

I JOLT BACK into my body and sink into the sofa, eyes closed, rubbing the sharp ache in my dead chest. Heartbreak, perhaps, after everything I have just learned. At least I now know what happened to my friends.

When I open my eyes, four faces are focused on me.

"He's safe," I croak. I glance at my watch: I've been under for only two minutes. We have plenty of time to reach him. "He's on his way to see his father. The Grand Master is in this building—" I give them the address. "But the guards will drop him here at two a.m." I provide the alternate drop-off location.

Harrison straightens, all business. "Can we go and fetch him?"

"Yes," I say. "But we must avoid the other vampires. We

don't need to trigger any problems for Valdarr, so it will be just the two of us, and we will need to time it perfectly."

No one questions me. Whenever someone throws a sidelong glance, James jabs them in the ribs and growls "Oracle" for good measure. They remain wary, but that is preferable to their thinking I'm an undercover spy. A progress of sorts.

I leave with Harrison, and we reach the drop-off point without incident, parking a little way down the road to stay out of sight. Tall, narrow buildings loom on either side, and the street is wide and unnervingly quiet. The perfect place for a handover.

We wait. The silence stretches, and I doubt Harrison quite believes me until the car finally pulls up.

"Please stay here."

I step onto the pavement just as Valdarr climbs from the other vehicle and tears off his hood.

The moment he sees me, he smiles.

I walk straight to him, and he gathers me into his arms.

"Did you catch all that?" he whispers against my ear.

"Yes," I murmur.

He cups my face, tilting my head until our eyes meet. "How do you feel? Any after-effects?"

"Just tired."

"How many visions did you risk?"

"Only one. I still can't believe you let them hood you." I playfully slap his arm. "You practically smiled at them. You should have seen the horror on their faces."

A wry smile touches his lips. "I wasn't happy, just confident I could handle them; they didn't even bind my hands.

Besides, I felt you, you touched my hand." He glances at his fingers with an odd look.

"I've no idea how I did that. Must be a mate thing. I feel ridiculous checking on you like that. You had the meeting with your father under control; you didn't need me to rescue you."

What I don't add is how afraid I am that I may have wasted our only chance to foresee what will happen with the Vampirical Council.

"I had that meeting under control because I knew you were watching, and I didn't want to let you down. When he spoke about you, your friends, and Simone, I wanted to launch myself across the table and rip his head off—but I didn't, because of you.

"I didn't want to disappoint you. You make me want to be a better man. When I'm with you, I feel human. I don't need to be unnecessarily violent. And now, after more than a thousand years, I finally have someone to live for."

I swallow a huge lump in my throat. "How do you always say the right thing?"

Valdarr grins.

Harrison has climbed out of the car. He doesn't look pleased that we are standing in the street talking.

"Come on. We don't have long before the guards raise the alarm." I tug him back towards the car. "Why would he give you the title of Grand Master?"

Valdarr shakes his head. "He's lying; he will never relinquish power. He thinks everyone wants to rule, so he can't understand the appeal of an easy life. He'd hand me the title so I would clean up his mess, then snatch it back or use it to discredit and kill me.

"He's always seen me as competition, while pushing me towards politics, wanting me by his side. I never wanted that. It's probably why I'm still alive. I have never openly opposed him. For now, until we know what he's planning, we shall play by his rules—if you agree?"

I nod.

If possible, he grows more serious. "We need to talk about what happened to your friends."

I stare at my feet. "There's nothing to say," I whisper. "I wanted answers and got them. I asked questions, played detective, and got myself killed." What a fool I am.

"He will pay for his crimes, Fred."

"No. Not if it puts you or your clan at risk. We both know life is not fair. Sometimes the monsters win." I close my eyes so they won't fill with tears. I have done enough crying for a lifetime. "First, we have to deal with the Vampirical Council and my illegal turning."

"We have faced them before—and won."

"About that..." I swallow, nerves fluttering. "I'm not sure whether I'm tapped out after the first council session vision marathon or whether my power works only once every twenty-four hours. I might not be able to see what happens tomorrow."

He squeezes my hand. "We will manage." He pats Harrison's arm as we climb inside. "Thanks for picking me up and keeping Fred safe."

In the car, I lean against him. His arms tighten around me, and I feel safe, even though I'm already worrying about tomorrow. I consider forcing another vision, but it isn't worth the risk. If I rest now, perhaps my power will recharge before we go back to court.

Maybe. This magic stuff is bloody complicated.

Chapter Forty-One

The worst thing happens. Bloody sod's law. I don't know whether it's performance anxiety or fate refusing to cooperate, but the next evening, as soon as the sun sets and I try to have a vision, nothing happens. I worry this power is going to drive me insane.

Why isn't it working?

"I should find more self-help podcasts," I grumble to James as he walks past.

If we survive, I might even try meditation. I've never been more terrified, and every time I say that, something else goes horribly wrong.

I really must learn not to tempt fate.

Baylor, curled at my feet, sneaks out his tongue and licks my ankle. He ate something that smelled suspiciously like fox poo on our walk, and his breath is minging. I wrinkle my nose at the rapidly drying spit.

James hands me his bottle of hand sanitiser. "Thank you," I say as I douse my leg and give it back.

"Did you know there are vampire podcasts? Actual podcasts made for vampires. Of course, they're not on human channels, and it takes a vampire with far too much time on his hands to know where to find them."

I stare at James, utterly flabbergasted. "This is... this is amazing."

"I know," he whispers back.

I grab my phone, and with his help, I find and start downloading the app as though my life depends on it.

He clears his throat. "So... any updates on your oracle thing? Do we know what's happening tonight?"

"No. My power is on the fritz."

He plonks himself beside me and whips out his tablet. "It says here that oracles can burn out if they overdo it. You've probably drained your magical reserves. Maybe we could try a circle, like you are doing with the stake?"

I lift my eyes from my phone and fix him with a look. "The stake."

"Yeah, it's sentient, right? Just like your talking house. You're not telling me it was you who went all vampire hunter on those human assassins. Simone said you couldn't fight for shit. I watched the footage back, and when it was over, you sat on the steps and cried."

"Bloody Sherlock Holmes," I mumble. "The stake is going to be furious when she finds out everyone knows about her. She's very... stabby-stabby."

He shrugs. "She must like us. That's why she protected us from the assassins. We're clearly the good guys."

"How can you be so sure?"

"Ah, because I'm right." He gives me that infuriatingly smug look.

I give him my best unimpressed stare.

"My life's not ending because a sentient stake decides I'm a bad guy."

"Well, you were a bad guy when we first met. She was dying to stab you."

"Yeah, but I'm not now, am I? I'm a great guy once you get to know me."

I roll my eyes. "Sure, James."

"So, what are you planning to do?"

"With what?"

"The visions, obviously."

"Well, I'm completely tapped out. I managed to see Valdarr, but that was it. Now I'm wondering if I wasted the chance."

"No, you didn't. You did the right thing. We've had so many changes; with our liege missing it was impossible not to panic. Clans need a powerful leader to keep everyone safe. The average lifespan of a newly turned vampire is three years, because our world is so dangerous."

I shake my head; I knew things were bad, but not that bad.

"Vampires are volatile. Something in the genetics means many of us lose our humanity; we become psychopaths. You might think I'm a fuddy-duddy, obsessed with rules and procedure, but I've watched friends change. Even when that doesn't happen, living so long wrecks a brain that was never built for it. It's like vampire Alzheimer's—eventually they go blood-crazy."

Like the Grand Master.

"Look, about the visions... I don't know how your power works, but if anything had happened to My liege last night, you'd never have forgiven yourself. At least you went all in."

I blow out a breath, my hair fluttering around my face. "It's just... if it were only me, I'd be fine. I wouldn't feel so—"

"—neurotic?" he offers.

"Anxious," I snap, though I can't help smiling. "But because it's Val—"

"You're terrified," he says gently. "You really do love him, don't you?"

"Yes. I do." I fold my arms across my chest, hugging myself. "Yes, even though his father is evil, Valdarr is still... a good man."

"He's good, but he's ruthless. You don't want to see him angry."

"Yeah, well, I guess you don't survive a thousand years by being soft."

"Or by being stupid," James mutters. "You've got to trust him to handle this now."

"But the difference is, the last time we went to The Hall of Silence, I saw us die—over and over—and nothing he did could protect us."

"Yet you protected him. You took over, dealt with the situation. That's what a good partnership does, each taking turns. Be that way again—calm, focused. And you are going to tell them, right? When you register as a day-walker, also register as an oracle. Do that proud know-it-all thing you do, and make them think you've already seen what's coming. If you stay calm and confident, they'll never risk killing us, because they'll assume you've foreseen it and changed the outcome. Reverse psychology." He taps his temple. "Make them think you've seen it all, even though you haven't. They'll be too busy panicking about what you might know."

"You know what? That's... actually genius."

"Of course it is. I'm basically a tactical mastermind."

I grin, and before I can stop myself, kiss him on the cheek. "Thanks, James. You are a superstar."

He splutters. "Don't be leaving your spit on me—my liege will know!"

"Your liege will know what?"

We both jump as my vampire strolls into the room, wearing an infuriatingly knowing grin.

"Have you been kissing my mate, James?"

"No! No, no, no!" James throws up a hand, tablet clutched to his chest. "I've been helping her with podcasts and giving her life tips. No kissing from me. None at all. Oh, look at the time. I need to finish the paperwork: Accord Codes 201.2, 206.1, and 208.4, mate-bond registration, day-walker certification, and oracular-precognition forms. MB-1, DW-3, OM-9. We'll need seals and signatures before we leave."

He bolts, practically tripping over himself as he leaves the room.

I watch him go and giggle. "That was hilarious."

Valdarr smiles faintly. "I'm glad you're getting along."

"Yeah, he's all right."

"Yeah. He is." He sits beside me and pulls me against his side.

"So," he murmurs, glancing at my phone, "what are you doing?"

"Have you seen this app? Podcasts! Motivational, helpful. Look at this one—" I scroll to something utterly ridiculous:

Bite Club Confidential, episode 8, "Confessions of a Vegan Vampire"—a candid interview with a vampire who claims to survive on beetroot juice and dark chocolate alone.

"That's a... very unusual topic," Valdarr says, deadpan.

"Yeah, but it's interesting."

I think back on what James said. It's so simple, yet so clever. "About the court, James thinks we should register me as an oracle."

"Yes, I noticed he's already filling out the forms." We share a grin. "I think it's a sound idea."

"Me too. Not that I'm much of an oracle; I still can't see what's going to happen tonight. James says I should act as though I know. I'm inclined to agree."

"We could try something else. A little power boost," he says, tilting his head and studying me.

"What sort of power boost?" I narrow my eyes.

"Well... vampires can drink from each other."

"Oh," I squeak. I have no idea what to say.

Valdarr simply waits—calm, unbothered—giving me space to work it out.

I have read enough about vampire culture to know that drinking from one another is... normal. It's part of their nature and their society. It isn't taboo or monstrous—at least, not to them.

Yet my human brain recoils. It whispers *disgusting, inhuman, wrong*.

Except, I don't see Valdarr as a monster, and I don't see myself as one either.

So, if we are not monstrous, why should this be?

"I know it's natural," I murmur, taking a deep breath. "It's normal."

"It is."

"Will it weaken you?"

"No. It will strengthen us both," he says softly, "and deepen our bond."

I nod. "Then... yes. I've never bitten anyone before. I mean, I tried a peach once."

Valdarr pulls a face. "Bet that wasn't very good."

"Disgusting," I agree. "So... do I just bite? Is there a preferred spot?"

"The wrist isn't ideal." He gestures to the side of his neck. "Here is better. Or the femoral artery in the upper thigh, but that might feel a little... personal."

My mind goes straight there. I wonder who he's bitten or who has bitten him. I growl before I can stop myself.

He chuckles, eyes sparkling.

"Sorry. So... do you want to bite me as well?"

"It would be good to exchange," he says.

"Right." I nibble my lip.

"You can go first," he adds gently. "Maybe the power boost will help your visions."

"Okay then." I shift closer on the sofa.

He unbuttons his shirt and slides it off one shoulder, revealing golden skin, muscles and his intricate tattoos.

Oh bloody hell.

"So I just bite?"

"Yes."

"And it's not going to hurt you?"

"No."

He taps a spot on his neck. "Here."

I swallow hard and lean in. His scent—musk, power, and a faint metallic note of power—fills my nose. I brush his skin; he doesn't even breathe. My hand trembles.

He rubs small, soothing circles on my back. "It's all right, let the vampire part of you take over. Your instincts know what to do."

He taps the spot again. "Just bite."

Oh, gosh. I'm really going to do this.

But he's my mate, and this will strengthen the bond. I press a brief kiss to his neck, then steel myself. *It is going to be fine.*

Fangs out, I sink them in.

His flesh parts easily, as if made for this. Rich, powerful blood surges into my mouth, fizzing with something electric. It tastes nothing like the blood I've tried before. His blood is alive with magic.

I take only a mouthful; I don't want to be greedy. When I draw back, I gently lick the wound clean, sealing it, and press a kiss to his neck.

I didn't frenzy. I didn't lose control. It was... nice—pleasant, even. Who am I kidding? It was mind-bendingly incredible!

He looks pained, and I panic.

"V—Valdarr, are you all right? Did I hurt you? I'm so sorry if—"

"No," he says hoarsely. "You didn't hurt me, sunshine. It's just... a lot. Having my mate bite me. It's intense."

"Oh," I whisper. "Well... would you like to bite me now?"

"Yes," he says, "but give me a moment."

He sits motionless, eyes closed. When he opens them, they're violet—glowing, vibrant, wild. I haven't seen them like that since he was furious.

I brush my fingers across his cheek; he leans into my palm and kisses it.

"Are you ready," I ask softly, "to seal the bond?"

He nods, smiling.

He gathers me onto his lap. The evidence of how much he enjoyed my bite presses against me, and I do my best to ignore it.

I slip off my top, leaving me in only my bra. I feel shy when he looks at me, and I cannot meet his eyes.

"You are so beautiful," he whispers. Valdarr leans in, nose tracing the line of my neck, lips brushing my skin.

He doesn't rush.

I can feel the smile tugging at his mouth. Then—slowly, carefully—he bites.

Power floods me; emotions crash in, some mine, some his. It feels as though the universe pauses and says, *"There. That's them."*

The bond wraps around us like a steel cable. I feel his love, his need, and my own answering feelings rise to meet them.

It's not just the bite; it's a joining of souls.

He drinks only a little, then seals the wound with a kiss. He also kisses the scar on my neck.

"Wow," I whisper.

"Wow, indeed," he replies.

Chapter Forty-Two

I DRESS in a navy trouser suit and a pale-pink silk blouse. My hair is pinned *just so*, and my makeup is flawless. Whenever I do my makeup, I think of House. I need to try to locate her again. Everything just keeps getting in the way.

Valdarr has people looking, but by now, she could be anywhere in the world. We have no way to contact her. She might be stuck wherever she is for years. No—*with* her magic, if she wanted to reach me, she probably could. House is powerful. So her silence must be part of some greater plan, though that doesn't stop me worrying.

Once this council visit is over—*if* we survive it—I will find my friend and help her for a change.

Beryl is warmer now; I'm sure she will be all right. She sits in the magic inside pocket of my jacket. Harrison has had a mage magically modify our clothing. When she wakes, we will have a long talk about boundaries, and I will apologise for outing her.

I just hope the bloodthirsty stake won't stab me.

Valdarr enters, dressed in a perfectly tailored suit. Somehow we have coordinated—same colour, same understated elegance—and he looks devastatingly handsome. He shoots me a silent question, and I shake my head. He nods. He already knows there's nothing I can do to summon a vision. Unless I manage to force one while we are in the car, we have run out of time.

I leave Baylor with security. Roger—the guard who helped me with Theresa—is on duty and delighted to dogsit. The guards adore my boy, and I don't want him upset when we leave, not in such a fancy house. He hates being left alone.

The drive to the curved, black-glass skyscraper is mercifully uneventful, yet I spend the whole ride gripping the seat, knuckles white. The attacks we faced last time have turned me into a nervous wreck.

Inside, the entrance now resembles an airport. Extra guards, magical scanners, weapons logged and removed. Pointless, really, when vampires are walking weapons. Harrison makes a show of being most put out when a few of his weapons are found, but the rest of us have nothing to surrender. I've seen the clan fight, and they use whatever they seize from their attackers.

They do not find Beryl.

The open-plan atrium gleams, spotless. It's as if the battle and executions never happened. Every trace has been repaired. So many deaths, and for the vampires, it was just another day in court.

What *has* changed is that the sweeping bone-white tiers of seating are crammed, as though every clan has gathered to watch my trial. Perhaps my accusation against the Grand Master is the true attraction—some want him to win, most want him to fail, and the rest are here for the spectacle.

The packed, curving white seats turn the hall into a modern coliseum. Once seen, the image won't leave me. I half-expect a lion.

We wait in silence, the clan at our backs. Valdarr's expression is unreadable.

I steady my breathing—though I don't need it—and recall every lesson: be direct, be respectful. James's reverse psychology advice echoes in my head.

Last time I was here, I listened to hours of council debate to our advantage. Now, the not-knowing is all-consuming, but I did this once, I can do it again.

The Vampirical Council file in and take their seats. The Grand Master settles on his throne, wearing a smug smile.

The Herald of Silence enters in royal blue, ceremonial staff in hand. He bows—first to the Grand Master, then to the assembled Council.

"Order!" he bellows. "The Court is in session."

The room falls silent as the staff slams down. I brace myself for the bone-crushing wave of magic. Stronger than before, the power booms through the chamber; a fresh ward seals the Hall and steals the air from my lungs.

"I, the Herald of Silence, speak as the voice of the Council. Winifred Crowsdale of Clan Blóðvakt, stand forth and be heard."

We step into the centre.

"Three nights past," the Herald intones, "you entered a

plea of guilty to unlicensed turning and failure to register, in breach of Accord Code 675.3 and the attendant registry provisions. You alleged, under oath and Accord Code 101.4, that the Grand Master was your sire."

A ripple passes through the tiers.

"*Let the Silence record*: Pursuant to Accord Code 101.4: Right of Blood Provenance and Mandatory Sire Verification, the Ministry of Magic conducted a bloodline assay. Result: bite signature—Grand Master confirmed; sire of record—no binding lineage detected. Result inconclusive. In parallel, by Protocol EM-12 under Accord 208.4, an Ethereal Memory Capture was performed. The ocular imprint corroborates the act of fatal feeding by the Grand Master. Your allegation is verified as to the bite and death. The question of siring remains unproven."

"I have no objection," the Grand Master replies smoothly. "I was unaware of the turning. Had I known, I would have begged leniency for my son's mate. Winifred Crowsdale was an unregistered living vampire, and my bite contributed to her death and raising."

Liar—I lack the DNA to be a living vampire.

I keep my expression neutral. I understand why he says it and why the Council, all nodding along, allow it.

Lander—though I hate to admit it—was right. No one must discover that magic-infused houses can bypass death and twist the change, turning a pure human into a vampire. If they did, every mage on earth would be pressed into service to bottle immortality.

This fiction protects us all.

They forget that true living vampires show obvious

signs—heightened senses, strength—but if the Vampirical Council decrees it, the majority accepts it.

Then I realise something else, and relief floods me so sharply it almost brings me to my knees. They are giving me an out, an alibi, explaining everything away. If they are willing to spin this story, we just might survive.

Let them lie all they like, so long as we live.

"As we all know, magic is wild and unpredictable," the Grand Master continues. "No one is to blame for this oversight. Yet, before my peers and subjects, I admit my mistake: no one is above our laws—least of all me."

He bows his head, hand to his chest. "My heir and I have reached an understanding: he will assume my role as Grand Master; I will step down and uphold the Accord's strictures regarding humans."

The vampires watch, rapt with fascination.

The Herald inclines his head. "The Council will confer on remedy and sanction under Accord 675.3 and on matters of succession noticed this night pursuant to Accord 401.1: Continuity of Office. The Hall will hold its silence."

A fresh sheet of warding rises around the councillors; sound dies, and the bone-white tiers lean forward to listen to nothing at all.

This time I can't eavesdrop; like everyone else, I must wait. My anxiety climbs, yet the discussion appears calm—no anger, little dissent. They reach a decision quickly.

Good or bad? I can't tell.

The ward falls.

The Herald steps forward, staff in hand. His voice rings out—

Chapter Forty-Three

"We, the Vampirical Council, having conferred, now speak judgment. As to your plea of guilty to unlicensed turning and failure to register breaches of Accord Code 675.3 and the attendant registry provisions: by findings entered this night, Ministry bloodline assay under Accord 101.4 and Ethereal Memory Capture under Accord 208.4, the victim of record. *Let the Silence record*: Winifred Crowsdale is adjudged to have been a living vampire at the material time. Under Accord 675.3(b), the Living Condition Exception, the prohibition on unlicensed turning does not attach. The plea is amended to not guilty by operation of law.

"As to registry, the Council grants immediate cure and grace under Accord 910.2(f) for anomalous states: your status and gifts shall be entered forthwith upon proper filing."

A hush tightens, then trembles.

"As to the Grand Master: the Ministry's instruments confirm his bite and fatal feeding upon the living vampire Winifred Crowsdale; however, no binding sire-line is detected. The Human Compact at Accord 3.1 does not apply to the death of one adjudged living vampire, and the predicate for capital sanction under Accord 221.9, Unlawful Predation is here mitigated by extenuation, admission, and succession settlement. The Council enters a formal censure and no further charge."

The Grand Master inclines his head, eyes glittering. "I thank the Council for its wise judgement."

He has played us and the Vampirical Council masterfully. He gets away with everything. But at least we get away alive.

"The Grand Master has noticed his intent to abdicate pursuant to Accord 401.1 and 401.4. Grand Master, do you withdraw?"

"I do not. My heir's ascension stands, if the Council permits."

"We, the Vampirical Council, accept your abdication and the heir's investiture. *Let the Silence record:* by your motion and with our assent, this is honour, not penalty, recorded under Accord 401.4."

The ceremonial staff slams against marble; power thrums through bone and stone.

"Hear the Silence," the Herald booms, "and mark the record: Valdarr Blóðvakt, Master of Clan Blóðvakt, Raven of the North, is henceforth Grand Master—first among fang and law, steward of the Accord."

A heavy wave of magic rolls the tiers. The bone-white

ranks rise as one, then drop to one knee, heads bowed to the new Grand Master.

Silence holds. Every gaze lifts to Valdarr.

"Council. Herald. I accept."

The Herald waits; everyone seems to expect more—perhaps a speech. Just before the silence turns awkward, he dips his head. "Grand Master."

James steps forward, bearing a stack of thick, cream-coloured parchment edged in gold and pricking with enchantment.

"By leave of the Council," Valdarr says, "we file the following registrations: pursuant to Accord 910.7, Mating Bonds and Claim Marks, the mate-bond between Valdarr Blóðvakt and Winifred Crowsdale; pursuant to Accord 502.3, Non-conforming Daylight Physiology, day-walker designation."

The Grand Master nods and smiles; everything is going to plan.

"And pursuant to Accord 910.2 and Accord 903.1, Oracle Designation and Handling, registry of gifts—Oracle."

Silence takes the Hall. A councillor or two forgets to blink.

The Herald clears his throat. "The Council receives and enters the filings. Day-walker and oracle statuses shall be provisionally recorded pending Ministry countersignature under Accord 903.1 and 502.3. Clan Blóðvakt, you are most... fortunate."

An aide bows, lifts the parchment from James, and bears it toward the lectern.

"Stop!"

The Grand Master's roar splits the chamber like a thunderclap. Every figure freezes.

Everyone freezes—everyone but Valdarr.

While I watched the Herald, he never once took his eyes off his father. Mine was the mistake; his wasn't. Valdarr's father is livid.

"An oracle?" he snarls. "Why was I not told? She is *mine*. I brought her into this life, I should benefit from her gifts."

The Herald turns, blue robes whispering. "Former Grand Master, the record reflects a duly filed mate-bond under Accord 910.7 and provisional Oracle designation under Accord 903.1. Further, Accord 112.6 Prohibition on Prior Claim against a Bonded Mate—extinguishes any antecedent assertion. You have no standing. By your abdication under Accord 401.4, you retain no claim and no recourse."

"I have a claim!" The old monster's voice cracks like a whip.

"Former Grand Master," the Herald warns, staff lifting, "Accord 12.9, Sanctity of Court. Stand down."

His fingers flick—a familiar, deadly gesture.

Oh no.

Chapter Forty-Four

The ward separating the seated vampires does not fail this time; it strengthens.

"You will all obey!" The Grand Master's words drop like a magical bomb. The air shifts. Power knifes through the hall; glass trembles, balconies shudder, lights gutter and dim. The command rolls through the room, and I can almost see it spreading—first hitting the council, then rippling outward.

It bounces off the Herald but continues like a wave from a stone thrown into a pond. It hits the guards, then smashes through the ward, sweeping over every single vampire.

He's compelled them all, taken over their minds.

The Herald steps forward to intervene, but the same aide who collected the paperwork slashes at him with a knife. He clutches his throat as blood spurts between his fingers, then collapses, choking.

The Grand Master's eyes burn as they lock on me. "You will do as I say."

The command slams into my head; my body almost nods on instinct. Valdarr's grip tightens on my hand, anchoring me.

He's growling.

"Bring her to me," his father orders.

I have no time to flinch before a hand clamps around my arm and yanks me forward away from Valdarr.

"Tony? What are you—"

His eyes are glazed, empty. Horror chills me: he's been compelled, too.

"Stop him," the Grand Master demands. As Valdarr lunges, my name on his lips, Ralph bear-hugs him from behind. Harrison piles on, then James. Even together they barely hold him. He roars, muscles straining, teeth bared.

Tony's iron grip drags me across the floor towards the platform. I am strong, but I'm still only a baby vampire and no match for him. "Tony, let go! You are hurting me!"

The Grand Master smiles, smug and cruel. He drifts closer, a ripple of compulsion sweeping the air like heat lightning.

"You are mine now," he says. His power slams into my mind like a wave. "You love me. I am your mate."

"You love me. I am your mate," I echo.

I love him.

He is my mate.

I glance at my mate on the platform. Why does despair and fear coil inside me?

Why... why won't my body move of its own accord?

Why am I being dragged across the room, a vampire's grip bruising my arm?

Why does my hand stretch behind me, clawing at the air, reaching for something?

Reaching for...

I look back and see *him*—beautiful, fierce—a handsome vampire. He's fighting two, no, three opponents, his movements a blur of strength and precision. He lifts his head, and his violet-grey eyes lock on mine.

And I remember.

Flash—the yellow door.

Flash—the hoodie.

Flash—the rescue at the border station.

Flash—the kiss.

Flash. Flash. Flash. The memories slam into me. His voice echoes in my mind: *"You, Winifred Crowsdale, are perfection. My sunshine in the dark."*

Our bond blazes to life. His blood, singing in my veins, ignites, not with pain but with power. My head pounds as Valdarr's strength floods through me, wrapping me in steel, shielding my mind.

I bare my fangs at the Grand Master. "No. Not happening."

"Oh, it will," he says, licking his lips. The burgundy has swallowed his dark grey irises; his eyes are entirely red. "I still remember how you tasted. You are mine. Your mate—my useless son—will be dead in moments."

"No," I growl. "I will stop you."

"You? You can't stop me. You can't do anything. You are nothing, just a freak of magic, an abomination dressed in borrowed gifts. Day-walking, foresight—all of it... *mine*. With your visions, my plans will unfold perfectly. The world will burn under my command, and I will rebuild it in my image."

His smile twists.

"I will start with the humans. They will be locked up where they belong: entertainment, food, nothing more. I will sweep through every country, enslaving them, breeding them like livestock, plucking the finest from the herd until they are broken husks."

He lifts his gaze to the audience, his tone swelling with dark triumph.

"I will do whatever I please, because I can. Nobody can stop me."

The vampires around us continue to stand silent, frozen in his web of power. I hadn't realised how powerful he truly is until now. How do you fight someone like this?

"I will make us strong again," he says, his voice rising like a war cry. "I will destroy the shifters and shatter the magic-users until they crawl like pets at our feet. I will reshape this world in blood and fire. And you..."

His gaze locks on me, his smile dark and consuming.

"You will be my weapon."

He steps closer, each movement deliberate—a predator stalking prey.

"And you will watch as I kill your mate."

Another vampire seizes my other arm. Pinned between two vampires, I can barely move at all.

My dead heart plummets.

Valdarr screams my name, thrashing against his clan,

while the rest of the hall watches, enthralled by the Grand Master's power.

Through the crowd another familiar figure advances, eyes as glazed as the rest: the executioner, ready to take Valdarr's head.

We are losing.

No. We have already lost.

Chapter Forty-Five

My whole body trembles. Is this what my life will be now? He will kill Valdarr and then—then the world ends. My world ends with a sword strike. The thought is unthinkable.

I have to protect him.

I can't. Two vampires pin my arms; the bones in my shoulders creak. The executioner stands ready, sword loose in his grip. He gives it a lazy practice swing, as though gauging the weight before the killing blow.

"It's either you or her, son. Give up," the Grand Master snarls.

Valdarr stops struggling. His eyes blaze—violet lit from within—brighter than I have ever seen. Despair burns in that light. If not for his own clan restraining him, I think he'd tear the room apart.

Forcing them to hold him is a cruelty beyond comprehension.

Valdarr could hurl them aside, kill them, but the ring of enthralled guards along the tiers stands waiting, mouths slack, eyes glazed, blades half-drawn. He might stop a handful. He cannot stop them all.

"You or your miracle?" the Grand Master taunts, chin jerking toward the executioner.

"Her," Valdarr says. "Always her."

"Good choice." A flick of fingers. "Proceed."

Tony's grip tightens on my arm. I can only watch as Ralph and Harrison force Valdarr to his knees. He bows his head and bares his neck, and still he doesn't take his gaze off me.

The sword rises in a perfect arc.

And just as the world narrows to a single downward stroke—

—my jacket stirs.

If you want something done right, Beryl drawls, *you have got to do it yourself.*

She rockets from my pocket like a fired bolt, wood humming, carves a corkscrew through the air and hits the Grand Master square in the chest.

A dull thud. A wet, awful squelch.

He looks down, astonished, at the stake buried to the hilt. His hands lift—hesitate—as if reality needs a moment to catch up. Beryl keeps boring, the magic vibration rattling my teeth from across the hall, shredding his heart.

He coughs. Thick, tar black blood sluices over his lips and chin, creosote and rot hitting the air. He staggers and drops to his knees.

Beryl bursts from his back in a spray of gore, a victorious, vicious little spear. He makes one final strangled sound and pitches face-first onto the platform.

The compulsion breaks like glass.

It rushes out of the room in a pressure wave; every glazed eye clears. Vampires on the tiers flinch as though waking from a nightmare. A dozen blades clatter to the marble. The hall inhales in one collective, horrified breath.

The Herald, still clutching his throat, half-sits. Healing already knits the skin; his eyes jump from the corpse to Valdarr to me. Councillors scramble at their dais, slapping down sigils, tripping wards, panic splashing across ancient faces.

"This... this is unprecedented," an elder rasps. "He compelled the court!"

Tony's hold on me loosens as though he's been scalded. "Winifred, I—" The apology dies; I'm already gone.

I sprint. Valdarr catches me, folding me into him, twisting us clear of the executioner's blade. He smells of musk, metal, and the copper-sweet tang of battle.

"Are you hurt?" He frames my face in his hands, searching my eyes while his thumbs sweep my cheekbones, then he peppers me with light kisses.

"I'm all right," I whisper.

He lets out a deep, body-shuddering sigh and holds me tight.

"Do your duty," Valdarr says, voice flat. He points at the platform without looking. "Take the traitors head."

The executioner bows. "Of course, Grand Master." He crosses the distance in three strides and brings the sword down. Clean. Final. Then Valdarr's father's head rolls once, twice, and is still.

That was for Amy and Max. For all of us. My knees buckle, and only Valdarr's support—his strong arms around my waist—keeps me upright. Beryl's strike should have been enough, but with that monster, I trust nothing short of ash.

"I'll burn him," Valdarr says, reading my mind, gaze fixed on the ruin of his father. "Scatter him to the four winds, and salt the earth. He will never come back. He will never touch you again." When his eyes finally meet mine, they are fierce and unbearably sad. "I'm sorry I couldn't protect you."

"You did." My voice is wrecked and shaking. "The only reason I fought him is—you. Your blood in my veins. He tried to convince me I was his, that I loved him. For one horrible moment I almost believed it." I press my palm to Valdarr's chest, to the steady, unnecessary rise and fall. "But your blood sang, and my soul knew I could never be his. I love you and every part of me knows it."

I wrap my arms around his neck and hold on.

"I love you, Winifred. Thank you for saving me," he whispers into my hair. "And for bringing your friend."

Coated in gore, Beryl gives a dramatic shake, flinging droplets like confetti that freckle the dais with dots of villain. Then she zips toward me.

"Oh no, you don't." I dodge. "Absolutely not. You are covered in Grand Master goo. You are not going back in my pocket like that."

She laughs, bright and shameless. *Missed you too, kid. Also, you are welcome.*

"Thank you," I say, breathless and shaky and half-hysterical. "For dealing with him and rescuing us."

"Thank you, Beryl." Valdarr inclines his head.

As she talks, I translate as he can't hear her.

I've been trying to get that bastard for one hundred and fifty-seven years. She executes a mid-air pirouette, delighted with herself. *Who would have thought a baby vampire would give me the opening?*

"Who indeed."

If I had lungs, she says, *I'd sing "Ding-Dong, the Vampire's Dead." Shame I'm not sparkly and musical.*

"Beryl..."

What? Don't give me that look. I just saved your husband and this court of evil. A little appreciation won't kill you—though technically, it nearly did.

"You are impossible."

And you love me for it.

Around us, the hall remembers how to think. Guards stumble as the last threads of command unravel. Vampires in the bone-white tiers look at one another with dawning horror, understanding exactly what was done to them.

The Herald hauls himself upright, palm flat to his breastbone, voice ragged but steady enough to carry. He will make his proclamations soon. There will be ash to sweep and oaths to swear and laws to mend.

But in this breath between catastrophe and consequence, Valdarr tips his forehead to mine.

"We are alive."

"For now," I answer, because hope is a fragile thing and I don't know how to hold it yet. I also do not want to jinx anything. "Let's keep it that way."

His mouth curves, and the fear in my chest unclenches.

Across the dais, the corpse leaks darkness onto marble.

Beryl hums, satisfied.

I lace my fingers with Valdarr's and squeeze. "Let's go home," I whisper.

"Home," he says, as though he's tasted the word before and never found it sweet.

Beryl zips a smug loop. *I call shotgun.*

"Bath first," I tell her. "Then shotgun."

And for the first time since I died, I let myself believe in afters. In the space beyond terror and courts and kings. In a tomorrow where the villain stays dead, the stake gets a rinse, and the man I love comes home with me.

Chapter Forty-Six

Bonus Scene One - The First Delivery
Valdarr's point of view

The ward shivers a warning, human, alone, heartbeat quick from the jog up the path. Damn it, another delivery. James swore he had cancelled the daytime security's standing order. I told him no more. Hire an approved chef; Father's spies are everywhere.

I stand inside the threshold, the house dark at my back. Before the driver can knock, I yank the door open.

"Good afternoon." Head down, voice warm, professional, polite—the way humans speak when danger lurks on the other side of a door.

Sunlight halos her golden-blonde hair and freckles her

cheeks. She is delicate—tiny, in fact—and too busy with the app on her phone to meet my eyes.

I'm irrationally irritated. Approaching any house unwary is dangerous; she will get herself killed. *Look up, silly girl.* Sunlight licks the boards at my boots.

"Nice of you to turn up. What took you so long?" I snarl.

Takeaway grease, canine, and orange juice masks her natural scent. I draw a deeper breath and—

Everything in me goes silent—then roars.

The bond slams into me so hard I must brace against the doorframe. *Mine.* The word detonates through a thousand years of restraint. *Mine*, every feral instinct whispers. *My mate. Mine to guard, mine to cherish... mine to ruin if I'm not careful.*

No.

Human.

Fragile.

Wrong life. Wrong time.

"My apologies, sir," she says, placating. "The restaurant is on the other side of the border. A forty-minute drive. But please don't worry, the food is under a stasis spell, so it's still piping hot."

I school my face to boredom—predatory, unimpressed—anything but the panic battering my chest.

She finally lifts her face.

Not a girl. All woman, and my mate is *beautiful*. Her heart skips once—exactly once. Pale blue eyes flecked with silver, ringed in deep navy, lock on mine.

I memorise the moment.

I take the bag and spit the first ugly words that will

make her go. "No tip." Cruel. Necessary. No one can know, least of all her.

Her gaze flickers; she squares her shoulders and nods. "Tipping isn't mandatory, sir. Enjoy your meal." Calm, still kind.

Sir. Respectful to the brute at the door. "Whatever." I slam the door on the brightest thing I've seen in a century. In my life.

I press my forehead to the wood like a fool until her footsteps fade.

Harrison will have my head. I don't care. I text her car's registration. *Send our best team to watch the woman. Do not engage. Report only.*

Chapter Forty-Seven

Bonus Scene Two – The Border Station
Valdarr's point of view

Around-the-clock security has watched her for four weeks. It took a few days to assemble the right people, but three teams now cover her in shifts. Every report is the same: delivery runs, a dog walk, and she is home before dark. There is nothing concerning.

Then the call comes.

They have lost her.

"Someone small, fast, ran up and down the street," the guard says. "*Vampire fast*. Picked up by border patrol, leaving the Human Sector."

My someone.

My coat is on before the call ends. James tries to talk—

agenda, meetings, a complaint about knives in the dishwasher. I leave him speaking and take the stairs two at a time.

By the time I reach the station, she's already in custody.

The building reeks of bleach, blood, and old magic. The desk officer straightens as I cross the floor.

Her fear scents the air like a fine razor. She keeps her gaze down, posture defensive, yet the absence of a heartbeat hammers against my senses. Rage spikes so sharp my power flares.

No.

Unacceptable.

Someone has turned my mate.

Winifred was meant to live a long, safe, *human* life.

I force calm.

"Sir, this vampire was running from the Human Sector across the scrubland," a guard reports. "She tripped the wards, and we apprehended her."

"Did she resist?"

"No, sir. She ran, but once spelled, she cooperated. She hasn't spoken, though—clearly frightened. The problem, sir, is that she's unmarked."

I can feel the absence. My jaw aches.

"Look at me," I say, low.

She lifts her head like the bravest thing I have ever seen.

Sunlight in a dark place. Her expressive eyes hold fear, yes, but relief too. A scar mars her throat, weeks old. The mate bond punches through me—fierce and incandescent—and everything goes very, very cold.

"All right, gentlemen, I'll take it from here," I say. "Lose the paperwork. She was never here."

"Sir? Do you know her?" a guard asks.

One look ends the discussion.

"Of course, sir," the desk officer barks. "Bravo Team, daylight's coming. Lock everything down."

They scatter. I guide her into an interview room, privacy first, wards set, sound locked. A dampening rune hums; the walls haze—no ears, no eyes, just us.

I call Harrison. "I found her. I need a car at the station. Emergency Protocol One." Phone pocketed, I finally touch her. I cup her chin; the scar on her neck under my thumb is jagged, scavenger fast. Not a clean taking.

"Who did this to you?" I snarl.

She stares, proud despite fear.

"You were human, and now you're not. So I'll ask again. Who did this to you?" I drag a breath through my teeth, shove the rage elsewhere and spin the chair so her back is to the table. I brace her between my arms. Cage her with my body, yes, but also shield her from the door, the world.

"The spell gives us privacy," I manage, voice shaking. "Winifred Crowsdale, answer my question. Who. Did. This. To. You?"

She startles. "How do you know my name?"

Oh, sunshine, I know everything about you. She licks her lips; my fangs ache like she has put her mouth on them.

Focus.

"Please answer my question."

"A man ordered a takeaway to your house," she rasps.

"That's impossible." Reflex. No one should have been there. No one was scheduled.

"Impossible?" she shoots back, heat under the hoarseness.

"I'm not calling you a liar," I say, forcing my voice flat. "But no one should have been at that house."

"He answered the door in broad daylight. Like you, he was awake during the day."

An elder. There are so few of us.

"I'm telling you the truth. It was Sunday, the day after you lent me the hoodie."

I had people watching her... no, not on the Sunday—we had only assembled the complete team on the Monday.

"Someone placed a delivery at your address. I assumed it was you. I collected the food, returned your hoodie, and one of your friends decided I would make a good snack. He dragged me inside by my hair and tore out my throat. Shock and blood loss made me pass out or die; I'm not sure which."

She shrugs, as though it's unimportant.

"I woke up like this, in your body bin." Her voice cracks. "You really are a bunch of sick bastards with no self-control. I'm surprised the human government hasn't wiped you out."

She cannot publicly talk like that; the council and the clans would kill her.

"Wipe us out? Are you forgetting *you* are a vampire?"

"Indeed. Your pal murdered me. Thanks for that."

"We're getting off track. What did he look like?"

In a flat monotone she describes him: chalk-pale skin, a crimson mouth, dark grey eyes. The way he caught sunlight and burned; his clothes, his stance, the tone of his voice—and what followed.

Father. Of course.

A muscle twitches in my cheek. I turn away before rage shatters the table.

Calm. Think. Protect her.

This isn't about *me*. It is about Fred.

"How did you turn?" I ask, already building scenarios in my head. None make sense. She didn't carry the DNA markers. I checked. *Twice*.

"I have no idea." She takes a deep, unsteady breath.

The world narrows to bitter orange, cool iron and the wrongness in the way she still draws breath. I force myself to move away.

"You're still so new," I say, pacing to bleed off the violence. "Still breathing. You have been an unregistered vampire with no clan for more than a month. How many bodies?" I must ask; the law demands it.

"Bodies?" She glares. "As in people? None. Do you think I'm out here murdering humans? I'm nothing like you or your friends."

I deserve that. The corner of my mouth twitches despite the danger; my mate is all fire.

"It's less than an hour to dawn. I need to get you somewhere safe."

"I just want to pretend today never happened and go home."

"Where's home?"

"That is none of your business. I don't know you."

"I'm the only help you've got," I hear myself say, and hate how true it is.

She grimaces. The defensive anger melts into something

closer to defeat. "I'm sorry, I'm not trying to be rude. I'm just... frightened. It's been a lot."

A knock interrupts. I crack the door. "Cameras wiped, bribes arranged," Harrison says, handing over the clan Bloodbrand—no larger than a coin, carved with spells older than language. The iron pulses faintly, runes alive beneath its surface.

I nod, close the door, and turn back to her.

"Winifred, vampires aren't clanless. To survive, you must belong. There's no hiding and no running." Not from Father, not from his treatment of mistakes. "You have managed so far, but time's up. Let me help. Let me take over now."

"Take over how?"

My phone buzzes. I ignore it. My focus stays locked on her. I need to get this done. We are running out of time.

"I wish I could give you more time, but you have run out," I say, truth heavy on my tongue. If I hesitate, I will lose her. "Please forgive me. I won't let anything happen to you, and I *will not* let you fall into another clan's hands." I blur the distance, catch her wrist, flip it palm-up, and press the Bloodbrand to her skin.

She gasps. "Ow!" The sound guts me.

The sigil sears a red raven on a shield, blood beading at the beak. I fang nick my thumb, smear blood over the mark, sealing it. "You are now a member of my clan." Calm, cold, efficient—pretending it doesn't rip me apart to hurt her.

"It hurts."

"I know. It's for your protection." For mine. For my sanity.

"My protection? What about my consent?"

"There wasn't time." A lie of omission; I'd have branded her even with time. Later I will beg forgiveness with my life. I hold out my hand. "Come, I've arranged a safe house for you."

She hesitates.

If she says no...

Her hand slides into mine.

Chapter Forty-Eight

Bonus Scene Three – The Wedding
Valdarr's point of view

The ruby hums against my finger as I step from the car into full sun. Heat bites, but the ring drinks it in—old magic, dangerous and worth the risk. I smooth an invisible crease from my charcoal suit and follow the scent of champagne, hairspray, and smug entitlement around the hotel.

I intend to observe only.

Two guards watch the lane, a driver idles three streets away, and I have a quiet plan to extract her if anything goes wrong. I promised myself I would not interfere unless she asked.

Then he corners her.

I feel it in my bones—the way her body angles back, polite retreat rather than fear—yet I know where this leads. He steps in; his hand lands where it has no right to be. I cross the lawn.

"But you're my girl," the man whines.

"No, I'm not. I haven't been your girl for nearly seven months, and if we're honest, not for years. Melissa is your *wife*, and unlike you, I believe in commitment, in loyalty. I won't lower my standards—or my morals—for anyone, least of all you. Move back, now."

Fred's voice is fierce, and she means every word. Then her eyes snap to mine—wide, disbelieving.

"I think you'd better listen to the lady and step back before I make you," I say, moving past him. I'd rehearsed being gentle; I am not gentle now. "Apologies I'm late." I kiss her cheek. Warm. *Human*. Sun-warm orange peel and clean skin. Her pulse flickers against my senses.

The groom, her ex, puffs out his chest. "Who the fuck are you—" he begins.

I place myself between them and let the portable ward in my pocket swell: a soft shimmer that dulls curious ears and phones within three paces. A courtesy veil; neither of them notices the magic.

"Her attachment to you is what made you special—you realise that, right?" I keep it civil, barely. "You should have counted your blessings and cherished her. She's no longer yours. You are embarrassing yourself. Go back to your wife."

"I'm not gonna take advice from a punk with a lip ring," he sneers.

I give him the slow, lethal once-over and let him see

what looks back. He pales by degrees I might find amusing if he weren't breathing my sunshine's air.

"Here's the advice from a 'punk with a lip ring': learn the difference between *owning* and *honouring*. You tried the first. I'll be doing the second." I vow to *cherish* the incredible woman he squandered.

His mouth opens, shuts.

Behind me I hear Winifred's breath tighten.

I lower my voice and lean just enough that only he hears. The ward swallows the words. "If you touch her again, I will take your hands. If you smear her name again, I will take your tongue. If you so much as breathe in her direction, I will take your breath. Nod if you understand."

He nods.

Good. Fear plants lessons where pride cannot.

I turn to her. "Come, let me walk you to your car." I take her elbow as though this were a ballroom, not a battlefield of egos. We walk. It is surprisingly difficult not to reach for her hand.

She peers up. "What did you say to him?"

"Nothing important," I reply—true, technically. The important words are for her.

Up close I see the small details I crave: her elegant navy dress, bracelets hiding my mark on her wrist. She is a thousand small braveries bound in one woman; she came for closure and to clear her name like a warrior.

She stares at the sunlight glazing my suit sleeve. "I—I don't understand how you are here, in daylight, actually standing in the sun."

"I'm a gifted old vampire," I answer, lips tugging—truth adjacent. I lift my hand, stop before I touch her, ask without asking. She allows it. My thumb grazes her throat. There. That hummingbird beat. Alive. "What I don't understand," I admit, "is why you're awake and *breathing*. I can hear your heartbeat."

It skips.

"I don't know why I was turned, or how. I'm a vampire at night and... this during the day." She shrugs. Honest, unflinching. "I have no explanation."

"I will help you discover what happened to you if you will do me a small favour. Keep your daytime humanity secret. Don't trust anyone; no one is safe."

She nods, slips from under my hand, resumes walking.

At the car I take her keys before she can fumble, unlock the door—small courtesies I can't seem to stop. I open it and step back.

"You're not going to... take me?" she asks warily.

"No. I won't take you anywhere you do not wish to go," I say and mean it. If she wanted the world, I would open it like a door. If she wanted me gone, I would vanish into shadow.

"Why did you come?"

"I'm your clan," I say simply. "I'm yours. And, if we are honest, I've known where you were since the moment you ran from the safe house."

"You have people watching me?"

"Yes. You're a member of my clan living in the Human Sector, and we have protocols to follow." The truth tastes surprisingly good.

Her eyes widen; panic ripples through her scent.

I raise a hand. "Don't panic. I'm not coming after you,

your dog, or your magical house. I'm glad you are somewhere safe."

She looks as though she might cry and refuses.

"I learnt about the wedding from a background check. I came to ensure you were all right. I hadn't intended to interfere, but I couldn't allow his hands on you. You looked frightened."

She softens. "Thank you. I appreciate your help."

"Always."

I return the keys and, weak where she's concerned, kiss her again. Closer to the corner of her mouth this time. The line between restraint and selfishness frays in my hands when she's this near.

"Happy birthday. I will be seeing you soon, sunshine."

She slides into the seat—dazed.

Jay chose to marry on her birthday and had the audacity to invite her. I shall build a memorial to his losses. On this anniversary, year after year, I will claim something else: his assets, his reputation, and whatever remains thereafter. Today I begin with the family business.

I close the door, step back, and watch until she drives away.

Only then do I allow myself the memory of her pulse beneath my thumb and the taste she left on my lips. Worth every mile, every risk, every plan I have yet to make.

The wizard's house crashes to earth on the very edge of the Magic Sector, landing squarely atop a ley line. Raw power surges through its depleted walls, and the ensuing blast can be seen for miles. When the smoke clears, the house has vanished. In its place lies an unconscious woman.

Accord Code Index

COURT AND PROCEDURE

Accord Code 12.9—Sanctity of Court
What it means in Plain Fang: bars violence, compulsion, or magic that disrupts proceedings.
"Former Grand Master, Accord 12.9, Sanctity of Court. Stand down."

Accord Code 40.2—Silence Ward Authority
What it means in Plain Fang: authorises the Herald to seal the chamber with a silence/containment ward. "Silence in the hall" is literal.

Accord Code 104.1—Writ of Continuance
What it means in Plain Fang: permits a recess to gather evidence or await Ministry intervention.

Accord Code 117.5—Emergency Censure
What it means in Plain Fang: immediate rebuke/sanction for contempt within the Hall.

Accord Code 233.5—Council Silence Protocol
What it means in Plain Fang: "Silence in the hall" is literal. Authorises the Herald to drop a silence ward.

Accord Code 302.1—Hall Jurisdiction and Extraterritorial Reach
What it means in Plain Fang: your castle walls don't matter in here. Any act adjudicated inside the Hall supersedes clan sovereignty.

Accord Code 308.6—Sanctuary of the Hall
What it means in Plain Fang: violence or compulsion within the Hall of Silence is capital treason unless formally sanctioned by the Council.

Accord Code 312.0—Registry of Derivative Gifts
What it means in Plain Fang: all gifts and rare talents must be logged within thirty nights of discovery; failure triggers immediate sequestration.

Accord Code 312.1—Order of Sealing (Interim Measures)
What it means in Plain Fang: allows the Council to sequester evidence, witnesses, or filings pending review.
"By 312.1, the record is sealed and the evidence impounded."

Accord Code Index

Accord Code 347.9—Cross-Derivative Non-Interference
What it means in Plain Fang: clarifies when Council defers to other species' tribunals—unless Accord, Silence, or existential risks are triggered.

Accord Code 401.4—Abdication and Succession
What it means in Plain Fang: framework for voluntary abdication and lawful transfer of authority.
"By 401.4, abdication entered; the succession may proceed."

Accord Code 410.3—War Status Protocol
What it means in Plain Fang: declares "war status," enabling extraordinary security measures (device purge, hardened transport).

Accord Code 499.2—Neutrality of the Herald of Silence
What it means in Plain Fang: reaffirms the Herald's nonpartisan role and evidentiary voice.

Accord Code 902.1—Dissolution for Gross Malfeasance
What it means in Plain Fang: when a clan commits high crimes (e.g., daylight assault, mass compulsion), the Council may strike its name, seize its assets, and execute its elders.

BLOOD, TURNING AND SIRE MATTERS

Accord Code 101.4—Right of Blood Provenance and Mandatory Sire Verification
What it means in Plain Fang: compels sire identification via sanctioned assay. Any vampire may demand a Ministry-certified test to prove a sire. Results are binding; false claims invite censure or execution.
"I invoke 101.4. Let the blood speak."

Accord Code 101.5—Ethereal Memory Assay and Ocular Imprint
What it means in Plain Fang: authorises Ministry-run memory capture to corroborate blood findings.

Accord Code 103.2—Unlicensed Turning (Human to Vampire)
What it means in Plain Fang: defines the crime of turning a human without prior leave.

Accord Code 103.9—Living Vampire Exception (Genetic Anomaly)
What it means in Plain Fang: carves out a narrow lawful category for "living vampires" (rare DNA markers) and how they are treated retroactively.
Often used as a legal fiction to dispose of liability.

Accord Code 104.7—Prohibition on Rogue Turning
What it means in Plain Fang: elevates pattern or intent in unauthorised turnings to aggravated status.

Accord Code Index

REGISTRATION AND STATUS

Accord Code 137.2—Sentient Constructs and Sapient Houses
What it means in Plain Fang: recognises wizard houses and sapient artefacts as protected entities with restricted but real rights; interference requires a Council warrant.

Accord Code 601.2—Clan Transfer Protocol
What it means in Plain Fang: a vampire may change allegiance once per century with Council approval; bonded mates transfer automatically under this clause.

Accord Code 675.3—Unregistered Status Violation
What it means in Plain Fang: failure to register a new state (turning, clan, domicile) within the required timeframe. License to Turn and Registration of New Vampires. No human may be turned without a filed petition and Council writ. Paperwork must be lodged within 72 hours of rising.

Accord Code 703.8—Day-Walker Registration Requirements
What it means in Plain Fang: mandatory disclosure/registration of artefact-assisted or innate day-walking.

Accord Code 903.1—Oracle/Seer Designation and Disclosure
What it means in Plain Fang: procedure to recognise, record, and safeguard prophetic gifts.
"Oracle designation provisionally lodged under 903.1."

Accord Code 910.7—Mate-Bond Registration and Clan Standing
What it means in Plain Fang: formalises mate-bonds; confers standing and protections.

CONDUCT AND TERRITORY

Accord Code 112.6—Prohibition on Prior Claim against a Bonded Mate
What it means in Plain Fang: nullifies any antecedent "claim" once a lawful mate-bond is in force.

Accord Code 201.3—Consent in Feeding and Non-Lethal Protocols
What it means in Plain Fang: codifies voluntary feeding and bans lethal drains absent exigency.

Accord Code 212.4—Territorial Trespass and Safe-Conduct
What it means in Plain Fang: defines trespass; permits lenity for first-time/aid-motivated breaches.

Accord Code 212.9—Breach-of-Ward Restitution
What it means in Plain Fang: the clan that fractures another's standing ward must restore all damage *and* pay triple reparations in coin, blood, or territory.

Accord Code 765.375—Right of Self-Defence
What it means in Plain Fang: affirms lethal/non-lethal self-defence when facing imminent unlawful harm. Any derivative creature may use lethal force against an immediate, unlawful threat; immunity is automatic if intent is proven.
"Immunity claimed under 765.375."

Accord Code 780.2—Prohibition on Human Assassins (Diurnal)
What it means in Plain Fang: bars clans from employing human kill-teams in daylight operations.

WAR, SANCTIONS AND PROPERTY

Accord Code 501.6—Dissolution of Clan for Contempt and Uprising
What it means in Plain Fang: enables Council power to disband a clan for grave defiance or chamber violence.

Accord Code 520.1—Wartime Seizure and Restitution
What it means in Plain Fang: allows seizure of assets to remedy wartime or inter-clan harms.

Accord Code 540.9—Restitution for Damage to Council Holdings
What it means in Plain Fang: diverts dissolved assets to repair the Hall or Council property.
"Restitution ordered under 540.9."

Accord Code 560.4—Anti-Infiltration and Ward Sabotage
What it means in Plain Fang: criminalises tampering with wards, keys, or sigils securing a clan seat.

Accord Code 812.4—War Designation and Blackout Protocols
What it means in Plain Fang: authorises comms burn, asset concealment, compulsory relocation to safe houses.

INTER-DERIVATIVE AND MINISTRY LIAISON

Accord Code 600.1—Cross-Derivative Respect and Non-Interference
What it means in Plain Fang: sets baseline respect among vampires, shifters, mages; defines jurisdiction.

Accord Code 600.9—Ministry Liaison and Evidence Handling
What it means in Plain Fang: authorises referral to the Magical Ministry for technical assays (bloodline, ethereal memory).

PUNITIVE LADDER

Accord Code 800.1—Sentence of Final Death (Capital Sanction)
What it means in Plain Fang: defines capital punishment threshold.

Accord Code 802.3—Hall of Silence Execution Protocols
What it means in Plain Fang: method and order of executions conducted by Council warrant.

Accord Code 820.5—Clan Sanctions Ladder
What it means in Plain Fang: graduated penalties: fines, censures, host withdrawals, dissolution.

Accord Code 899.7—Mercy Stay and Commutation
What it means in Plain Fang: council power to stay/commute sentences on public-interest grounds.

Dear Reader,

Thank you for taking a chance on my book! I can't believe I've done it again. I hope you enjoyed the story as much as I loved writing it. If you did, I would be incredibly grateful if you could take a moment to leave a review or give it a rating.

Every single review makes a big difference—it helps other readers discover my work and supports me as an author.

Your kind words might even inspire me to keep writing more stories like this one. Who knows? Your review could even be featured in one of my marketing campaigns—how exciting would that be?

Thanks a million!

    Love,
    Brogan x

P.S. DON'T FORGET! Sign up on my VIP email list! You will get early access to all sorts of goodies, including: signed copies, private giveaways, advance notice of future projects and free stuff! The link is on my website at **www.brogan-thomas.com** your email will be kept 100% private, and you can unsubscribe at any time, with zero spam.

About the Author

Brogan lives in Ireland with her husband and their eleven furry children: five furry minions of darkness (aka the cats), four hellhounds (the dogs), and two traditional unicorns (fat, hairy Irish cobs).

In 2019 she decided to embrace her craziness by writing about the imaginary people that live in her head. Her first love is her husband, followed by her number-one favourite furry child Bob the cob, then reading. When not reading or writing, she can be found knee-deep in horse poo and fur while blissfully ignoring all adult responsibilities.

amazon.com/author/broganthomas
facebook.com/BroganThomasBooks
instagram.com/broganthomasbooks
goodreads.com/Brogan_Thomas
bookbub.com/authors/brogan-thomas

Also by Brogan Thomas

Creatures of the Otherworld series

Cursed Wolf (Forrest)

Cursed Demon (Emma)

Cursed Vampire (Tru)

Cursed Witch (Tuesday)

Cursed Fae (Pepper)

Cursed Dragon (Kricket)

Rebel of the Otherworld series

Rebel Unicorn (Tru)

Rebel Vampire (Tru)

The Bitten Chronicles

Bitten Shifter (Lark)

Bitten Vampire (Winifred)

Bitten by Magic (House)